Philip José Farmer was born in 1918. A part-time student at Bradley University, he gained a BA in English in 1950. Two years later he shocked the SF world with the publication of his novella *The Lovers* in *Startling Stories*. This won him a Hugo Award in 1953; his second Hugo came in 1968 for the story *Riders of the Purple Wage* written for Harlan Ellison's famous *Dangerous Visions* series; and his third came in 1972 for the first part of the acclaimed Riverworld series, *To Your Scattered Bodies Go*. Leslie Fiedler, eminent critic and Professor of English at the State University of New York at Buffalo, has said that Farmer 'has an imagination capable of being kindled by the irredeemable mystery of the universe and of the soul, and in turn able to kindle the imaginations of others – readers who for a couple of generations have been turning to science fiction to keep wonder and ecstasy alive'. Philip José Farmer lives and works in Peoria, Illinois.

PHILIP JOSÉ FARMER

Riverworld and Other Stories

GRAFTON BOOKS

A Division of the Collins Publishing Group

LONDON GLASGOW
TORONTO SYDNEY AUCKLAND

Grafton Books
A Division of the Collins Publishing Group
8 Grafton Street, London W1X 3LA

A Grafton UK Paperback Original 1981
Reprinted 1986, 1988

Copyright © Philip José Farmer 1979

ISBN 0-586-05379-4

Printed and bound in Great Britain by
Cox & Wyman Ltd, Reading

Set in Plantin

Acknowledgments

Contents

Riverworld

Foreword

The first of the Riverworld series was actually written in 1952. This was a 150,000-word novel originally titled Owe for the Flesh. It was written in one month so I could enter it in an international fantasy-science-fiction-award contest. It won, but because of circumstances I won't go into here, it was never published and I got only a fraction of the money due me. It was then not conceived as a series; the manuscript was a complete book in which the mystery of the Riverplanet was solved. After the distressing events connected with the contest were finished, I had ownership of the book. There wasn't at that time a market for very long s-f novels by someone who'd only sold a few magazine stories. I put the ms. in the proverbial trunk and forgot about it for some years.

In 1964 I took it out, dusted it off, and changed the title to Owe for a River. It went out to a couple of publishers, one of whom rejected it on the grounds it was just 'an adventure' story. This wasn't at all true. Also, curiously, the publisher making this comment had published my The Green Odyssey, which was far more an 'adventure' novel than Owe for a River.

Fred Pohl was at that time editor of Galaxy magazine and its sister s-f magazines. I sent the ms. to him, and he returned it to me with some very perceptive comments. It was, he said, too big a concept to confine even within such a long novel. He proposed that I write a series of novelettes for him. These could later be put into book form, if I wished. By then I'd done enough thinking about the Riverworld concept to know that he was right. A planet on which most of humanity living from 1,000,000 B.C. to the early twenty-first century had been resurrected along a ten-million- or perhaps twenty-million-mile-long river was too big a world to put *into one volume. And it had too many characters I'd like to write about.*

So I wrote Day of the Great Shout, *a novelette which appeared in Pohl's* Worlds of Tomorrow *in the January 1965 issue. Thirteen years had elapsed since the original story. In that, the action had started twenty years after the day on which thirty-five billion people from many different times and places on Earth had been raised from the dead in some mysterious but scientific manner. 'Day' began even before the general resurrection with the hero, Sir Richard Francis Burton, accidentally (or was it accidentally?) awakening in the pre-resurrection chamber, though only briefly.*

Day was later somewhat expanded and presented as Chapters 1-18 of the novel, To Your Scattered Bodies Go,* *1971.*

Its sequel, The Suicide Express, *appearing in the same magazine in March 1966, was expanded to make chapters 19-30 of* To Your Scattered Bodies Go.

I wrote the novelette Riverworld *shortly after* The Suicide Express, *but it appeared in* Worlds of Tomorrow *in January of the same year. I wasn't satisfied with it then, and I expanded it slightly for appearance in a collection of some of my shorter works in* Down in the Black Gang. *Still, I hadn't done what I should have done. The story seemed to me more an outline than a full-fleshed tale.*

So, this time, Riverworld *has been expanded from 12,000 to 33,750 words. I think I'll be satisfied with this version.*

When the fourth volume of the Riverworld series, The Magic Labyrinth,* *comes out, the mysteries set forth in the first three will be solved, and the series will have a definite conclusion. But, as I said in the foreword to the third,* The Dark Design,* *I do plan on writing a fifth and even sixth book dealing with matters which I didn't have space for in the first four volumes. These are what I call the 'mainstream' books of the series. The fifth and*

*Now available from Granada Paperbacks.

sixth will be in the 'sidestream' or 'tributary' tales.

Tom Mix will be in these, but the story at hand, Riverworld, won't be included. All of the tales in the fifth will be previously unpublished, brand new.

1

Tom Mix had fled on Earth from furious wives, maddened bulls, and desperate creditors. He'd fled on foot, on horse, and in cars. But this was the first time, on his native planet or on the Riverworld, that he had fled in a boat.

It sailed down-River and downwind swiftly, rounding a bend with the pursuer about fifty yards behind. Both craft, the large chaser and the small chased, were bamboo catamarans. They were well-built vessels, though there wasn't a metal nail in them: double-hulled, fore-and-aft rigged and flourishing spinnakers. The sails were made of bamboo fiber.

The sun had two hours to go before setting. People were grouped by the great mushroom-shaped stones lining the banks. It would be some time before the grailstones would roar and spout blue electricity, energy which would be converted in the cylinders on top of the stones into matter. That is, into the evening meal and also, liquor, tobacco, marijuana, and dreamgum. But they had nothing else to do at this time except to lounge around, talk, and hope something exciting might happen.

They would soon be gratified.

The bend which Mix's boat had rounded revealed that the mile-wide River behind him had suddenly become a three-mile wide lake ahead. There were hundreds of boats there, all filled with fishers who'd set their cylinders on the stones and then put out to augment their regular diet with fish. So many were the craft that Mix suddenly found that there was even less room to maneuver than in the narrower stretch of water behind him.

Tom Mix was at the tiller. Ahead of him on the deck were

two other refugees, Bithniah and Yeshua. Both were Hebrew, tied together by blood and religion though separated by twelve hundred years and sixty generations. That made much difference. In some ways Bithniah was less a stranger to Mix than she was to Yeshua; in some ways, Yeshua was closer to Mix than to the woman.

All three, at the moment, shared bruises and contusions given by the same man, Kramer. He wasn't in the boat following their wake, but his men were. If they captured the three, they'd return them to 'The Hammer,' as Kramer had been called on Earth and was here. If they couldn't take the refugees alive, they'd kill them.

Mix glanced behind him. Every bit of sail on the two-masted catamaran was up. It was slowly gaining on the smaller craft. Mix's boat should have been able to keep its lead, its crew was far lighter, but, during the escape, three spears had gone through the sail. The holes were small, but their effect had accumulated during the chase. In about fifteen minutes the prow of the chaser could be touching the stern of his craft. However, Kramer's men wouldn't try to board from the bow of their boat. They'd come up alongside, throw bone grappling hooks, draw the vessels together, and then swarm over the side.

Ten warriors against three, one a woman, one a man who would run away but who refused on principle to fight, and one a man who'd been in many duels and mass combats but wouldn't last long against such numbers.

People in a fishing boat shouted angrily at him as he took the catamaran too near them. Mix grinned and swept from his head his ten-gallon white hat, made of woven straw fibers painted with a rare pigment. He saluted them with the hat and then donned it. He wore a long white cloak made of towels fastened together with magnetic tabs, a white towel fastened around his waist, and high-heeled cowboy boots of white River-serpent leather. The latter were, in this situation, both an affectation and a handicap. But now that fighting was close, he needed bare feet to get a better grip on the slippery deck.

He called to Yeshua to take over the tiller. His face rigid, unresponsive to Mix's grin, Yeshua hastened to him. He was five feet ten inches tall, exactly Mix's height, but considered tall among the people of his time and place on Earth. His hair was black but with an undercoating which shone reddish in the sun. It was cut just below the nape of the neck. His body was thin but wiry, covered only by a black loincloth; his chest was matted with curly black hair. The face was long and thin, ascetic, that of a beardless scholarly-looking Jewish youth. His eyes were large and dark brown with flecks of green, inherited, he'd said, from Gentile ancestors. The people of his native land, Galilee, were much mixed since it had been both a trade route and a road for invaders for several thousand years.

Yeshua could have been Mix's twin, a double who'd not been eating or sleeping as well as his counterpart. There were slight differences between them. Yeshua's nose was a trifle longer, his lips a little thinner, and Mix had no greenish flecks in his eyes nor red underpigment in his hair. The resemblance was still so great that it took people some time to distinguish between them – as long as they didn't speak.

It was this that had caused Mix to nickname Yeshua as 'Handsome.'

Now Mix grinned again. He said, 'Okay, Handsome. You handle her while I get rid of these.'

He sat down and took off his boots, then rose and crossed the deck to drop them and his cloak into a bag hanging from a shroud. When he took over the tiller, he grinned a third time.

'Don't look so grim. We're going to have some fun.'

Yeshua spoke in a deep baritone in a heavily accented English.

'Why don't we go ashore? We're far past Kramer's territory now. We can claim sanctuary.'

16

'Claiming's one thing,' Mix drawled in a baritone almost as deep. 'Getting's another.'

'You mean that these people'll be too scared of Kramer to let us take refuge with them?'

'Maybe. Maybe not. I'd just as soon not have to find out. Anyway, if we beach, so will they, and they'll skewer us before the locals can interfere.'

'We could run for the hills.'

'No. We'll give them a hard time before we take a chance on that. Get back there, help Bithniah with the ropes.'

Yeshua and the woman handled the sail while Mix began zigzagging the boat. Glances over his shoulder showed that the pursuer was following his wake. It could have continued on a straight line in the middle of the River, and so gotten ahead of Mix's craft. But its captain was afraid that one of the zigs or zags would turn out to be a straight line the end of which would terminate at the bank.

Mix gave an order to slacken the sail a little. Bithniah protested.

'They'll catch us sooner!'

Mix said, 'They think they will. Do as I say. The crew never argues with the master, and I'm the captain.'

He smiled and told her what he hoped to do. She shrugged, indicating that if they were going to be boarded, it might as well be sooner as later. It also hinted that she'd known all along that he was a little mad and this was now doubly confirmed.

Yeshua, however, said, 'I won't spill blood.'

'I know I can't count on you in a fight,' Mix said. 'But if you help handle the boat, you're indirectly contributing to bloodshed. Put that in your philosophical pipe and smoke it.'

Surprisingly, Yeshua grinned. Or perhaps his reaction wasn't so unexpected. He delighted in Mix's Americanisms, and he also liked to discuss subtleties in ethics. But he was going to be too busy to engage in an argument just now.

Mix looked back again. The fox – the chaser was the fox and he was the rabbit – was now almost on his tail. There was a gap of twenty feet between them, and two men at the bows of the double hull were poised, ready to hurl their spears. However, the rapid rise and fall of the decks beneath them would make an accurate cast very difficult.

Mix shouted to his crew – *some* crew! – and swung the tiller hard over. The prow had been pointed at an angle to the righthand bank of the River. Now it turned away suddenly, the boat leaning, the boom of the sail swinging swiftly. Mix ducked as it sang past his head. Bithniah and Yeshua clung to ropes to keep from being shot off the deck. The righthand hull lifted up, clearing the water for a few seconds.

For a moment, Mix thought the boat was going to capsize. Then it righted, and Bithniah and Yeshua were paying out the ropes. Behind him he heard shouting, but he didn't look back. Ahead was more shouting as the crews of two small one-masted fishing boats voiced their anger and fear.

Mix's vessel ran between the two boats in a lane only thirty feet wide. That closed quickly as the two converged. Their steersmen were trying to turn them away, but they had been headed inward on a collision path. Normally, they would have straightened this out, but now the stranger was between them, and its prow was angling toward the boat on the port.

Mix could see the twisted faces of the men and women on this vessel. They were anguished lest his prow crash into their starboard side near their bow. Slowly, it seemed too slowly, the prow of that boat turned. Then its boom began swinging as it was caught in the dead zone.

A woman's voice rose above the others, shrilling an almost unintelligible English at him. A man threw a spear at him, a useless and foolish action but one which would vent some of his anger. The weapon soared within a foot of Mix's head and splashed into the water on the starboard.

Mix glanced back. The pursuer had fallen into the trap.

Now, if only he could keep from being caught in his own.

His vessel slid by the boat to port, and the end of its boom almost struck the shrouds of the mast tied to the starboard edge of the deck. And then his boat was by.

Behind him, the shouting and screaming increased. The crash of wood striking wood made him smile. He looked swiftly back. The big catamaran had smashed bows first into the side of the fishing boat on his right. It had turned the much smaller single-hulled bamboo vessel around at right angles to its former course. The crew of both boats had been knocked to the deck, including the steersmen. Three of Kramer's men had gone over the side and were struggling in the water. Count them out. That left seven to deal with.

2

The rabbit became a fox; the attacked, the attacker. His craft turned as swiftly as Mix dared take it and began beating against the wind toward the two that had collided. This took some time, but Kramer's vessel was in no shape to countermaneuver. Both it and the fishing boat had stove-in hulls and were settling down slowly. Water was pouring in through the hulls. The captain of the catamaran was gesturing, his mouth open, his voice drowned by all those on his boat and the others, plus the yelling from the many other crafts. His men must have heard him, though, or interpreted his furious signs. They picked themselves up, got their weapons, and started toward the vessel they'd run into. Mix didn't understand why they were going to board it. That would be deserting a sinking ship for another, jumping from the boiling kettle into the fire. Perhaps it was just a reflex, a mindless reaction. They were angry, and they meant to take it out on the nearest available persons.

If so, they were frustrated. The two men and two women on the fisher leaped overboard and began swimming. Another boat sailed toward them to pick them up. Its sail slid down as it neared the swimmers, and men leaned over its side to extend helping hands. Two of Kramer's men, having gotten on the smaller vessel, ran to the other side and heaved spears at the people in the water.

'They must be out of their mind,' Mix muttered. 'They'll have this whole area at their throats.'

That was agreeable to him. He could leave the pursuers to the mercy of the locals. But he didn't intend to. He had a debt to pay. Unlike most debts, this would be a pleasure to discharge.

He told Yeshua to take over the tiller, and he got a war boomerang from the weapons box on the deck. It was two feet long, fashioned by sharp flint from a piece of heavy white oak. One of its ends turned at an angle of 30 degrees. A formidable weapon in the hand of a skilled thrower, it could break a man's arm even if hurled from five hundred feet away.

The weapons box contained three chert-headed axes, four more boomerangs, several oak spear shafts with flint tips, and two leather slings and two bags of sling-stones. Mix braced himself by the box, waited until his boat had drawn up alongside the enemy's on the portside, and he threw the boomerang. The up-and-down movement of the deck made calculation difficult. But the boomerang flew toward its target, the sun flashing off its whirling pale surface, and it struck a man in the neck. Despite the noise of voices, Mix faintly heard the crack as the neck broke. The man fell sidewise on the deck; the boomerang slid against the railing.

The dead man's comrades yelled and turned toward Mix.

The captain recalled the four men aboard the sinking fisher. They threw clubs and spears, and Mix and his crew dropped flat onto the deck. Some of the missiles bounced off the wood or stuck quivering in it. The nearest, a spear with a fire-hardened wooden point, landed a few inches from Yeshua's ear and slid off into the water.

Mix jumped up, braced himself, and when the starboard side of the craft rolled downward, hurled a spear. It fell short of its mark, the chest of a man, but it pierced his foot. He screamed and yanked the point loose from the deck, but he didn't have courage enough to withdraw it from his foot. He hobbled around the deck, shrilling his pain, until two men got him down and yanked the shaft out. The head was dislodged from the shaft and remained half-sticking out from the top of his foot.

Meanwhile, the second fisher, the one which Mix's boat had almost struck, had come alongside the sinking fisher. Three men leaped onto it and began securing ropes to lash the two boats together. Several rowboats and three canoes came up to the fisher, and their occupants climbed aboard it. Evidently, the locals were angry about the attack and intended to take immediate measures. Mix thought they would have been smarter to have waited until the big catamaran sank and then speared the crew members as they swam. On the other hand, by attacking Kramer's men, they were getting deeply involved. This could be the start of war. In which case, the refugees would be welcomed here.

However, a catamaran, because of its two hulls, didn't sink easily. It might even be able to get away, if not back to its homeport, at least out of this area. The locals didn't want this to happen.

The enemy captain, seeing what was coming, had ordered his men to attack. Leading them, he boarded the sinking fisher, crossed it, and hurled himself at the nearest man on the fisher. A woman whirled a sling above her head, loosed one end, and the stone smashed into the captain's solar plexus. He fell on his back, unconscious or dead.

Another of Kramer's warriors fell with a spear sticking through his arm. His comrade stumbled over him and received the point of a spear with the full weight of its wielder behind it.

The woman who'd slung the stone staggered backward with a spear sticking out of her chest and toppled into the water.

Then both sides closed, and there was a melee.

Yeshua brought the catamaran up alongside the portside of Kramer's while Bithniah and Mix let the sail down and then threw grappling hooks onto the railing. While Bithniah and Yeshua sweated to tie the two boats together, Tom Mix used his sling. He had practiced on land and water for hundreds of hours with this weapon, and so he worked smoothly with great speed and finesse. He had to wait until an enemy was separated from the crowd to prevent accidentally hitting a local. Three times he struck his target. One stone caught a man in the side of his neck. Another hit the base of a spine. The third smashed a kneecap, and the writhing man was caught and held down by some locals while a flint knife slashed his jugular.

Mix threw a spear which plunged deep into a man's thigh. Then, gripping a heavy axe, he leaped onto the catamaran and his axe rose and fell twice on the backs of heads.

The two enemy survivors tried to dive overboard. Only one made it. Mix picked up the boomerang from the deck, lifted it to throw at the bobbing head, then lowered it. Boomerangs were too hard to come by to waste on someone who was no longer dangerous.

Suddenly, except for the groaning of the wounded and the weeping of a woman, there was silence. Even the onlookers, now coming swiftly toward the scene of the battle, were voiceless. The battlers looked pale and spent. The fire was gone from them.

Mix liked to be dressed for the occasion, and this was one of victory. He returned to his boat, winked at Yeshua and Bithniah, and put on his boots and cloak. His ten-gallon hat had remained on his head throughout. He returned to the fisher, removed his hat with a flourish, grinned, and spoke.

'Tom Mix, Esquire, at your service, ladies and gentlemen. My heartfelt thanks for your help, and my apologies for any inconvenience our presence caused you.'

The captain of the rescue boat said, 'Bare bones o' God, I scarce comprehend your speech. Yet it seems to be somewhat English.'

Mix put his hat back on and rolled his eyes as if asking for help from above.

'Still in the seventeenth century! Well, at least I can understand your lingo a little bit.'

He spoke more slowly and carefully. 'What's your handle, amigo?'

'Handle? Amigo?'

'Your name, friend. And who's your boss? I'd like to offer myself as a mercenary. I need him, and I think he's going to need me.'

'John Wickel Stafford is the lord-mayor of New Albion,' a woman said. She and others were looking strangely at him and Yeshua.

He grinned and said, 'No, he's not my twin brother, or any sort of brother to me, aside from the kinship that comes from being human. And you know how thin that is. He was born about one thousand eight hundred and eighty years before me. In Palestine. Which is a hell of a long way off from my native Pennsylvania. It's only a trick of fate he resembles me so. A lucky one for him, otherwise he might not've slipped the noose Kramer'd tied around his neck.'

Apparently, some of his audience understood some of what he'd said. The trouble was not so much vocabulary, though there were some significant differences, as with the intonation and the pronunciation. Theirs somewhat resembled the speech of some Australians he'd met. God knew what they thought his was like.

'Any of you know Esperanto?' he said.

The captain said, 'We've heard of that tongue, sir. It is being taught by some of that new sect, the Church of the Second Chance, or so I understand. So far, though, none has come into this area.'

'Too bad. So we'll make do with what we have. My friends and I have had a tough time the last couple of days. We're tired and hungry. I'd like permission to stay in your spread for a few days before we go on down the River. Or maybe join up with you. Do you think your boss, uh, lord-mayor, would object?'

'Far from it, sir,' the woman said. 'He welcomes good fighting men and women in the hope they'll stay. And he rewards them well. But tell us, those men, Kramer's they must be, why were they so hot for your blood? They chased you here, yet they knew they were forbidden to come here under pain of death.'

'That's a long story, ma'am,' Mix said.

He smiled. His smile was very attractive, and he knew it. The woman was pretty, a short blonde with a buxom figure, and possibly she was unattached at the moment or thinking of being so. Certainly, there was nothing shy about her.

'You evidently are acquainted with Kramer the Hammer, Kramer the Burner. These two, Bithniah and Yeshua, were prisoners of his, ripe for the stake because they were heretics, according to his lights, and that's what counts in his land. Also they were Jewish, which made it worse. I got them loose, along with a bunch of others. We three were the only ones made it to a boat. The rest you know.'

The captain decided he might as well introduce himself.

'I am Robert Nickard. This woman is Angela Doverton. Be not deceived by her immodest manner, Master Mix. She talks boldly and without regard to her sex, unmindful of her place. She is my wife, though there is neither giving nor taking of marriage in heaven or hell.'

Angela smiled and winked at Mix. Fortunately, the eye was turned away from Nickard.

'As for this business of heretics, New Albion does not care – officially, anyway – what the religion of a man or woman be. Or indeed if he be an atheist, though how any could be after having been resurrected from the dead, I cannot understand. We welcome all as citizens, so they be hard-working and dutiful, clean and comparatively sober. We even accept Jews.'

'That must be quite a change from when you were alive,' Mix said.

Quickly, before Nickard could comment on that, he said, 'Where do we report, sir?'

Nickard gave him directions. Mix told his crew to return to their craft. They untied the ropes, retrieved the grappling hooks, hoisted sail, and departed down-River. Not, however, before Mix saw Angela Doverton slip him another wink. He had already decided to steer clear of her, desirable though she was. He didn't believe in making love to another man's mate. On the other hand, if she were to leave Nickard, which seemed likely, then...no, she seemed like a troublemaker. Still...

Behind him the business of getting the two damaged boats in to shore before they sank had begun. The lone survivor of the Kramer force had been pulled out of the water and was being taken, bound, to the shore. Mix wondered what would happen to him, not that he cared.

The woman Bithniah steered the catamaran while Yeshua took care of the ropes. Tom Mix stood in the prow, one hand on a shroud to support himself, his long white cloak flapping. He must seem a strange and dramatic figure to the locals. At least, he hoped so. Wherever he was, if he found drama lacking, he drummed up some.

3

As almost everywhere in the never-ending valley, both sides of the River were bordered with plains. These were usually from a mile to a mile and half wide. They were as unbumpy as the floor of a house but sloped gently toward the foothills. A shortbladed grass that no amount of trampling could kill covered them. Here and there were some trees.

Beyond the plains, the hills started out as mounds twenty feet high and sixty feet broad. As they neared the mountains, they became broader and higher and finally converged. The hills were thick with forest. Eighty out of every hundred were usually the indestructible 'irontrees,' deep-rooted monsters the bark of which resisted fire and shrugged off the edge of even steel axes – though very few of these existed in this metal-poor world. Beneath the trees grew long-bladed grass and bamboos – some only two feet high, some over a hundred. Unlike every other area he'd been in, this lacked ash and yew trees and so the bow and arrow were seldom seen. Most of the bows were made from the mouth of a huge fish, but apparently the people here had not caught many of these. Even the bamboo here wasn't suitable for use as bows.

Beyond the hills, the mountains soared. The lower parts were rugged with small canyons and fissures and little plateaus. At the five-thousand-foot height, the mountains became unbroken cliffs, smooth as glass. Then they climbed straight up for another five thousand feet or leaned outward near the top. They were unclimbable. If a man wished to get to the valley on the other side of them, he'd have to follow The River, and that might take him years. The Rivervalley was a world-snake, winding down from the headwaters at the North Pole and around the South Pole and back up the other hemisphere to the mouth at the North Pole.

Or so it was said. Nobody had yet proved it.

In this area, unlike some he'd been in, huge vines encircled the trees and even some of the bamboo stands. From the vines grew perennial flowers of many sizes, shapes, and exhibiting every shade of the spectrum.

For ten thousand miles the Rivervalley would be a silent, frozen explosion of color. Then, just as abruptly as it had started, the trees would resume their unadorned ascetic green.

But this stretch of The River trumpeted a flourish of hue.

A mile from the scene of the battle, Mix ordered that Bithniah steer toward the lefthand bank. Presently, Yeshua lowered the sail, and the catamaran slid its nose up onto a slope of the bank. The three got off, and many hands among the crowd grabbed the hulls and pulled it entirely on land. Men and women surrounded the newcomers and asked many questions. Mix started to answer one from a good-looking woman when he was interrupted by soldiers. These wore fish-leather bone-reinforced helmets and cuirasses, modeled after those used in the time of Charles I and Oliver Cromwell. They carried small round shields of leather-covered oak and long stone-tipped or wooden-ended spears or heavy war-axes or big clubs. Thick fish-leather boots protected their legs to just above the knees.

Their ensign, Alfred Regius Swinford, heard Mix's report halfway through. Mix interrupted himself then, saying, 'We're hungry. Couldn't we wait until we charge our buckets?'

He gestured at the nearest mushroom-shaped stone, six feet high and several feet broad. The bottoms of the gray cylinders of the bystanders were inserted in the depressions on its top.

'Buckets?' the ensign said. 'We name them copias, stranger. Short for cornucopia. Give me your copias. We'll charge them for you, and you can fill your bellies after Lord Stafford's talked to you. I'll see that they're properly identified.'

Mix shrugged. He was in no position to argue, though, like everybody else, he was uneasy if his 'holy bucket' was out of his sight. The three walked among the soldiers across the plain toward a hill. They went past many one-room bamboo huts. On top of the hill was a larger circular wall of logs. They went through the gateway into a huge yard. The Council House, their destination, was a long triangular log building in the center of the stockade. There were many observation towers and a broad walkway behind the outer walls. The sharp-pointed logs towered above this, but windows and slits for defenders to throw spears or pour out burning fish oil on attackers were plentiful. There were also wooden cranes which could be swung over the walls to dump nets full of large rocks.

Mix saw ten large wooden tanks filled with water and sheds which he supposed held stores of dried fish and acorn bread and weapons.

Out of one of the sheds, though, came men carrying baskets of earth. These would be digging a secret underground tunnel to the outside for escape or for a rear attack on the enemy. It wasn't much of a secret if they allowed strangers to see evidence of it. He felt chilled momentarily. Perhaps no stranger who knew of the tunnel would be allowed to leave.

Mix said nothing. He might as well play dumb, though he doubted that the ensign would think he was that unobservant. No. He should try something, however weak.

'Digging a well,' he said. 'That's a good idea. If you're besieged, you needn't worry about water.'

'Exactly,' Swinford said. 'We should have dug it a long time ago. But then we were shorthanded for a while.'

Mix didn't think that he'd fooled the ensign, but at least he'd tried. By then the sun had reached the peaks of the western mountain range. A moment later it sank, and the valley thundered with the eruption of the copiastones along the banks. Dinner was ready.

Stafford and his council were sitting at a round table of pine on a platform at the far end of the hall. Between this and the entrance was a long rectangular table with many bamboo chairs around it. Trap doors in the ceiling were open to let in the light, but this was fading fast. Pine torches impregnated with fish oil had already been lit and set in brackets on the walls or in stands on the dirt floor. The smoke rose toward the high blackened beams and rafters, and the stench of fish heavied the air. Underlying it was another stink – unwashed human bodies. Mix thought that there might have been an excuse for this uncleanliness in seventeenth-century England, but there was none here. The River was within comfortable walking distance. However, he knew that old habits clung hard, despite which they were changing slowly. With the constant passage of people who came from cultures which did bathe frequently, a sense of cleanliness and the shame associated with uncleanliness were spreading. In ten or fifteen years these Englishmen would be soaping regularly in The River. Well, most of them would be, anyway. There were always persons in every culture who would think that water was for drinking only.

Actually, aside from the offensiveness of body odor and the esthetics of a clean body, there was no reason why they should wash frequently. There were no diseases of the body on the Riverworld. Plenty of diseases of the mind, though.

The ensign halted below the platform and reported to Stafford. The others at the table, twenty in all, stared at the newcomers. Many smoked copia-supplied cigarettes or cigars, unknown to them in their time on Earth when pipes only were used.

Stafford rose from the table to greet his guests courteously. He was a tall man, six feet two inches, broad-shouldered, long-armed, slimly built. His face was long and narrow, his eyebrows very thick and tangled, his eyes gray, his nose long and pointed, his lips thin, his chin out-thrusting and deeply cleft. His brownish hair hung to just below his shoulders and was curled at the ends.

In a pleasant voice thick with a Northern burr – he was a

native of Carlisle, near the Scotch border – he asked them to sit at the table. He offered them their choice of wine, whiskey, or liqueur. Mix, knowing that the supply was limited, took the offer as a good sign. Stafford would not be so generous with expensive commodities to those he thought were hostiles. Mix sniffed, smiled at the scent of excellent bourbon, and sipped. He would have liked to pour it down, but this would have meant that his hosts would have to offer him another immediately.

Stafford asked Tom Mix to make his own report. This involved a long tale, during which fires were lit in the two great hearths on each side of the central part of the hall. Mix noticed that some of those bringing in the wood were short, very swarthy Mongolianish men and women. These, he supposed, were from the other side of The River, which was occupied by Huns. From what he'd heard, these had been born about the time Attila had invaded Europe, the fifth century A.D. Whether they were slaves or refugees from across The River, he could not know.

Stafford and the others listened to Mix with only a few comments while they drank. Presently, their copias were brought in, and all ate. Tom was pleasantly surprised by this evening's offering of his bucket. It was Mexican: tacos, enchiladas, burritos, a bean salad, and the liquor was tequila with a slice of lemon and some salt. It made him feel more at home, especially when the tobacco turned out to be some slim-twisted dark cigars.

Stafford didn't seem to like the liquor he got. He smelled it, then looked around. Mix interpreted his expression correctly. He said, 'Would you like to trade?'

The lord-mayor said, 'What is it you have?'

This made for an extended explanation. Stafford had lived when North America was first being colonized by the English, but he knew very little of it. Also, in his time, Mexico was an area conquered by the Spanish, and he had almost no data on it. But after listening to Mix's lengthy exposition, he handed his cup to Mix.

Tom sniffed at it and said, 'Well, I don't know what it is, but I ain't afraid of it. Here, try the tequila.'

Stafford followed the recommended procedure: the drink at once succeeded by the salt and the lemon.

'Zounds! It feels as if fire were leaping from my ears!'

He sighed and said, 'Most strange. But most pleasant and exhilarating. What about yours?'

Mix sipped. 'Ah! I don't know what the hell brand it is! But it tastes great, though it's a little gross. Whatever its origin, it's wine – of a sort. Maybe it's what the ancient Babylonians used to push. Maybe it's Egyptian, maybe it's Malayan or early Japanese saki, rice wine. Did the Aztecs have wine? I don't know, but it's powerful stuff, and it's rank yet appealing.

'Tequila is a distilled spirit gotten from the heart-sap of the century or agave plant. Well, here's to international brotherhood, no discrimination against foreign alcohol, and your good health.'

'Hear, hear!'

Having finished his supply from the copia, Stafford ordered a keg of lichen liquor in. This was composed of alcohol distilled from the green-blue lichen that grew on the mountain cliffs and then cut with water, the flavor provided by powdered dried leaves from the tree-vines. After quaffing half a cupful, Stafford said, 'I don't know why Kramer's men were so eager to kill you that they dared trespass on my waters.'

Speaking carefully and slowly, so that they could understand him easier, Mix began his story. Now and then Stafford nodded to an officer to give Mix another drink. Mix was aware that this generosity was not just based on hospitality. If Stafford got his guest drunk enough, he might, if he were a spy, say something he shouldn't. Mix, however, was a long way from having enough to make him loose-tongued. Moreover, he had nothing to hide. Well, not much.

'How far do you want me to go back in my story?'

Stafford laughed, and his slowly reddening eyes looked merry.

'For the present, omit your Earthy life. And condense it previously to your first meeting with Kramer.'

'Well, ever since All Souls' Day' – one of the names for the day on which Earthpeople had first been raised from the dead – 'I've been wandering down The River. Though I was born in 1880 A.D. in America and died in 1940, I wasn't resurrected among people of my own time and place. I found myself in an area occupied by fifteenth-century Poles. Across The River were some sort of American Indian pygmies. Until then I hadn't known that such existed, though the Cherokee Indians have legends of them. I know that because I'm part Cherokee myself.'

That was a lie, one which a movie studio had originated to glamorize him. But he'd said it so often that he half believed it. It couldn't hurt to spread it on a little.

Stafford belched, and said, 'I thought when I first saw you that you had some redskin blood in you.'

'My grandfather was a chief of the Cherokees,' Mix said. He hoped that his English, Pennsylvania Dutch, and Irish ancestors would forgive him.

'Anyway, I didn't hang around the Poles very long. I wanted to get to some place where I could understand the language. I shook the dust off my feet and took off like a stripe-assed ape.'

Stafford laughed and said, 'What droll imagery!'

'It didn't take me long to find out there weren't any horses on this world, or any animals except man, earthworms, and fish. So I built me a boat. And I started looking for folks of my own time, hoping I'd run into people I'd known. Or people who'd heard of me. I had some fame during my lifetime; millions knew about me. But I won't go into that now.

'I figured out that if people were strung along The River according to when they'd been born, though there were many exceptions, me being one, the twentieth-century people ought to be near the River's mouth. That, as I found out, wasn't necessarily so. Anyway, I had about ten men and women with me, and we sailed with the wind and the current for, let's see, close to five years. Now and then we'd stop to rest or to work on land.'

'Work?'

'As mercenaries. We picked up extra cigarettes, booze, good food. In return, we helped out people that needed helping real bad and had a good cause. Most of the men were veterans of wars on Earth and so were some of the women. I'm a graduate of Virginia Military Institute...'

Another movie prevarication.

'Virginia I've heard about,' Stafford said. 'But...'

Tom Mix had to pause in his narrative to ask just how much Stafford knew of history since his death. The Englishman replied that he'd gotten some information from a wandering Albanian who'd died in 1901 and a Persian who'd died in 1897. At least, he supposed they had those dates right. Both had been Moslems, which made it difficult to correlate their calendar with the Christian. Also, neither had known much about world history. One had mentioned that the American colonies had gained their independence after a war. He hadn't known whether or not to believe the man. It was so absurd.

'Canada remained loyal,' Mix said. 'I see I have a lot to tell you. Anyway, I fought in the Spanish-American War, the Boxer Rebellion, the Philippine Insurrection, and the Boer War. I'll explain what these were later.'

Mix had fought in none of these, but what the hell. Anyway, he would have if he'd had a chance to do so. He'd deserted the US cavalry in his second hitch because he wanted to get to the front lines and the damned brass had kept him home.

'A couple of times we were captured by slavers when we landed at some seemingly friendly place. We escaped, but the time came when I was the only one left of the original group.

33

The rest were either killed or quit because they were tired of traveling. My lovely little Egyptian, a daughter of a Pharaoh . . . well, she was killed, too.'

Actually, Miriam was the child of a Cairo shopkeeper and was born sometime in the eighteenth century. But he was a cowboy, and cowboys always embellished the truth a little. Maybe more than a little. Anyway, figuratively, she was a daughter of the Pharaohs. And what counted in this world, as in the last one, was not facts but what people believed were the facts.

He said, 'Maybe I'll run into her again someday. The others, too. They could've just as well been re-resurrected down-River as up-River.'

He paused, then said, 'It's funny. Among the millions, maybe billions of faces I've seen while sailing along, I've not seen one I knew on Earth.'

Stafford said, 'I met a philosopher who calculated that there could be at least thirty-five billion people along The River.'

Mix nodded.

'Yeah, I wouldn't be surprised. But you'd think that in five years just one . . . well, it's bound to happen someday. So, I built this last boat about five thousand miles back, a year ago. My new crew and I did pretty well until we put in at a small rocky island for a meal. We hadn't used our buckets for some time because we'd heard the people were mighty ornery in that area. But we were tired of eating fish and bamboo shoots and acorn bread from our stores. And we were out of cigarettes and the last booze we'd had had been long gone. We were aching for the good things of life. So, we took a chance on going ashore, and we lost. We were brought before the local high muckymuck, Kramer himself, a fat ugly guy from fifteenth-century Germany.

'Like a lot of nuts, and begging your pardon if there's any like him among you, he hadn't accepted the fact that this world isn't near what he thought the afterlife was going to be. He was

34

a bigshot on Earth, a priest, an inquisitor. He'd burned a hell of a lot of men, women, and children after torturing them for the greater glory of God.'

Yeshua, sitting near Mix, muttered something. Mix fell silent for a moment. He was not sure that he had not gone too far.

Although he had seen no signs of such, it was possible that Stafford and his people might just be as lunatic in their way as Kramer was in his. During their Terrestrial existence, most of the seventeenth-centurians had had a rock-fast conviction in their religious beliefs. Finding themselves here in the strange place neither heaven nor hell, they had suffered a great shock. Some of them had not yet recovered.

There were those adaptable enough to cast aside their former religion and seek the truth. But too many, like Kramer, had rationalized their environment. Kramer, for instance, maintained that this world was a purgatory. He had been shaken to find that not only Christians but all heathens were here. He had insisted that the teaching of the Church had been misunderstood on Earth. They had been deliberately perverted in their presentation by Satan-inspired priests. But he clearly saw The Truth now.

However, those who did not see the truth as he did must be shown it. Kramer's method of revelation, as on Earth, was the wheel and the fire.

When Mix had been told this, he had not argued with Kramer's theory. On the contrary, he was enthusiastic – outwardly – in offering his services. He did not fear death, because he knew that he would be resurrected twenty-four hours later elsewhere along The River. But he did not want to be stretched on the wheel and then burned.

He waited for his chance to escape.

One evening a group had been seized by Kramer as they stepped off a boat. Mix pitied the captives, for he had witnessed Kramer's means of changing a man's mind. Yet there was nothing he could do for them. If they were stupid enough to refuse to pretend that they agreed with Kramer, they must suffer.

'But this man Yeshua bothered me,' Mix said. 'In the first place, he looked too much like me. Having to see him burn would be like seeing myself in the flames. Moreover, he didn't get a chance to say yes or no. Kramer asked him if he was Jewish. Yeshua said he had been on Earth, but he now had no religion.

'Kramer said he would have given Yeshua a chance to become a convert, that is, believe as Kramer did. This was a lie, but Kramer is a mealymouthed slob who has to find justification for every rotten thing he does. He said that he gave Christians and all heathens a chance to escape the fire – except Jews. They were the ones who'd crucified Jesus, and they should all pay. Besides, a Jew couldn't be trusted. He'd lie to save his own skin.

'The whole boatload was condemned because they were all Jews. Kramer asked where they'd been headed, and Yeshua said they were looking for a place where nobody had ever heard of a Jew. Kramer said there wasn't any such place; God would find them out no matter where they went. Yeshua lost his temper and called Kramer a hypocrite and an anti-Christ. Kramer got madder than hell and told Yeshua he wasn't going to die as quickly as the others.

'About then, I almost got thrown into prison with them. Kramer had noticed how much we looked alike. He asked me if I'd lied to him when I told him I wasn't a Jew. How come I looked like a Jew if I wasn't? Of course, this was the first time he thought of me looking like a Jew, which I don't. If I was darker, I could pass for one of my Cherokee ancestors.

'So I grinned at him, although the sweat was pouring out of me so fast it was trickling down my legs, and I said that he had it backwards. Yeshua looked like a Gentile, that's why he resembled me. I used one of his own remarks to help me; I reminded him he'd said Jewish women were notoriously adulterous. So maybe Yeshua was half-Gentile and didn't know it.

'Kramer gave one of those sickening belly laughs of his; he drools until the spit runs down his chin when he's laughing. And he said I was right. But I knew my days were numbered. He'd get to thinking about my looks later, and he'd decide that I was lying. To hell with that, I thought, I'm getting out tonight.

'But I couldn't get Yeshua out of my mind. I decided that I wasn't just going to run like a cur with its tail between its legs. I was going to make Kramer so sick with my memory his pig's belly would ache like a boil every time he thought of me. That night, just as it began to rain, I killed the two guards with my axe and opened the stockade gates. But somebody was awake and gave the alarm. We ran for my boat, had to fight our way to it, and only Yeshua, Bithniah and I got away. Kramer must have given orders that the men who went after us had better not return without our heads. They weren't about to give up.'

Stafford said, 'God was good enough to give us eternal youth in this beautiful world. We are free from want, hunger, hard labor, and disease. Or should be. Yet men like Kramer want to turn this Garden of Eden into hell. Why? I do not know. One of these days, he'll be marching on us, as he has on the people to the north of his original area. If you would like to help us fight him, welcome!'

'I hate the murdering devil!' Mix said. 'I could tell you things...never mind, you must know them.'

'To my everlasting shame,' Stafford replied. 'I must confess that I witnessed many cruelties and injustices on Earth, and I not only did not protest, I encouraged them. I thought that law and order and religion, to be maintained, needed torture and persecution. Yet I was often sickened. So when I found myself in a new world, I determined to start anew. What had been right and necessary on Earth did not have to be so here.'

'You're an extraordinary man,' Mix said. 'Most people have continued to think exactly what they thought on Earth. But I think the Riverworld is slowly changing a lot of them.'

4

The food from the copias had been put on wooden plates. Mix, glancing at Yeshua, saw that he had not eaten his meat. Bithniah, catching Mix's look, laughed.

'Even though his mind has renounced the faith of his fathers, his stomach clings to the laws of Moses.'

Stafford, not understanding her heavily accented English, asked Mix to translate. Mix told him what she'd said.

Stafford said, 'But isn't she Hebrew, too?'

Mix said that she was. Bithniah understood their exchange. She spoke more slowly.

'Yes, I am a Hebrew. But I have abandoned my religion, though, to tell the truth, I was never what you would call devout. Of course, I didn't voice any doubts on Earth. I would've been killed or at least sent into exile. But when we were roaming the desert, I ate anything, clean or unclean, that would fill my belly. I made sure, though, that no one saw me. I suspect others were doing the same. Many, however, would rather starve than put an unclean thing in their mouths, and some did starve. The fools!'

She picked up a piece of ham on her plate and, grinning, offered it to Yeshua. He turned his head away with an expression of disgust.

Mix said, 'For Christ's sake, Yeshua. I've told you time and

38

again that I'll trade my steak for your ham. I don't like to see you go hungry.'

'I can't be sure that the cow was slaughtered or prepared correctly,' Yeshua said.

'There's no kosher involved. The buckets must somehow convert energy into matter. The power that the bucketstones give off is transformed by a mechanism in the false bottom of the bucket. The transformer is programmed, since there's a different meal every day.

'The scientist that explained all that to me said, though he admitted he was guessing, that there are matrices in the buckets that contain models for certain kinds of matter. They put together the atoms and molecules formed from the energy to make steaks, cigars, what have you. So, there's no slaughter, kosher or unkosher.'

'But there must have been an original cow that was killed,' Yeshua said. 'The beef which was the model for the matrix came from a beast which, presumably, lived and died on Earth. But was it slaughtered in the correct manner?'

'Maybe it was,' Mix said. 'But the meat I just ate isn't from the cow. It's a reproduction, just matter converted into energy. Properly speaking, it was made by a machine. It has no direct connection with the meat of the beast. If what that scientist said was true, some kind of recording was made of the atomic structure of the piece of beef. I've explained what recordings and atoms are to you. Anyway, the meat in our buckets is untouched by human hands. Or nonhuman, for that matter.

'So, how can it be unclean?'

'That is a question which would occupy rabbis for many centuries,' Yeshua said. 'And I suppose that even after that long a time they would still disagree. No. The safest way is not to eat it.'

'Then be a vegetarian!' Mix said, throwing his hands up. 'And go hungry!'

'Still,' Yeshua said, 'there was a man in my time, one who

was considered very wise and who, it was said, talked to God, who did not mind if his disciples sat down with dirty hands at the table if there was no water to wash them or there were mitigating circumstances. He was rebuked by the Pharisees for this, but he knew that the laws of God were made for man and not man for the laws.

'That made good sense then and it makes good sense now. Perhaps I am being overstrict, Pharasaical, more devoted to the letter than to the spirit of the law. Actually, I should pay no attention to the law regarding what is ritually clean and what unclean. I no longer believe in the law.

'But even if I should decide to eat meat, I could not put the flesh of swine in my mouth if I knew what it was. I would vomit it. My stomach has no mind, but it knows what is fit for it. It is a Hebrew stomach, and it is descended from hundreds of generations of such stomachs. The tablets of Moses lie as heavy as a mountain in it.'

'Which doesn't keep Bithniah from eating pork and bacon,' Mix said.

'Ah! That woman! She is the reincarnation of some abominable pagan!'

'You don't even believe in reincarnation,' Bithniah said, and she laughed.

Stafford had understood part of the conversation. He said, eagerly, 'Then you, Master Yeshua, lived in the time of Our Lord! Did you know him?'

'As much as I know of any man,' Yeshua said.

Everybody at the table began plying him with many questions. Stafford ordered more lichen-liquor brought in.

How long had he known Jesus?

Since his birth.

Was it true that Herod massacred the innocents?

No. Herod wouldn't have had the authority if he had wished to do so. He would have been removed by the Romans and perhaps executed. Moreover, such a deed would have caused a violent revolution. No. That tale, which he had never heard until he came to The Riverworld, was not true. It must be a folk story which had originated after Jesus was dead. Probably, though, it was based on an earlier tale about Isaac.

Then that meant that Jesus, Joseph, and Mary did not flee to Egypt?

They didn't. Why should they?

What about the angel who appeared to Mary and announced that she would give birth though she was a virgin?

How could that be when Jesus had older brothers and sisters, all fathered by Joseph and borne by Mary? Anyway, Mary, whom he knew well, had never said anything about an angel.

Mix, observing that the redness of some faces was not wholly caused by the liquor, leaned close to Yeshua.

'Careful,' he whispered. 'These guys may have decided that their religion was false, but they still don't like to hear denied what they were taught all their life was true. And a lot of them are like Kramer. They believe, even if they won't say it, that they're in a kind of purgatory. They're still going to Heaven. This is just a way station.'

Yeshua shrugged and said, 'Let them kill me. I will rise again elsewhere in a place neither worse nor better than this.'

One of the councilors, Nicholas Hyde, began banging his stone mug on the table.

'I don't believe you, Jew!' he bellowed. 'If you *are* a Jew! You are lying! What are you doing, trying to create dissension among us with these diabolical lies? Or perhaps you are the *devil?*'

Stafford put his hand on Hyde's arm. 'Restrain yourself, dear sir. Your accusations make no sense. Just the other day I heard you say that God was nowhere on The River. If He isn't here, then Satan is also absent. Or is it easier to believe in Old Nick than in the Creator? This man is here as our guest, and as long as he is such, we will treat him courteously.'

He turned to Yeshua. 'Pray continue.'

The questions were many and swift. Finally, Stafford said, 'It's getting late. Our guests have gone through much today, and we have much work tomorrow. I'll allow one more.'

He looked at a tall distinguished-looking youth who'd been introduced as William Grey.

'Milord, care you to put it?'

Grey stood up somewhat unsteadily.

'Thank you, my lord-mayor. Now, Master Yeshua, were you present when Christ was crucified? And did you see him when he had risen? Or talk to someone reliable who had seen him, perhaps on the road to Emmaus?'

'That is more than one question,' Stafford said. 'But I'll allow it.'

Yeshua was silent for a moment. When he spoke, he did so even more slowly.

'Yes, I was present when he was crucified and when he died. As for events after that, I will testify only to one thing. That is, he did not rise from the dead on Earth. I have no doubt that he rose here, though.'

A clamor burst out, Hyde's voice rising above the others and demanding that the lying Jew be thrown out.

Stafford stood up, banging a gavel on the table, and cried, 'Please, silence, gentlemen! There will be no more questions.'

He gave orders to a Sergeant Channing to conduct the three to their quarters. Then he said, 'Master Mix, I will speak with you three in the morning. God gives you a pleasant sleep.'

Mix, Yeshua, and Bithniah followed the sergeant, who held a torch, though it was not needed. The night sky, blazing with giant star clusters and luminous gasclouds, cast a brighter light than Earth's full moon. The River sparkled. Mix asked the soldier if they could bathe before retiring. Channing said that they could do so if they hurried. The three walked into the water with their kilt-towels on. When with people who bathed nude, Mix did so also. When with the more modest, he observed their proprieties.

Using soap provided by the copias, they washed the grime and sweat off. Mix watched Bithniah. She was short and dark, full-bosomed, narrow-waisted, and shapely-legged. Her hips, however, were too broad for his tastes, though he was willing to overlook this imperfection. Especially now, when he was full of liquor. She had long, thick, glossy blue-black hair and a pretty face, if you liked long noses, which he did. His fourth wife, Vicky Forde, had had one, and he'd loved her more than any other woman. Bithniah's eyes were huge and dark, and even during the flight they had given Mix some curious glances. He told himself that Yeshua had better watch her closely. She radiated the heat of a female alleycat in mating season.

Yeshua now, he was something different. The only resemblance he had to Mix was physical. He was quiet and withdrawn, except for that one outburst against Kramer, and he seemed to be always thinking of something far away. Despite his silence, he gave the impression of great authority – rather, of a man who had once had it but was now deliberately suppressing it.

Channing said, 'You're clean enough. Come on out.'

'You know,' Mix said to Yeshua, 'shortly before I came to Kramer's territory, something puzzling happened to me. A little dark man rushed at me crying out in a foreign tongue. He tried to embrace me; he was weeping and moaning, and he kept repeating a name over and over. I had a hell of a time convincing him he'd made a mistake. Maybe I didn't. He tried to get me to take him along, but I didn't want anything to do with him. He made me nervous, the way he kept on staring at me.

'I forgot about him until just now. I'll bet he thought I was you. Come to think of it, he did say your name quite a few times.'

Yeshua came out of his absorption. 'Did he say what his name was?'

'I don't know. He tried four or five different languages on

43

me, including English, and I couldn't understand him in any of them. But he did repeat a word more than once. Mattithayah. Mean anything to you?'

Yeshua did not reply. He shivered and draped a long towel over his shoulders. Mix knew that something inside Yeshua was chilling him. The heat of the daytime, which reached an estimated 80 F. at high noon (there were no thermometers), faded away slowly. The high humidity of the valley (in this area, anyway) retained the heat until the invariable rains fell a few hours after midnight. Then the temperature dropped swiftly to an estimated 65 F. and stayed there until dawn.

Channing led them to their residences. These were two small square one-room bamboo huts, the roofs thatched with the huge leaves of the irontree. Inside each was a table, several chairs, and a low bed, all of bamboo. There were also wooden towel racks and a rack for spears and other weapons. A baked-clay nightjar stood in one corner. The floor was a slightly raised bamboo platform. Real class. Most huts had bare earth floors.

Yeshua and Bithniah went into one hut; Mix, into the other. Channing started to say good night, but Mix asked him if he minded talking a little while. To bribe the sergeant, he gave him a cigar from his grail. At one time on Earth Mix had smoked, but he had given up the habit to preserve his image as a 'cleancut' hero for his vast audiences of young movie-goers. Here, he alternated between long stretches of indulgences or abstinences. For the past year, he had laid off tobacco. But he thought it might make the sergeant chummier if he smoked with him. He lit up a cigarette, coughed, and became dizzy for a moment. The tobacco certainly tasted good, though.

Micah Shepstone Channing was a short, muscular, and heavy-boned redhead. He'd been born in 1621 in the village of Havant, Hampshire, where he became a parchment maker. When the civil war broke out, he'd joined the forces against Charles I. Badly wounded at the battle of Naseby, he returned home, resumed his trade, married, had eight children of whom

44

four survived to adulthood, and died of a fever in 1687.

Mix asked him a number of questions. Though his interest was mainly to establish a friendly feeling, he was curious about the man. He liked people in general.

He then went on to other matters, the personalities of the important men of New Albion, the setup of the government, and the relations with neighboring states, especially Kramer's Deusvolens, which the Albions pronounced as Doocevolenz.

During the English Civil War, Stafford had served under the Earl of Manchester. But, losing a hand from an infected wound, he went to live in Sussex and became a beekeeper. In time he became quite prosperous and branched out from honey to general merchandising. Later, he specialized in naval provisions. In 1679 he died during a storm off Dover. He was, Channing said, a good man, a born leader, quite tolerant, and had from the first been instrumental in establishing this state.

'Twas he who suggested that we do away with titles of nobility or royalty and elect our leaders. He's now serving his second term as lord-mayor.'

'Are women allowed to vote?' Mix said.

'They weren't at first, but last year they insisted they get their rights, and after some agitation, they got them. There's no holding them,' Channing said, looking somewhat sour. 'They can pick up any time they want and leave, since there's little property involved and no children to take care of and blessed little housework or cooking to do. They've become mighty independent.'

Anglia, on the south border of New Albion, had a similar system of government, but its elected chief was titled the sheriff. Ormondia, to the north, was inhabited chiefly by those royalists who'd been faithful to Charles I and Charles II during the troubles. They were ruled by James Butler, first Duke of Ormonde, lord-lieutenant of Ireland under Charles I and Charles II, and chancellor of Oxford University.

'It's *milord* and *your grace* in Ormondia,' Channing said.

'Ye'd think that England had been transplanted from old Earth to The River. Despite which, the titles are mainly honorary, ye might say, since all but the duke are elected, and their council has in it more men born poor but honest and deserving than nobles. What's more, when their women found out ours was getting the vote, they set up a howl and there was nothing His Grace could do but swallow the bitter pill and smile like he was enjoying it.'

Though relations between the two tiny states had never been cordial, they were united against Kramer. The main trouble was that their joint military staffs didn't get along too well. The duke didn't like the idea of having to consult the lord-mayor or deferring to him in any way.

'Far as that goes, I don't like it either,' Channing said. 'There should be one supreme general during a war. This is a case where two heads be not better than one.'

The Huns across The River had caused much trouble in the early years, but for some time now they'd been friendly. Actually, only about one-fourth of them were Huns, according to Channing. They'd fought among themselves for so long they'd killed off each other. These had been replaced by people from other places along The River. They spoke a Hunnish pidgin with words from other languages making up a fourth of the vocabulary. The state directly across from New Albion was at the moment ruled by a Sikh, Govind Singh, a very strong military leader.

'As I said,' Channing said, 'for three hundred miles along here on this side the people resurrected were mainly British of the 1600's. But there's some ten-mile stretches where they aren't. Thirty miles down are some thirteenth-century Cipangese, fierce little slant-eyed yellow bastards. And there's Doocevolenz, which is fourteenth-century and half-German and half-Spanish.'

Mix thanked him for the information and then said that he had to turn in. Channing bade him a good night.

5

Mix fell asleep at once. Sometime during the night he dreamed that he was making love to Victoria Forde, his fourth wife, the one woman whom he still loved. Drums and blarings from many fish-bone horns woke him up. He opened his eyes. It was still dark, but its paleness indicated that the sun would soon come up over the mountains. He could see through the open window the graying sky and fast-fading stars and gas clouds.

He closed his eyes and drew the edge of the double blanket-length towels over his head. Oh, for a little more sleep! But a lifetime of discipline as a cowboy, a movie actor, and a circus star on Earth, and as a mercenary on this world, got him out of bed. Shivering in the cold, he put on a towel-kilt and splashed icy water from a shallow fired-clay basin onto his face. Then he removed the kilt to wash his loins. His dream-Vicky had been as good in bed as the real Vicky.

He ran his hand over his jaw and cheeks. It was a habit he'd never overcome despite the fact that he did not have to shave and never would. All men had been resurrected permanently beardless. Tom didn't know why. Maybe whoever had done it didn't like facial hair. If so, they had no distaste for pubic or armpit hairs. But they had also made sure that hair didn't grow in the ears and nose hairs only grew to a certain length.

The unknowns responsible for the Riverworld had also made certain adjustments in the faces and bodies of some. Women who'd had huge breasts on Earth had wakened from death here to find that their mammaries had been reduced in size. Women with very small breasts had been given 'normal'-sized breasts. And no woman had sagging breasts.

Not all were delighted. By no means. There were those who'd liked what they had had. And of course there had been societies in which huge dangling breasts were much admired and others in which the size and shape of the female breast meant nothing at all in terms of beauty or sex. They were just there to provide milk for the babies.

Men with very small penises on Earth here had penises which would not cause ridicule or shame. Mix had never heard any complaints about this. But a man who'd secretly yearned on Earth to be a woman had once, while drunk, poured his grievances into Mix's ear. Why couldn't the mysterious beings who'd corrected so many physical faults have given him a female body?

'Why didn't you tell them what you wanted?' Mix had said and he'd laughed. Of course, the man couldn't have informed the Whoevers. He'd died, and then awakened on the banks of The River, and in between he'd been dead.

The man had hit Tom in the eye then and given him a black whopper. Tom had had to knock him out to prevent further injury to himself.

Other deficiencies or deviations from the 'normal' had also been corrected. Tom had once met a very handsome, perhaps too handsome Englishman – eighteenth century – who'd been a nobleman. From the groin upward, he'd been perfect, but his legs had been only a foot and a half long. Now he stood six feet two inches high. No complaints from him. But his grotesqueness on Earth had seemingly twisted his character. Though now a beautiful man in body, he was still embittered, savagely cynical, insulting, and, though he was a great 'lover,' hated women.

Tom had had a run-in with him, too, and broken the limey's nose. After they'd recovered from their injuries, they became friends. Strangely, now that the Englishman's handsomeness was ruined by the flat and askew nose, he'd become a better person. Much of his hatefulness had disappeared.

It was often hard to figure out human beings.

While Tom had been drying himself, he'd been thinking about what the Whoevers had done in the physical area to people. Now he wrapped himself in a cloak made of long towels held together with magnetic tabs inside the cloth, and he picked up a roll of toilet paper. This, too, had been provided by the copias, though there were societies who didn't use it for the intended purpose. He left the hut and walked toward the nearest latrine. This was a ditch over which was a long bamboo hut. It had two entrances. On the horizontal plank above each, a crude figure of a man, full-face, had been incised. The women's crapper was about twenty yards distant from it, and over its entrances crude profiles of women had been cut into the wood.

If the custom of daily bathing was not yet widespread in this area, other sanitation was enforced. Sergeant Channing had informed Mix that no one was allowed to crap just anywhere he or she pleased. (He did not use the word 'crap,' however, since this had been unknown in the seventeenth century.) Unless there were mitigating circumstances, a person caught defecating outside the public toilets was exiled – after his or her face had been rubbed in the excrement.

Urinating in public was lawful under certain situations, but the urinator must take care to be unobserved if the opposite sex was present.

'But it's a custom more honored in the breach than in the observance,' Channing had said, quoting Shakespeare without knowing it. (He'd never heard of the Bard of Avon.) 'In the wild lawless time just after the resurrection, people became rather shameless. There was little modesty then, and people, if you'll pardon the phrase, just didn't give a shit. Haw, haw!'

At regular intervals, the latrine deposits were hauled up to the mountains and dropped into a deep and appropriately named canyon.

'But some day it's going to be so high that the wind'll bring the stink down to us. I don't know what we'll do then. Throw it into The River and let the fish eat it, I suppose. That's what those disgusting Huns across The River do.'

'Well,' Mix had drawled, 'that seems to me the sensible way to do it. The turds don't last long. The fish clean them up right away, almost before the stuff hits the water.'

'Yes, but then we catch the fish and eat them!'

'It don't affect their taste any,' Mix had said. 'Listen, you said you lived on a farm for a couple of years, didn't you? Well, then you know that chickens and hogs eat cow and horse flop if they get a chance, and they often do. That didn't affect their taste when they were on the table, did it?'

Channing had grimaced. 'It don't seem the same. Anyway, hogs and chickens eat cow manure, and there's a big difference between that and human ordure.'

Mix had said, 'I wouldn't really know. I never ate either.'

He paused. 'Say, I got an idea. You know the big earthworms eat human stuff. Why don't you people drag them out of the ground and throw them into the shit pit? They'd get rid of the crap, and the worms'd be as happy as an Irishman with a free bottle of whiskey.'

Channing had been amazed. 'That's a splendid idea! I wonder why none of us thought of it?'

He'd then complimented Mix on his intelligence. Mix hadn't told him that he'd been through many areas in which his 'new' idea was a long-standing practice.

These places, like this one, had been lacking in sulfur. Otherwise, they would have processed nitrate crystals from the excrement and mixed it with charcoal and sulfur to make gunpowder. The explosive was then put into bamboo cases to be used as bombs or warheads for rockets.

Mix went into the latrine shed and sat down on one of the twelve holes. During the short time he was there, he picked up some gossip, mostly about the affair one of the councilmen was having with a major's woman. He also heard a dirty joke he'd never heard before, and he'd thought he'd heard them all on Earth. After washing his hands in a trough connected to a nearby stream, he hastened back to his hut. He picked up his grail and walked forty yards to Yeshua's hut. He'd intended to knock on the door and invite the couple to go with him to the nearest charging stone. But he halted a few paces from the door.

Yeshua and Bithniah were arguing loudly in heavily accented English of the seventeenth century. Mix wondered why they weren't using Hebrew. Later, he would find out that English was the only language they had in common, though they could carry on a very limited conversation in sixteenth-century Andalusian Spanish and fourteenth-century High German. Though Bithniah's native tongue was Hebrew, it was at least twelve hundred years older than Yeshua's. Its grammar was, from Yeshua's viewpoint, archaic, and its vocabulary was loaded with Egyptian loanwords and Hebrew items which had dropped out of the speech long before he was born.

Moreover, though born in Palestine of devout Jewish parents, Yeshua's native tongue was Aramaic. He knew Hebrew mainly as a liturgical tool, though he could read the Torah, the first five books of the Old Testament, with some difficulty.

As it was, Mix had some difficulty in understanding half of what they said. Not only did their Hebrew and Aramaic pronunciations distort their words, they had learned their English in an area occupied by seventeenth-century Yorkshire people, and that accent further bent their speech. But Mix could fill in what he didn't grasp. Usually.

'I'll not go with you to live in the mountains!' Bithniah was shouting. 'I don't want to be alone! I hate being alone! I have to have many people around me! I don't want to sit on top of a rock with no one but a walking tomb to talk to! I won't go! I won't go!'

'You're exaggerating, as usual,' Yeshua said loudly but much more quietly than Bithniah. 'In the first place, you will have to go down to the nearest foothill copiastone three times a day. And you may go down to the bank and talk whenever you feel like it. Also, I don't plan to live up there all the time. Now and then I'll go down to work, probably as a carpenter, but I don't . . .'

Mix couldn't understand the rest of what the man said even though he spoke almost as loudly as before. He had no trouble comprehending most of Bithniah's words, however.

'I don't know why I stay with you! Certainly it's not because no one else wants me! I've had plenty of offers, let me tell you! And I've been tempted, very tempted, to accept some!

'I do know why you want me around! It's certainly not because you're in love with my intelligence or my body! If it were, you'd delight in them, you'd be talking to me more and have me on my back far more than you do!

'The only reason you stick with me is that you know that I knew Aharon and Mosheh, and I was with the tribes when we left Egypt and when we invaded Canaan! Your only interest in me is to drain me of all I know about your great and holy hero, Mosheh!'

Mix's ears figuratively stood up. Well, well! Here was a man who'd known Christ, or at least claimed to, living with a woman who'd known Aaron and Moses, or at least claimed to. One or both of them, however, could be liars. There were so many along The River. He ought to know. It took one to recognize one, though his lies were mainly just harmless prevarications.

Bithniah screamed, 'Let me tell you, Yeshua, Mosheh was a louse! He was always preaching against adultery and against lying with heathen women, but I happen to know what he practiced! Why, he even married one, a Kushi from Midian! And he tried to keep his son from being circumcised!'

'I've heard all that many times before,' Yeshua said.

'But you don't really believe I'm telling the truth, do you? You can't accept that what you believed so devoutly all your life is a bunch of lies! Why should I lie? What would I gain by that?'

'You like to torture me, woman.'

'Oh, I don't have to lie to do that. There are plenty of other ways! Anyway, it's true that Mosheh not only had many wives, he would take other men's women if he got a chance! I should know; I was one of them. But he was a real man, a bull! Not like you! You can only become a real man when you've taken dreamgum and are out of your mind! What kind of a man is that, I ask you?'

'Peace, woman,' Yeshua said softly.

'Then don't call me a liar!'

'I have never done that.'

'You don't have to! I can see in your eyes, hear in your voice, that you don't believe me!'

'No. Though there are times – most of the time, in fact – when I wish I'd never heard your tales. But great is the truth, no matter how much it hurts.'

He continued in Hebrew or Aramaic. The tone of his voice indicated that he was quoting something.

'Stick to English!' Bithniah screamed. 'I got so disgusted with the so-called holy men always quoting moral proverbs, and all the time their own sins stank like a sick camel! You sound like them! And you even claim to have been a holy man! Perchance you were! But I think that your devoutness ruined you! I wouldn't know, though! You've never actually told me much about your life! I found out more about you when you were talking to the councilmen than you've ever told me!'

Yeshua's voice, which had been getting lower, suddenly became so soft that Mix couldn't make out a word of it. He glanced at the eastern mountains. A few minutes more, and the sun would clear the peaks. Then the stones would give up their thundering, blazing energy. If they didn't hurry, they'd have to go breakfastless. That is, unless they ate dried fish and acorn bread, the thought of which made him slightly nauseated.

He knocked loudly on the door. The two within fell silent. Bithniah swung the door open violently, but she managed to smile at him as if nothing had occurred.

'Yes, I know. We'll be with you at once.'

'Not I,' Yeshua said. 'I don't feel hungry now.'

'That's right!' Bithniah said loudly. 'Try to make me feel guilty, blame your upset stomach on me. Well, I'm hungry, and I'm going to eat, and you can sit here and sulk for all I care!'

'No matter what you say, I am going to live in the mountains.'

'Go ahead! You must have something to hide! Who's after you? Who are you that you're so afraid of meeting people? Well, *I* have nothing to hide!'

Bithniah picked up her copia by the handle and stormed out. Mix walked along with her and tried to make pleasant conversation. But she was too angry to cooperate. As it was, they had just come into sight of the nearest mushroom-shaped rock, located between two hills, when blue flames soared up from the top and a roar like a colossal lion's came to them. Bithniah stopped and burst into her native language. Obviously she was cursing. Mix contented himself with one short word.

After she'd quieted down, she said, 'Got a smoke?'

'In my hut. But you'll have to pay me back later. I usually trade my cigarettes for liquor.'

'Cigarettes? That's your word for pipekins?'

He nodded, and they returned to his hut. Yeshua was not in sight. Mix purposely left his door open. He trusted neither Bithniah nor himself.

Bithniah glanced at the door.

'You must think me a fool. Right next door to Yeshua!'

Mix grinned.

'You never lived in Hollywood!'

He gave her a cigarette. She used the lighter that the copia had furnished; a thin metallic box which extended a whitely glowing wire when pressed on the side.

'You must have overheard us,' she said. 'Both of us were shouting our fool heads off. He's a very difficult man. Sometimes he frightens me, and I don't scare easily. There's something very deep – and very different, almost alien, maybe unhuman, about him. Not that he isn't very kind or doesn't understand people. He does, too much so.

'But he seems so aloof most of the time. Sometimes, he laughs very much, and he makes me laugh, for he has a wonderful sense of humor. Other times, though, he delivers harsh judgments, so harsh they hurt me because I know that I'm included in the indictment. Now, I don't have any illusions about men or women. I know what they are and what to expect. But I accept this. People are people, although they often pretend to be better than they are. But expect the worst, I say, and you now and then get a pleasant surprise because you don't get the worst.'

'That's pretty much my attitude,' Mix said. 'Even horses aren't predictable, and men are much more complicated. So you can't always tell what a horse or a man's going to do or what's driving him. One thing you can bet on. You're Number One to yourself, but to the other guy, Number One is himself or herself. If somebody acts like you're Number One, and she's sacrificing herself for you, she's just fooling herself.'

'You sound as if you'd had some trouble with your wife.'

'Wives. That, by the way, is one of the things I like about this world. You don't have to go through any courts or pay any alimony when you split up. You just pick up your bucket, towels, and weapons, and take off. No property settlements, no in-laws, no kids to worry about.'

'I bore twelve children,' she said. 'All but six died before they were two years old. Thank God, I don't have to go through that here.'

'Whoever sterilized us knew what he was doing,' Mix said. 'If we could have kids, this valley'd be jammed tight as a pig-trough at feeding time.'

He moved close to her and grinned.

'Anyway, we men still have our guns, even if they're loaded with blanks.'

'You can stop where you are,' she said, although she was still smiling. 'Even if I leave Yeshua, I may not want you. You look too much like him.'

'I might show you the difference,' he said.

But he moved away from her and picked up a piece of dried fish from his leather bag. Between bites, he asked her about Mosheh.

'Would you get angry or beat me if I told you the truth?' she said.

'No, why should I?'

'Because I've learned to keep my mouth shut about my Earthly life. The first time I told about it, that was less than a year after the Day of the Great Shout, I was badly beaten and thrown into The River. The people who did it were outraged, though I don't know why they should have been. They knew that their religion was false. They had to know that the moment they rose from the dead on this world. But I was lucky not to have been tortured and then burned alive.'

'I'd like to hear the real story of the exodus,' he said. 'It won't bother me that it's not what I learned in Sunday school.'

'You promise not to tell anybody else?'

'Cross my heart and hope to fall off Tony.'

6

She looked blank.

'Is that an oath?'

'As good as any.'

She was, she said, born in the land of Goshen, which was in the land of Mizraim, that is, Egypt. Her tribe was that of Levi, and it had come with other tribes of Eber into Mizraim some four hundred years before.

Famine in their own land had driven them there. Besides, Yoseph – in English, Joseph – had invited them to come. He was the vizier of the Pharaoh of Egypt and so was able to get the tribes into the land of plenty just east of the great delta of the Nile.

Mix said, 'You mean, the story of Joseph is true? He *was* sold into slavery by his brothers, and he *did* become the Pharaoh's righthand man?'

Bithniah smiled and said, 'You must remember that all that happened four hundred years before I was born. It may or may not have been true, but that was the story I was told.'

'It's hard for me to believe that a Pharaoh would make a nomadic Hebrew his chief minister. Why wouldn't he choose an Egyptian, a civilized man who'd know all the complicated problems of administering a great nation?'

'I don't know. But the Pharaoh of lower Egypt then, when my ancestors came into Egypt, was not an Egyptian. He was a foreigner, one of those invaders from the deserts whom the English call the shepherd-kings. They spoke a language much like Hebrew, or so I was told. He would have regarded Joseph as more or less a cousin. One of a kindred people, anyway, and more to be trusted than a native Egyptian. Still, I don't know if the story is true, since I did not see Joseph with my own eyes, of course. But while my people were in Goshen, the people of upper Egypt conquered the shepherd-kings and set up one of their own as Pharaoh of all Egypt.'

That, said, Bithniah, was when the lot of the sons of Eber and of Jacob began to worsen. They had entered Mizraim as free men, working under contract, but then they became slaves, in effect if not officially.

'Still, it was not so bad until the great Raamses became Pharaoh. He was a mighty warrior and a builder of forts and cities, and the Hebrews were among the many people set to build these.'

'Was this Raamses the first or the second?' Mix said.

'I don't know. The Pharaoh before him was named Seti.'

'He would have been Raamses II,' Mix said. 'So *he* was the Pharaoh of the Oppression! And was the man who succeeded him named Merneptah?'

'You pronounce his name strangely, but, yes, it was.'

'The Pharaoh of the exodus.'

'Yes, the going-forth. We were able to escape our bondage because Mizraim was in turmoil then. The people of the seas, as the English call them, and as they were called in my time, invaded. They were, I hear, beaten back, but during the time of troubles we took the opportunity to flee Mizraim.'

'Moses, I mean Mosheh, didn't go to the Pharaoh and demand that his people be allowed to go free?'

'He wouldn't have dared. He would have been tortured and then executed. And many of us would have been slain as an example.'

'You've heard of the plagues visited upon the Egyptians by God because of Moses' requests? The Nile turning to blood, the plague of frogs, the slaying of the firstborn male children of all the Egyptians and the marking with blood of the doorposts of the Hebrews so that their sons might be spared?'

She laughed and said, 'Not until I came to this world. There was a plague raging throughout the land, but it killed Hebrew as well as Egyptian. My two brothers and a sister died of it, and I was sick with it, but I survived.'

Mix questioned her about the religion of the tribes. She said that there was a mixture of religions in the tribes. Her mother had worshipped, among others, El, the chief god that the Hebrews had brought with them when they had entered the land of Goshen. Her father had favored the gods of Egypt, especially Ra. But he had participated in offering sacrifices to El, though these were few. He couldn't afford to pay for many.

She had known Mosheh since she was very young. He was a wild kid (her own words), half-Hebrew, half-Mizraimite. The mixture was nothing unusual. The women slaves were often raped by their masters or gave themselves willingly to get more food and creature comforts. Or sometimes just because they liked to have sexual intercourse. There was even some doubt about whether or not one of her sisters had a Hebrew or an Egyptian father.

There was also some doubt about the identity of Mosheh's father.

'When Mosheh was ten years old he was adopted by an Egyptian priest who'd lost his two sons to a plague. Why would the priest have adopted Mosheh instead of an Egyptian boy unless the priest was Mosheh's father? Mosheh's mother had worked for the priest for a while.'

When Mosheh was fifteen, he had returned to the Hebrews and was once again a slave. The story was that his fosterfather had been executed because he was secretly practicing the forbidden religion of Aton, founded by the accursed Pharaoh Akhenaton. But Bithniah suspected that it was because Mosheh was suspected by his father of lying with one of his concubines.

'Didn't he have to flee to Midian later on when he killed an Egyptian overseer of slaves? He is supposed to have murdered the man when he caught him maltreating a Hebrew slave.'

Bithniah laughed.

'The truth is probably that the Egyptian caught him with his wife, and Mosheh was forced to kill him to keep from being killed. But he did escape to Midian. Or so he said when he returned some years later under a false name.'

'Moses must have been horny as hell,' Mix said.

'The kid grows up to be a goat.'

On returning with his Midianite wife, Mosheh announced that the sons of Eber had been adopted by a god. This god was Yahweh. The announcement came as a surprise to the Hebrews, most of whom had never heard of Yahweh until then. But Yahweh had spoken from a burning bush to

Mosheh, and Mosheh had been charged to lead his people from bondage. He was inspiring and spoke with great authority, he seemed truly to burn as brightly with the light of Yahweh as the burning bush he described.

'What about the parting of the Red Sea and the drowning of Pharaoh and his soldiers when they pursued you Hebrews?'

'Those Hebrews who lived long after we did and wrote those books I've been told about were liars. Or perchance they weren't liars but just believed tales that had been told for many centuries.'

'What about the golden calf?'

'You mean the statue of the god that Mosheh's brother Aharon made while Mosheh was on the mountain talking to Yahweh? It was a calf, the Mizraimite god Hapi as a calf. But it wasn't made of gold. It was made of clay. Where would we get gold in that desert?'

'I thought you slaves carried off a lot of loot when you left?'

'We were lucky to have our clothes and our weapons. We left in a hurry, and we didn't want to be burdened down any more than we could help, if the soldiers came after us. Fortunately, the garrisons were undermanned at that time. Many soldiers had been called to the coast to fight against the people of the sea.'

'Moses did make the tablets of stone?'

'Yes. But there weren't ten commandments on them. And they were in Egyptian sign-writing. I couldn't read them; three-fourths of us couldn't. Anyway, there wasn't room on the tablets to write out ten commandments in Egyptian signs. And the writing didn't last long. The paint was poor, and the hot winds and the sand soon flaked the paint off.'

7

Mix wanted to keep on questioning her, but a soldier knocked on the doorpost. He said that Stafford wanted to see the three at once. Mix called Yeshua out of his hut, and they followed the soldier to the council hall. Nobody said a word all the way.

Stafford said good morning and asked them if they intended to stay in New Albion.

The three said that they would like to be citizens.

Stafford said, 'Very well. But you have to realize that a citizen owes the state certain duties in return for its protection. I'll enumerate these later. Now, what position in the army or navy are you particularly fitted for? If any?'

Mix had already told him what his skills were, but he repeated them. The lord-mayor told him that he would have to start as a private, though his experience qualified him to be a commissioned officer.

'I apologize for this, but it is our policy to start all newcomers at the botttom of the ranks. This prevents unhappiness and jealousy among those who've been here for a long time. However, since you have stone weapons of your own, and these are scarce in this area, I can assign you to the axeman squad. Axemen are treated as elite, as something special. After a few months, you may be promoted to sergeant if you do well, and I'm sure you will.'

'That suits me fine,' Tom said. 'But I can also make boomerangs and instruct your people in throwing them.'

Stafford said 'Hmm!' and drummed his fingers on the desk for a moment.

'Since that'll make you a specialist, you deserve to be sergeant immediately. But when you're with the axe squad, you'll still have to take orders from the corporals and sergeants. Let's see. It's an awkward situation. But...I can make you a nonactive sergeant when you're in the squad and an active sergeant when you're in the capacity of boomerang instructor.'

'That's a new one on me,' Mix said grinning. 'Okay.'

'What?' Stafford said.

'Okay means "all right." It's agreeable with me.'

'Oh! Very well. Now, Yeshua, what would you like to do?'

Yeshua said that he had been a carpenter on Earth and had also done considerable work in this field here. In addition, he had learned how to flake stone. Moreover, he had a small supply of flint and chert. The boat they'd fled in happened to have a leather bag full of unworked stone brought down from a distant area.

'Good!' Stafford said. 'You can start by working with Mr Mix. You can help him make boomerangs.'

'I'm sorry,' Yeshua said. 'I can't do that.'

Stafford's eyes widened. 'Why not?'

'I am under a vow not to shed the blood of any human being nor to take part in any acitivity which results in the shedding of blood.'

'But what about when you were running away? Didn't you fight then?'

'No, I did not.'

'You mean that if you'd been captured you would not have defended yourself? You'd have just stood there and allowed yourself to be slain?'

'I would.'

Stafford drummed his fingers again while his skin became slowly red. Then he said, 'I know little of this Church of the Second Chance, but I have heard some reports that its members refuse to fight. Are you one of them?'

Yeshua shook his head.

'No. My vow is a private one.'

'There isn't any such thing,' Stafford said. 'Once you've told others of your vow, it becomes a public thing. What you mean is that you made this vow to your god.'

'I don't believe in gods or a God,' Yeshua said in a low but firm voice. 'Once I did believe, and I believed very strongly. In fact, it was more than a belief. It was knowledge. I *knew*. But I was wrong.

'Now I believe only in myself. Not because I know myself. No man really knows anything, including himself, or perhaps I should say that no man knows much. But I do know this. That I can make a vow to myself which I will keep.'

Stafford gripped the edge of his desk as if he were testing its reality.

'If you don't believe in God, then why make such a vow? What do you care if you shed blood while defending yourself? It would only be natural. And where there is no God, there is no sin. A man may do what he wants to do, no matter how he harms others, and it is right because all things are right or all things are wrong if there is no Upper Law. Human laws do not matter.'

'The vow is the only true thing in the world.'

Bithniah laughed and said, 'He's crazy! You won't get any sense out of him! I think that he refuses to kill to keep from being killed because he wants to be killed! He would like to die, but he doesn't have guts enough to commit suicide! Besides, what good would it do! He'd only be resurrected some other place!'

'Which,' Stafford said, 'makes your vow meaningless. You can't really kill anybody here. You can put out a person's breath, and he will become a corpse. But twenty-four hours later, he will be a new body, a whole body, though he had been cut into a thousand pieces.'

Yeshua shrugged. 'That doesn't matter. Not to me, anyway. I have made my vow, and I will not break it.'

'Crazy!' Bithniah said.

'You're not intending to start a new religion, are you?' Mix said.

Yeshua looked at Mix as if he were stupid.

'I just said that I don't believe in God.'

Stafford sighed. 'I don't have time to dispute theology or philosophy with you. This issue is easily disposed of, however. You can leave our state at once, and I mean this very minute. Or you can stay here but as an undercitizen. There are ten such living in New Albion now. They, like you, won't fight, though for different reasons from yours. But they have their duties, their work, just like all citizens. They do not, however, get any of the bonuses given to citizens every three months by the state, the extra cigarettes, liquor, and food. They are required to contribute a certain amount from their copias to the state treasury. And they must work extra shifts as latrine-cleaners. Also, in case of war, they will be kept in a stockade until the war is over. This is so they will not get in the way of the military. Another reason for this is that we can't be sure of their loyalty.'

'I agree to this,' Yeshua said. 'I will build you fishing boats and houses and anything else that is required as long as they are not directly connected with the making of war.'

'That isn't always easy to discern,' Stafford said. 'But, never mind, we can use you.'

After they were dismissed and had gone outside, Bithniah stopped Yeshua.

Glaring, she said, 'Goodbye, Yeshua. I'm leaving you. I can't endure your insanity any longer.'

Yeshua looked even sadder. 'I won't argue with you. It will be best if we do separate. I was making you unhappy, and it is not good to thrust one's unhappiness upon another.'

'No, you're wrong about that,' she said. Tears trickled down her cheeks. 'I don't mind sharing unhappiness if I can help relieve it, if I can do something about it. But I can't help you. I tried, and I failed, though I don't blame myself for failing.'

Yeshua walked away.

Bithniah said, 'Tom, there goes the unhappiest man in the

world. I wish I knew why he is so sad and lonely.'

Mix glanced at his near-double, walking swiftly away as if he had some place to go, and said, 'There but for the grace of God go I.'

And he wondered again what strange meeting of genes had resulted in two men, born about one thousand and eighty years apart in lands five thousand miles apart, of totally different ancestry, looking like twins. How many such coincidences had happened during man's existence on Earth?

Bithniah left to report to a woman's labor force. Mix looked up a Captain Hawkins and transmitted Stafford's orders to him. He spent an hour in close-order drill with his company and the rest of the morning practicing mock-fighting with axe and shield and some spear-throwing. That afternoon, he showed some craftsmen how to make boomerangs. In a few days he would be giving instruction in the art of throwing the boomerang.

Several hours before dusk, he was dismissed. After bathing in The River, he returned to his hut. Bithniah was in hers, but Yeshua had left.

'He went up into the mountains,' she said. 'He said something about purifying himself and meditating.'

Mix said, 'He can do what he wants with his free time. Well, Bithniah, what about moving in with me? I like you, and I think you like me.'

'I'd be tempted if you didn't look so much like Yeshua,' she said, smiling.

'I may be his spitting image, but I'm not a gloomy cuss. We'd have fun, and I don't need dreamgum to make love.'

'You'd still remind me of him,' she said. Suddenly she began weeping, and she ran into her hut.

Mix shrugged and went to the nearest stone to put his copia upon it.

8

While eating the goodies provided by his copia, holy bucket, miracle pail, grail, or whatever, he struck up a conversation with a pretty but lonely-looking blonde. She was Delores Rambaut, born in Cincinnati, Ohio, in 1945. She'd been living in the state across The River until this very afternoon. Her hutmate had driven her crazy with his unreasonable jealousy, and so, after putting up with him for a long time, she'd fled out of the hut, but he was likely to try to kill her.

'How was it living with all those Huns?' he said.

She looked surprised.

'Huns? Those people aren't Huns. They're what we call Scythians. At least, I think they are. They're mostly a fairly tall white-skinned people, Caucasians. They were great horsemen on Earth, you know, and they conquered a wide territory in southern Russia. In the seventh century B.C., if I remember right what I read about them.'

'The people here call them Huns,' he said. 'Maybe it's just an insulting term and has no relation to their race or nationality. Or whatever. Anyway, I'm glad you're here. I don't have a mate, and I'm lonely.'

She laughed and said, 'You're kind of rushing it, aren't you? Tom Mix, heh? You couldn't be...?'

'The one and only,' he said. 'And just as horseless as the ancient Scythians are now.'

'I should have known. I saw enough pictures of you when I was a child. My father was a great admirer of yours. He had a lot of newspaper clippings about you, an autographed photo, and even a movie poster. *Tom Mix in Arabia*. He said it was the greatest movie you ever made. In fact, he said it was one of the best movies he ever saw.'

'I kind of liked it myself,' he said smiling.

'Yes. It was rather sad, though. Oh, I don't mean the movie. I mean about all your movies. You made...how many?'

'Two hundred and sixty – I think.'

'Wow! That many? Anyway, my father said, oh, it was years later, when he was a very old man, that all of them had disappeared. The studios didn't have any, and the few still existing were privately owned and fading fast.'

Tom winced, and he said, '*Sic transit gloria mundi.* However, I made a hell of a lot of money and enjoyed blowing it. So, what the hell!'

Delores had been born five years after he'd rammed his car into a barricade near Florence on the highway between Tucson and Phoenix. He'd been traveling as advance agent for a circus and was carrying a metal suitcase full of money with which to pay bills. As usual, he was driving fast, ninety miles an hour at the time. He'd seen the warning on a barrier that the highway was being repaired. But, also as usual, he'd paid no attention to the sign. One moment, the road was clear. The next...there was no way he could avoid the crashing into the barricade.

'My father said you died instantly. The suitcase was behind you, and it snapped your neck.'

Tom winced again.

'I always was lucky.'

'He said the suitcase flew open, and there were thousand-dollar bills flying all over the place. It was a money shower. The workmen didn't pay any attention to you at first. They were running around like chickens with a fox loose in the henhouse, catching the money, stuffing it in their pockets and under their shirts. But they didn't know who you were until later. You got a big funeral, and you were buried in Forest Lawn Cemetery.'

'I had class,' he said. 'Even if I did die almost broke. Was Victoria Forde, my fourth wife, at the funeral?'

'I don't know. Well, what do you know? I'm eating and talking with a famous movie star!'

Tom had felt hurt that the workers had been more interested in scooping up the money that was whirling like green snowflakes than in finding out whether he was dead or not. But he quickly smiled to himself. If he'd been in their skins, he might have done the same thing. The sight of a thousand-dollar bill blown by the wind was very tempting – to those who didn't earn in ten years what he'd made in a week. He couldn't really blame the slobs.

'They put up a monument at the site of the accident,' she said. 'My father stopped off to see it when he took us on a vacation trip through the Southwest. I hope knowing that makes you feel better.'

'I wish the locals knew what a big shot I was on Earth,' he said. 'Maybe they'd give me a rank higher than sergeant. But they hadn't heard of movies until they came here, of course, and they can't even visualize them.'

After two hours, Delores decided that they'd known each other long enough so that he was no longer rushing it. She accepted his invitation to move into his hut. They had just reached its door when Channing appeared. He'd been sent to summon Mix at once to the lord-mayor.

Stafford was waiting for him in the Council Hall.

'Master Mix, you know so much about Kramer and have such an excellent military background that I'm attaching you to my staff. Don't waste time thanking me.

'My spies in Kramer's land tell me he's getting ready for a big attack. His military and naval forces are completely mobilized, and only a small force is left for defense. But they don't know where the invasion will be. Kramer hasn't told even his staff, as yet. He knows we have spies there, just as he has his spies here.'

'I hope you still don't suspect that I might be one of his men,' Mix said.

Stafford smiled slightly.

'No. My spies have reported that your story is true. You're

not a spy unless you're part of a diabolically clever plot to sacrifice a good boat and some fighting men to convince me you're what you claim to be. I doubt it, for Kramer is not the man to let go of Jewish prisoners for any reason whatsoever.'

Stafford, Mix learned, had been impressed by the showing of Mix in the fight on The River and by the reports of Mix's superiors. Also, Mix's Earthly military experiences had given Stafford some thought. Tom felt a little guilty then, but it quickly passed. Moreover, Mix knew the topography and the defenses of Deusvolens well. And he had said the night before that the only way to defeat Kramer was to beat him to the punch.

'A curious turn of phrase but clear in its meaning,' Stafford had said.

'From what I've heard,' Mix said, 'Kramer's method of expansion is to leapfrog one state and conquer the one beyond it. After he consolidates his conquest, he squeezes the bypassed area between his two armies. That's fine, but it wouldn't work if the other states would unite against Kramer. They know he's going to gobble them all up eventually. Despite which, they're so damned suspicious they don't trust each other. Maybe they got good reason, I don't know. Also, as I understand it, no one state's willing to submit itself to another's general. I guess you know about that.

'I think that if we could deliver one crippling blow, and somehow capture or kill Kramer and his Spanish sidekick, Don Esteban de Falla, we would weaken Deusvolens considerably. Then the other states would come galloping in like Comanches so they could really crush Deusvolens and grab all the loot that's for the grabbing.

'So, my idea is to make a night raid, by boat, of course, a massive one that would catch Kramer with his pants down. We'd burn his fleet and burst in on Kramer and de Falla and cut their throats. Knock off the heads of the state, and the body surrenders. His people would fall apart.'

'I've sent assassins after him, and they've failed,' Stafford said. 'I could try again. If we make enough diversion, they might succeed this time. However, I don't see how we could carry this off. Sailing up-River is slow work, and we couldn't reach Kramer's land while it's still dark if we left at dusk. We'd be observed by his spies long before we got there, most probably when we amassed our boats. Kramer would be ready for us. That would be fatal for us. We have to have surprise.'

'Yeah,' Mix said. 'But you're forgetting the Huns across The River. Oh, by the way, I just found out they're not really Huns, they're ancient Scythians.'

'I know that,' Stafford said. 'They were mistakenly called Huns in the old days because of their savagery and our ignorance. The terminology doesn't matter. Stick to the relevant points.'

'Sorry. Well, so far, Kramer has been working on this side of The River only. He's not bothered the Huns. But they aren't dumb, according to what I've just heard.'

'Ah, yes, from the woman, Delores Rambaut,' Stafford said.

Tom Mix tried to repress his surprise. 'You've got spies spying on your own people.'

'Not officially. I don't have to appoint people to spy on their own countrymen. There are enough volunteers to come running to me with accounts of everything that goes on here. They're gossips, and they're nuisances. Occasionally, though, they tell me something important.'

'Well, what I meant when I said the Huns weren't dumb was that they know that Kramer's going to attack them when he has enough states on this side of The River under his belt. They must know he'll move against them then so he can consolidate this whole area. They know it'll be some years from now, but they know it's coming. So, they might be receptive to some ideas I've been hatching. Here's what we could do.'

They talked for another hour. At the end, Stafford said that he'd do what he could to develop Mix's plan. It was a desperate one, in his opinion, chiefly because of the very little time left to carry it out. It meant staying up all night and working hard. Every minute that passed gave Kramer's spies just that much more opportunity to find out what was happening. But it had to be done. He didn't intend to sit passively and wait for Kramer to attack. It was better to take a chance than *to let Kramer call the shots*. Stafford was beginning to pick up some of Mix's twentieth-century Americanisms.

9

Intelligence reported that Kramer was not using his entire force. Though he theoretically had available enough soldiers and sailors to overwhelm both New Albion and Ormondia, in fact he was afraid to withdraw many from his subject states. His garrisons there were composed of a minority of men from Deusvolens and a majority of collaborators in the occupied states. They kept the people terrorized and had built earth and wooden walls on the borders and stationed troops in forts along these. The copias of most citizens were stored in well-guarded places and only passed out during charging times. Anyone who wished to flee either had to steal his copia or kill himself and rise somewhere else on The River with a new copia. The former was almost impossible to do, and the latter course was taken only by the bravest or most desperate.

Nevertheless, if Kramer weakened the garrisons too much, he would have a dozen revolutions at once.

From what Stafford's spies said, Kramer had quietly taken

two out of every ten of his soldiers and sailors in the subject states and brought them to Deusvolens and Felipia, the state adjoining his north border. His fleet was stationed along the banks of The River in a long line. But the soldiers and the boats might be amassed at any time during the night. What night was, of course, unknown.

'Kramer's spies know that you and Yeshua and Bithniah are here,' Stafford said to Mix. 'You think that he'll attack New Albion just to get you three back. I don't believe it. Why should you three be so important to him?'

'Others have escaped him,' Mix said, 'but never in such a public manner. The news has gotten around, he knows it, and he feels humiliated. Also, he's afraid that others might get the same idea. However, I think that he's been planning to extend his conquests, and we've just stimulated him to act sooner than he'd intended.

'What he'll do, he'll bypass Freedom and Ormondia and attack us. If he takes New Albion, he'll then start his squeeze play.'

Messengers had been sent to Ormondia, and the duke and his council had met Stafford and his council at the border. Half the night had been spent in trying to get the duke to agree to join in a surprise attack. The rest of the night and all morning had been taken up in arguing about who the supreme general should be. Finally, Stafford had agreed that Ormonde should be in command. He didn't like to do so, since he thought the duke wasn't as capable as himself. Also, the New Albionians would not be happy about serving under him. But Stafford needed the Ormondians.

Not stopping for even a short nap, Stafford then crossed The River to confer with the rulers of the two 'Hunnish' states. Their spies had informed them that Kramer was planning another invasion. They hadn't been much concerned about it, since Kramer had never attacked across The River. Stafford finally convinced them that Kramer would get to them eventually. They bargained, however, for the majority of the loot. Stafford and the duke's agent, Robert Abercrombie, reluctantly agreed to this.

The rest of the day was taken up in making plans for the disposition of the Hunnish boats. There was much trouble about this. Hartashershes and Dherwishawyash, the rulers, argued about who would take precedence in the attack. Mix suggested to Stafford that he suggest to them that the boats carrying the rulers should sail side by side. The two could then land at the same time. From then on it would be every man for himself.

'But all of this may go awry,' he said to Mix. 'Who knows what Kramer's spies have found out? There may even be some in my own staff or among the Huns. If not, the watchers in the hills will have observed us.'

Soldiers in New Albion and Ormondia were scouring the hills, searching for spies. These would be hiding, unable to light signal fires or beat on their relay drums. Some would have slipped through the hunters to carry their information on foot or by boat. That, however, would take time.

Meanwhile, envoys from New Albion had gone to three of the states south of its border. They would attempt to get these to furnish personnel and craft in the attack.

Tom had, by the end of the night, been commissioned a captain. He was supposed to don the leather, bone-reinforced casque and cuirass of the Albionian soldier, but he'd insisted that he keep his cowboy hat. Stafford was too weary to oppose him.

Two days and nights passed. During this time, Mix managed to get some sleep. In the afternoon of the third day, he decided that he'd like to get away from all the bustle and noise. There was so much going on that he could find no quiet place to sleep. He'd go up into the hills and find a silent spot to snooze, if that was possible. There were still search parties there.

First, though, he stopped at Bithniah's to see how she was

doing. She was, he found, now living with a man whose mate had been killed during the River-fight. She seemed fairly happy with him. No, she hadn't seen 'the crazy monk,' Yeshua. Mix told her he'd seen him at a distance now and then. Yeshua had been cutting down some pine trees with a flint axe, but Mix didn't know for what purpose.

On the way to the hills, he ran into Delores. She was on a work party which was hauling logs of the giant bamboo down to the banks. These were being set up to reinforce the wooden walls lining the waterside of New Albion's border. She looked tired and dirty and not at all happy. It wasn't just the hard labor that made her glare at Mix, however. Not once had they had time or the energy to make love.

Tom grinned at her and called, 'Don't worry, dear! We'll get together after this is all over! And I'll make you the happiest woman alive!'

Delores told him what he could do with his hat.

Tom laughed and said, 'You'll get over that.'

She didn't reply. She bent her back to the rope attached to the log and strained with the other women to get it up over the crest of the hill.

'It'll be all downhill from now on,' he said.

'Not for you it won't,' she called back.

He laughed again, but, when he turned away, he frowned. It wasn't his fault that she'd been drafted into a work party. And he regretted as much as she, maybe more, that they hadn't had a honeymoon.

The next hill was busy and loud with the ring of stone axes chopping at the huge bamboo plants, the grunting of the choppers, and the shouted orders of the foremen and forewomen. Presently, he was on a still higher hill, only to discover that it, too, was far from conducive to sleep. He continued, knowing that when he got to the mountain itself, he would run into no human beings there. He was getting tired and impatient, though.

He stopped near the top of the last hill to sit down and catch his breath. Here the great irontrees grew closely together, and among them were the tall grasses. He could see no one, but he could hear the axes and the voices faintly. Maybe he should just lie down here. The grass was not soft, and it was itchy, but he was so fatigued that he wouldn't mind that. He'd spread out his cloak and put his hat over his face and pass out quickly into a much-deserved sleep. There were no insects to crawl over him or sting him, no pestiferous ants, flies, or mosquitoes. Nor would any loud bird cries disturb him.

He rose and removed his white cloak and placed it on the grass. The sun's hot rays came down between two irontrees on him; the long grass made a wall around him. Ah!

Stafford might be looking for him right now. If so, it was just too bad.

He stretched out, then decided he'd take his military boots off. His feet were hot and sweating. He sat up and slid one boot from his right foot and started to remove the woven-grass sock. He stopped. Had he heard a rustle in the grass not made by the wind?

His weapons lay by him, a chert tomahawk and a flint knife and a boomerang, all in straps in his belt. He took all three out, laying the boomerang on the cloak, and he held the tomahawk in his right hand and the knife in his left.

The rustling had stopped, but after a minute it resumed. He rose cautiously and looked over the top of the grass. There, twenty feet away, toward the mountain, the grass was bending down, then springing up. For a while he couldn't see the passerby. Either he was shorter than the tall blades or he was bending over.

Then he saw a head rise above the green. It was a man's, dark-skinned, black-haired, and Spanish-featured. That wasn't significant, since there were plenty like him in the area, good citizens all, some of them refugees from Deusvolens and Felipia. The stealthiness of the man, however, indicated that he wasn't behaving like one who belonged here.

He could be a spy who'd eluded the search parties.

The man had been looking toward the mountain, presenting his profile to the watcher. Mix ducked down before the stranger turned his head toward him. He crouched, listening. The rustling had stopped. After a while, it started again. Was the man aware that somebody else was here and so was trying to locate him?

He got down on his knees and put his ear to the ground. Like most valleydwellers, the fellow was probably barefooted or wore sandals. But he might step on a twig, though there weren't too many of those from the bushes. Or he might stumble.

After a minute of intent listening, Mix got up. Now he couldn't even hear the noise of the man's passage. Nor was there any movement of the grass caused by anything except the breeze. Yes! There was! The fellow had resumed walking. The back of his head was moving away from Mix.

He quickly strapped on his belt, fastened his cloak around his neck, and put the boot back on. With his white hat held by the brim in his teeth, the knife in one hand, the tomahawk in the other, he went after the stranger. He did so slowly, however, raising his head now and then above the grass. Inevitably, the followed and the follower looked at each other at the same time.

The man dropped at once. Now that he'd been discovered, Mix saw no reason to duck down. He watched the grass as it waved, betraying the crawler beneath as water disturbed by a swimmer close to the surface. He breasted the grass, striding swiftly toward the telltale passage but ready to disappear himself if the green wake ceased.

Suddenly, the dark man's head popped up. Surprisingly, he placed a finger on his lips. Mix stopped. What in hell was he doing? Then the man pointed beyond Mix. For a second, Mix refused to look. It seemed too much like a trick, but what could the man gain by it? He was too far away to get any advantage by charging when Mix was looking behind him.

Trick or not, Mix had too much curiosity. He turned to look over the territory. And there was the grass moving as if an invisible snake were crawling over it.

He considered the situation quickly. Was that other person an ally of the dark man and sneaking up on himself? No. If he were, the dark man wouldn't be pointing him out. What had happened was that the dark man was an Albionian who had detected a spy. He'd been trailing him when Mix had mistaken him for a spy.

Mix had no time then to think about how he might have killed one of his own people. He dropped down and began approaching the place where the third person was – had been, rather, since by the time he got there the unknown would probably be some place else. Every twelve feet or so he rose to check on the unknown's progress. Now the ripples were moving toward the mountain, away from both himself and the dark man. The latter, as indicated by the moving grass, was crawling directly toward where Mix had been.

Tired of the silent and slow play, sure that a sudden and violent action would flush out the quarry, Mix whooped. And he ran through the grass as swiftly as it would allow him.

The afternoon was certainly full of surprises. Two heads shot up where he had expected one. One was blond, and the other was a redhead. The woman had been in front of the man as they had crawled and crouched and risen briefly like human periscopes, though he hadn't actually seen them coming up to observe.

Mix stopped. If he'd made a mistake about the identity of the first person, could he be doing the same with these two?

He shouted to them, telling them who he was and what he was doing here. The dark man then called out, saying that he was Raimondo de la Reina, a citizen of New Albion. The redhead and the blonde then identified themselves: Eric

Simons and Guindilla Tashent, also citizens of the same state.

Mix wanted to laugh at this comedy of errors, but he still wasn't sure. Simons and Tashent might be lying so that the others would let down their guard.

Tom stayed where he was. He said, 'What were you two doing here?'

'For God's sake,' the man said, 'we were making love! But please do not bruit this about. My woman is very jealous, and Guindilla's man would not be very pleased if heard about this, either!'

'Your secret is safe with me,' Mix called.

He turned toward de la Reina, who was walking toward him. 'What about you, pard? There isn't any reason to say anything about this, is there? Especially since it makes all of us look like fools?'

There was another problem. The two lovers were probably shirking their duties. This could be a serious, a court-martial business, if the authorities learned about it. Mix had no intention of reporting it, but the Spaniard might feel that it must be brought to the attention of the authorities. If he insisted, then Mix couldn't argue with him. Not too strongly, anyway.

He, Simons, and Tashent hadn't moved. De la Reina was plowing through the grass toward him, probably to talk the situation over with him. Or perhaps he thought that the pair wasn't to be trusted. Which made sense, Mix thought. They could be spies who'd invented this tale when found out. Or, more likely, prepared it in case they were discovered.

But Mix didn't really think this was so.

Presently, the Spaniard was a few feet from him. Now Mix could clearly see his features, long and narrow, aquiline, a very aristrocratic Hispanic face. He was as tall as Mix. Through the bending grass Mix glimpsed a green towel-kilt, a leather belt holding two flint knives, and a tomahawk. One hand was behind his back; the other was empty.

Mix wouldn't allow anybody to get near him who hid one hand. He said, 'Stop there, amigo!'

De la Reina did so. He smiled but at the same time looked puzzled.

'What's the matter, friend?'

He spoke seventeenth-century English with a heavy foreign accent, and it was possible that he had trouble understanding Mix's twentieth-century American pronunciation. He was given the benefit of the doubt, though not very much.

Tom spoke slowly. 'Your hand. The one behind your back. Bring it out. Slowly.'

He chanced to look at the others. They were moving toward him, though slowly. They looked scared.

The Spaniard said, 'Of course, friend.'

And de la Reina was leaping toward him, shouting, the hand now revealed, clutching a flint blade. There were only a few inches showing, but there was enough to slash a jugular vein or a throat. If the Spaniard had been smarter, he could have concealed the entire weapon in his hand and let the hand swing naturally. But he had been afraid to do that.

Tom Mix swung the tomahawk. Its edge cracked against de la Reina's temple. He dropped. The blade fell from his grip.

Tom called to the two. 'Stop where you are!'

They looked at each other uneasily, but they halted.

'Hold your hands up,' he said. 'High above your heads!'

The hands went up as high as they could go. Simons, the redhead, said, 'What happened?'

'Get over under that irontree!'

The two started to walk toward the indicated place. An abandoned hut stood under it, but the grass around it had been recently cut. It had grown back to a height of a foot, enabling Mix to see if they carried weapons or not.

He bent down and examined the Spaniard. The fellow was still breathing, though harshly. He might or might not recover, and if he did, he might never have all his wits about him. It would be far better for him if he died, since he was bound to be tortured. That was the fate of all spies in this area who failed to kill themselves when facing inevitable capture. This one would be stretched over a wooden wheel until the ropes on his wrists and ankles pulled his joints apart. If he wouldn't give any worthwhile information or he was thought to be lying, he'd be suspended naked over a low fire and slowly seared.

During his turnings on the spit, he might have one eye or both poked out or an ear sliced off. Should he still refuse to talk, he'd be taken down and cooled off with water. Then his fingernails and toenails might be pulled out or tiny cuts made in his genitals. A hot flint tip might be thrust up his anus. One finger at a time might be severed and the stump immediately thereafter cauterized with a hot rock.

The list of possible tortures was long and didn't bear thinking about by any sensitive imaginative person.

Mix hadn't seen the Albionians put any spies to the question. But he had witnessed some inquisitions while Kramer's prisoner, and so he knew too well the horrors awaiting the Spaniard.

What could this poor devil tell that was worth hearing? Nothing, Mix was sure.

He straightened up to check on Simons and Tashent. They were under the branches of the tree now, standing near the hut.

He stooped and slashed the man's jugular vein. Having made sure that he was dead and having collected the valuable weapons, he walked toward the tree. The fellow would be resurrected in a whole body somewhere along The River far from here. Maybe someday Mix would run into him again, and he could tell him about his act of mercy.

Halfway toward the tree, he halted. From above, somewhere on the mountain, the wild skirling of a bamboo syrinx floated down.

Who could be up there wasting time when everybody was supposed to be working hard? Another pair of lovers, one of whom was entertaining the other with music between the couplings? Or was the skirling some sort of signal by a spy? Not very likely but he had to consider all possibilities.

The blonde and the redhead still had their hands up. Both were naked. The woman certainly had a beautiful body, and her thick pubic hair was just the red-gold that especially excited him. She reminded him of a starlet he'd run around with just after his divorce from Vicky.

'Turn around,' he said.

Simons said, 'Why?' But he obeyed.

'Okay,' Mix said. 'You can put your hands down now.'

He didn't tell them that he'd once been stabbed by a naked prisoner who'd gripped a knife between the cheeks of his buttocks until he was close to his captor.

'Now, what happened?'

Events had been much as he'd thought. The two had sneaked off from a work-party to make love in the grass. While lying in the grass between bouts, getting ready to light up cigarettes, they'd heard the spy walking nearby. Picking up their weapons, they'd started to trail him. They were sure that the stranger was up to no good.

Then they'd seen Mix following de la Reina and were just about to join him when the Spaniard had seen them. He'd been a quick thinker in trying to deceive Mix into believing that they were the spies.

'He might've succeeded if he hadn't tried to kill me at once instead of waiting for a better time,' Tom said. 'Well, you two get back to your duty.'

Guindilla said, 'You aren't going to tell anybody about this, are you?'

Tom said, grinning, 'Maybe, maybe not. Why?'

'If you keep quiet about this, I could make it worth your while.'

Eric Simons snarled, 'Guin! You wouldn't, would you?'

She shrugged, causing intriguing ripples.

'What could it hurt? It'd be just this once. You know what'll happen if he turns us in. We'll be put on acorn bread and water for a week, publicly humiliated, and... well, you know how Robert is. He'll beat me, and he'll try to kill you.'

'We could just run off,' Simons said.

He looked very nasty. 'Or would you like to tumble this man, you slut!'

Tom laughed again, and said, 'If you got caught while deserting, you'd be executed. Don't worry. I'm not a blackmailer, a lecherous hard-hearted Rudolf Rassendale.'

They looked blank. 'Rassendale?' Simons said.

'Never mind. You wouldn't know. You two get going. I'm not telling anybody the whole truth. I'll just say I was alone when I discovered the Spaniard. But tell me, who's playing the syrinx up there?'

They said they had no idea. As they walked away into the grass to retrieve their weapons and clothes, they quarreled loudly. Mix didn't think their passion for each other would survive this incident.

When their wrangling voices faded out, Tom turned to the mountain. Should he go back to the plain and report that he'd killed a spy? Go up the mountain to check out the syrinx player? Or do what he had come here for, that is, sleep?

Curiosity won out. It always did with him.

Telling himself he should have been a cat, one who'd already used up one of his nine lives, he began climbing. There were fissures along the face of the mountain, ledges, little plateaus, and steep narrow paths. Only a mountain goat or a very determined or crazy person would use these to get up the cliff, however. A sensible man would look up it and perhaps admire it, but he'd stay below and loaf or sleep or roll a pretty woman in the grass. Best of all, he'd do all three, not to mention pouring down some good bourbon or whatever his copia gave him in the way of booze.

Sweating despite the shade, he pulled himself over the edge of one of the small plateaus. A building that was more of an enclosed leanto than a hut was in the middle of the tablerock. Beyond it was a small cascade, one of the many waterfalls that presumably originated from unseen snows on top of the mountains. The cascades were another mystery of this planet, which had no seasons and thus should rotate at an unvarying 90 degrees to the ecliptic. If the snows had no thawing period, where did the water come from?

Yeshua was by the waterfall. He was naked and blowing on the pan's pipe and dancing as wildly as one of the goat-footed worshippers of The Great God. Around and around he spun. He leaped high, he skipped, he bent forward and backward, he kicked, he bent his legs, he pirouetted, he swayed. His eyes were closed, and he came perilously close to the edge of the plateau.

Like David dancing after the return of the ark of God, Mix thought. But Yeshua was doing this for an invisible audience. And he certainly had nothing to celebrate.

Mix was embarrassed. He felt like a window-peeper. He almost decided to retreat and leave Yeshua to whatever was possessing him. But the thought of the difficulty of the climb and the time he had taken made him change his mind.

He called. Yeshua stopped dancing and staggered backward as if an arrow had struck him. Mix walked up to him and saw that he was weeping.

Yeshua turned, kneeled and splashed the icy water from a pool by the side of the cataract, then turned to face Mix. His tears had stopped, but his eyes were wide and wild.

'I was not dancing because I was happy or filled with the glory of God,' he said. 'On Earth, in the desert by the Dead Sea, I used to dance. No one around but myself and The Father. I was a harp, and His fingers plucked the strings of ecstasy. I was a flute, and He sounded through my body the songs of Heaven.

'But no more. Now I dance because, if I do not, I would scream my anguish until my throat caught fire, and I would leap over the cliff and fall to a longed-for death. What use in that? In this world, a man cannot commit suicide. Not permanently. A few hours later, he must face himself and the world again. Fortunately, he does not have to face his god again. There is none left to face.'

Mix felt even more embarrassed and awkward.

'Things can't be that bad,' he said. 'Maybe this world didn't turn out to be what you thought it was going to be. So what? You can't blame yourself for being wrong. Who could possibly have guessed the truth about the unguessable? Anyway, this world has many good things that Earth didn't have. Enjoy them. It's true it's not always a picnic here, but when was it on Earth? At least, you don't have to worry about growing old, there are plenty of good-looking women, you don't have to sit up nights wondering where your next meal is coming from or how you're going to pay your taxes or alimony. Hell, even if there aren't any horses or cars or movies here, I'll take this world anytime! You lose one thing; you gain another.'

'You don't understand, my friend,' Yeshua said. 'Only a man like myself, a man who has seen through the veil that the matter of this physical universe presents, seen the reality beyond, felt the flooding of The Light within...'

He stopped, stared upward, clenched his fists, and uttered a long ululating cry. Mix had heard only one cry like that – in Africa, when a Boer soldier had fallen over a cliff. No, he hadn't really heard any Boer soldier. Once more, he was mixing fantasy with reality. 'Mix' was a good name for him.

'Maybe I better go,' Mix said. 'I know when there's nothing to be done. I'm sorry that –'

'I don't want to be alone!' Yeshua said. 'I am a human being; I need to talk and to listen, to see smiles and hear laughter, and know love! But I cannot forgive myself for being...what I was!'

Mix wondered what he was talking about. He turned and started to walk to the edge of the plateau. Yeshua came after him.

'If only I had stayed there with the Sons of Zadok, the Sons of Light! But no! I thought that the world of men and women needed me! The rocks of the desert unrolled before me like a scroll, and I read therein that which must come to pass, and soon, because God was showing me what would be. I left my brothers in their caves and their cells and went to the cities because my brothers and sisters and the little children there must know, so that they would have a chance to save themselves.'

'I got to get going,' Mix said. 'I feel sorry for whatever's riding you, but I can't help you unless I know what it is. And I doubt that I'd be much help then.'

'You've been sent to help me! It's no coincidence that you look so much like me and that our paths crossed.'

'I'm no brain doctor,' Mix said. 'Forget it. I can't straighten you out.'

Abruptly, Yeshua dropped the hand held out to Mix, and he spoke softly.

'What am I saying? Will I never learn? Of course you haven't been sent. There's Nobody to send you. It's just chance.'

'I'll see you later.'

He began climbing down. Once he looked upward, and he saw Yeshua's face, his own face, staring down at him. He felt angry then, as if he should have stayed and at least given some encouragement to the man. He could have listened until Yeshua talked himself into feeling better.

By the time he had reached the hills and started walking back, he had a different attitude. He doubted that he could really aid the poor devil.

Yeshua must be half cracked. Certainly he was half baked. And that was a peculiar thing about this world and the resurrection. Everybody else had not only been awakened from the dead with the body of a twenty-five-year-old – except, of course, for those who had died on Earth before that age – but all who had suffered a mental illness on Earth had been restored mentally whole.

However, as time passed, and the problems of the new world pressed in, many began to sicken again in their minds. There wasn't much schizophrenia; but he understood from talking to a twentieth-centurian that at least three-quarters of schizophrenia had been proved to be due to a physical imbalance and was primarily genetic in origin.

Nevertheless, five years of life in the Rivervalley had produced a number of insane people, though not in the relative proportions known on Earth. And the resurrection had not been successful in converting the majority of the so-called sane to a new viewpoint, a different attitude, one that phased in with reality.

Whatever reality was.

As on Earth, most of humanity was often irrational, though rationalizing, and was impervious to logic it didn't like. Mix had always known the world was half mad and behaved accordingly, usually to his benefit.

Or so he had thought then. Now, since he had time sometimes to contemplate the Terrestrial past, he saw that he had been as half-mad as most people. He hoped he'd learned his lessons, but there were plenty of times when he doubted it. Anyway, except for a few deeds, he'd been able to forgive himself for his sins.

But Yeshua, miserable fellow, could not forgive himself for whatever he had been or had done on Earth.

10

After telling Stafford about de la Reina, he went to his hut, and he drank the last of his whiskey, four ounces.

Whoever would have thought that there'd be a dead ringer for Tom Mix, and an ancient Jew at that, for Christ's sake? It was too bad Yeshua hadn't been born at the same time as he had. Yeshua could have made good money as his stand-in.

Despite the noise still swirling around the hut, he managed to sleep well. The rest didn't last long, though. Two hours later, Channing woke him up. Tom told him to shove off. Channing continued to shake his shoulder, then gave up on that method of wakening, and emptied a skin-bucket full of water on his face. Sputtering, swearing, striking out with his fists, Mix came up off the bed. The sergeant ran out of the hut laughing.

The council lasted an hour, and he went back to the hut for some more shut-eye. He was roused momentarily when the copiastones thundered. Fortunately, he'd promised some cigarettes to a man if he'd place Mix's copia for him so he wouldn't go supperless.

Sometime later, Delores came in, set down their copias, and then tried to wake him up for their first, and possibly last, love-making. He told her to go away, but she did something that very few men could ignore. Afterward, they ate and then smoked a couple of cigarettes. Since he might not come out of the invasion alive, one coffin nail wouldn't hurt him. Anyway, Delores didn't like smoking alone after being plumbed.

The cigarette, however, made him cough, and he felt dizzy. He swore off again though the tobacco certainly had tasted delicious. A moment later, having forgotten his resolve, he lit up another.

A corporal came after him then. Tom kissed Delores. She cried and said that she was sure she'd never ever see him again.

'I appreciate your sentiments,' Tom said. 'But they aren't exactly comforting.'

The fleets of Anglia and New Cornwall, a neighboring state which had decided at the last minute to join the invasion, were approaching the New Albion shores. Tom, dressed in his ten-gallon hat, cloak, vest, kilt, and Wellington boots, got onto the flagship. It was the biggest man-of-war in New Albion, three-masted, carrying ten catapults. Behind it came the other largest boats, four men-of-war. After it trailed twenty frigates, as the two-masters were called, though they looked little like the frigates of Earth. After them came forty cruisers, single-masted warcanoes, hollowed out of giant bamboo logs.

The night-sky blazed down on a River in which the traffic of tacking vessels was thick. There were a few unavoidable collisions, but little damage resulted, though they caused a lot of shouting and cursing. The danger increased as the Hunnish, or Scythian, fleets put out. Bull's-eye lanterns burning fish oil signaled everywhere. An observer in the hills would have been reminded of the dance of fireflies on Earth. But if there were any spies left, they didn't light signal fires or beat drums. They were lying low, still hiding from the search parties. All the male soldiers left behind were manning the forts and other important posts. Armed women were beating the hills now.

The miles dropped by slowly. Then the Ormondian fleet sailed out to join them, the duke's flagship in the van. More signals were rayed out.

Just north of Ormondia was the determinedly neutral state of Jacobea. Stafford and Ormonde had debated inviting it to be an ally, but had finally decided against it. There was little chance of its joining, and even if it had, its security couldn't be trusted. Now, as the fleet ventured into Jacobean waters, the cries of sentinels came to it. Its crews saw torchlights flare up, and they heard the booming of the hollow-log and fish-skin drums. The Jacobeans, fearing an invasion, poured out of their huts, their weapons in hand, and began falling into formation.

Up in the hills, signal fires began building up. These were tended by Kramer's spies, which Jacobea allowed to operate unmolested.

However, the clouds were forming in the skies. Fifteen minutes later, they emptied their contents, drowning out the fires. If Stafford's planning went as hoped for, there would be no relay of warning signals to Kramer.

The signal-man on the duke's boat flashed a message to the Jacobeans. It identified the fleets and said that they intended no harm. They were sailing against Kramer, and if Jacobea cared to join them, they'd be welcome.

'They won't do it, of course,' Stafford said. He laughed. 'But it'll throw them into a frenzy. They won't know what to do, and they'll end up doing nothing. If they follow us into battle, and we lose, God forbid, then Kramer will take his vengeance on them. If we win by God's good will, then they will be in our bad graces, and we might invade them. 'Twould only be justice if we did, and it would serve the scurvy curs right. But we have no desire to bring more sorrow and bloodshed upon this land. They won't know that, though.'

'In other words,' Mix said, 'they won't know whether to shit or go blind.'

'What? Oh! I see what you mean. It's a powerful phrase but most distasteful. Just like the excrement you referred to.'

Grimacing, he turned away.

Whatever changes the Riverworld had made in Stafford, one had not been a tolerance for obscene language. He no longer believed in the god of the Old and New Testament, though he still used His name, but he reacted as strongly here as on Earth to 'dirty' words. Half a Nonconformist still lived within him. Which must give him daily pain, Mix thought, since the exroyalists and the ex-peasants in this area were not averse to earthy speech.

The boats passed the state just below Deusvolens as the fog rose up from The River and rolled down from the hills on schedule. From then on, the men in the crow's nests above the gray clouds directed the sailing by pulling on ropes. The men handling these on the decks told the steersmen which way to turn the tiller and when to expect the great booms to swing over. It was dangerous navigation, and twice Mix heard the crash of boats colliding.

After what seemed an endless time, the signal was given that Deusvolens had been sighted. At least, they hoped that it was their destination. Sailing so blindly, with the plains as well as The River concealed in fog, they could not be sure.

Shortly before the sky was due to turn pale under the greater blaze of the rising sun, the capital 'city' of Fides was sighted. One of the watchmen came down to report.

'There be great lights all over the place. Something's stirring, my lord-mayor.'

A moment later there was a cry from aloft.

'Boats! Many boats! They're heading straight for us! Beware, milord!'

Stafford revealed that he could curse as well as any when under great pressure.

'God's wounds! It's Kramer's fleet! The goddamned swine! He's setting out on his own invasion! What damnable timing! May he rot in the devil's ass forever!'

Ahead of them came the clamor of war, men shouting, the blowing of flutes, beating of drums, then, faintly, the sound of great vessels in the vanguard ramming into each other, screams as men fell into the water or were speared, knifed, clubbed, or axed.

Stafford ordered that his craft ignore the Kramerian fleet, if possible, and head for Fides. He also commanded that signals be sent by his watchman to the other Albionian boats.

'Let the duke and the Cornishmen and the Huns take care of the enemy on the water!' he said. 'We'll storm ashore as planned!'

As the sun cleared the mountains on their left, it disclosed a high earth and rock rampart on top of which was a wall of upright logs extending as far as the eye could see. At its base the fog was a woolen covering, but this would soon be burned away by the sun. There were thousands of helmeted heads behind the wall and above them the heads of thousands of spears. The huge alarm-drums were still booming, the echoes rolling back from the mountain behind it.

Amidst the deafening bruit, the flagship, *Invincible*, pulled up alongside the main gate, just past the end of the piers, and loosed, one by one, great stones from its catapults. These smashed in the main gates. Other boats, in Indian file, came up and loosed their boulders. Some struck too high, some too low. Nevertheless, five other huge holes were breached in the wooden walls and a few defenders smashed.

Instead of turning around to use the catapults on the other sides, a maneuver that would have taken much time, the boats sailed along the banks. They had to tack some to keep from grounding and so being rammed by those behind them. When the flagship had gone far enough to give room for its followers to stop, its sails were dropped, and its bow turned toward shore. Anchors, large stones tied to ropes, dropped into the shallows. At once, the small boats were launched, and since there was no room in them for all those aboard, many soldiers leaped into the water.

They swarmed ashore under a hail of spears, clubs, slingstones, and axes onto the strip of land between the bases of the ramparts and the edge of the banks. They ran toward the smashed gateway, many carrying tall ladders.

Mix was among those in the lead. He saw men fall in front and on both sides of him, but he escaped being struck. After a minute, he was forced to slow his pace. The gateway was still a half mile away; he'd be too tired to fight at once if he ran full speed. The strategy of Stafford and the Council didn't seem so good now. They were losing too many men trying to amass at the breaches for a massive assault. Still, if the plans had gone as hoped, they might have worked quite well. The other fleets were to sail along the walls and throw the big rocks at intervals above and below where Stafford's vessels were. Thus, fifty different breaches could have been stormed and the Deusvolentians would have had to spread out their forces to deal with these.

If only Kramer's fleet hadn't decided to set out just before the big attack came. If only. . . that was the motto of generals, not to mention the poor devils of soldiers who had to pay for the if-only's.

As he ran he glanced now and then toward The River. The fog was almost gone now. He could see. . .

The deafening thunder of the copiastones erupting almost made his heart stop. He'd completely forgotten about them. They were inside the earth walls, set within log wells. At least the enemy wasn't going to have time to eat breakfast.

He looked to his right again. Out in The River were at least fifty vessels grappled in pairs, the crews of each trying to board the other. Many others were still maneuvering, trying to run alongside the foe so that they could release missiles: fish-oil firebombs, stones, spears hurled by atlatls, clubs, stones tied to wooden shafts. It was too bad that there hadn't been time to make boomerangs and train men how to use them. They would have been very effective.

He couldn't determine how the battle on the water was going. Two ships were on fire. Whether they were enemy or friend, he didn't know. He saw a big warcanoe sink, a hole in its bottom made by a boulder cast by a catapult. A frigate was riding over the stern of a large catamaran. It was too early to say on whom Victory was smiling. She was a treacherous bitch, anyway. Just as you thought you couldn't lose, she slipped in something that resulted in you running like hell to get away from the defeated-suddenly-become-conquerors.

Now the attackers had joined in front of the gateway or before the other breaches. He had to catch his breath, and so did most of the others. However, men who'd landed from boats that had stopped close to these were already storming up the rampart and going through the holes in the walls. Trying to, anyway. Many dead or wounded lay on the slopes and in the entrances. Above them the Kramerians cast spears or hurled stones or poured burning fish oil from leather buckets into down-tilted stone troughs.

Tom cast his spear and had the satisfaction of seeing it plunge into one of the faces above the pointed ends of the log wall. He pulled his heavy axe from his belt and ran on.

Only so many defenders could get on the walkways behind the walls, and many of these had been struck by spears or large, unworked stones attached to wooden shafts.

On the ground behind the walls would be massed many soldiers, far outnumbering the invaders. At first, they'd crowded across the gateway, but now, as the first wave of Albionians crumbled, the Deusvolentians retreated. They were waiting for the next wave to come through. Then they would spread out, surround them, and close in.

A major shouted for the next charge to begin. Mix was glad that he couldn't be in that. Not unless those ahead of him were so successful that everybody got in.

Stafford, standing near Mix, shouted at the major to hold the attack. Two frigates were coming in. They'd be able to throw their catapults over the anchored ships and over the walls and into the men beyond them. The major couldn't hear him in the din. If he had, he wouldn't have been able to stop. Those behind forced him through the gate. Mix glimpsed him getting a spear in the chest, then he toppled forward out of sight.

Presently, Tom was being forced ahead by those axemen behind him. He fell once over a body, was kicked hard several times, struggled up, and began climbing up the steep slope of earth. Then he was through the gateway, walking over bodies, slipping, catching himself, and he was in a melee.

He fought as well as he could in the press, but he had no sooner engaged a spearman than he was whirled away, and he was fighting somebody else, a short dark man with a leather shield and a spear. Mix battened the man's shield aside with his axe and knocked the spear downward. He brought the axe upward, striking the man on the chin. The fellow reeled back, but something hit Mix's wrist, and he dropped his axe.

Quickly, Tom pulled out his tomahawk with his left hand and leaped on the man, knocking him down. Astride him, he brought the weapon down, splitting the skull between the eyes. He rose, panting. An Albionian staggered back and fell against him, flattening him. He writhed out from under and got to his feet. He wiped the blood from his eyes, not knowing if it was his or the soldier's who'd fallen over him. Certainly, he hadn't been aware of any head wound.

Panting, he glared around. The battle was going against the invaders. At least a fourth were casualties, and another fourth would soon be. Now was the time for a strategic withdrawal. But between him and the gateway were at least one hundred men, facing inward, their spears thrust out, waiting. The invaders were trapped.

Beyond them, at the other breaches, the fight was still going on. There were, however, so many Kramerians between him and the entrances that he couldn't make out the details.

Stafford, bloody, his helmet knocked off, his eyes wide, gripped his arm.

'We'll have to form men for a charge back through the gateway!'

That was a good idea, but how were they to do it?

Suddenly, by that unexplained but undeniable telepathy that exists among soldiers in combat, all the Albionians came to the same decision. They turned and fled toward those blocking the exit. They were speared in the back as they ran, hurled forward by clubs and axes from behind, or knocked over by weapons from the sides. Stafford tried to marshal them for a disciplined attack. He must have known that it was too late, though he tried valiantly nevertheless. He was bowled over by two men, rose, and fell again. He lay on his back, his mouth open, one eye staring up at the sky. The other was pierced by a spearhead.

Slowly, pulled by the weight of the shaft, his head turned, and his one eye was looking straight at Mix.

Something struck Tom in the back of the head and his knees loosened. He was vaguely aware that he was falling, but he had no idea who he was or where he was, and he had no time to try to figure it all out.

11

Tom Mix awoke, and he was sorry that he had.

He was lying on his back, a throbbing pain in the back of his head and a twisting in his stomach. The face looking down was blurry and doubled, wavering in and out. It was long and thin and hatchety, dark, black-eyed, a grim smile showing rows of white teeth in which the two front lower were missing.

Tom groaned. The face belonged to de Falla, Kramer's ramrod. The teeth had been knocked out by Tom himself while making his escape from this very place, Fides. He didn't think he'd be doing a repeat performance.

The Spaniard spoke in excellent only slightly accented English.

'Welcome to Deusvolens.'

Mix forced a smile.

'I don't suppose I bought a return ticket?'

De Falla said, 'What?'

Mix said, 'Never mind. So what kind of cards are you planning to deal me?'

'Whatever they are, you'll accept them,' de Falla said.

'You're in the driver's seat.'

He sat up and leaned on one arm. His vision wasn't any better, and the movement made him want to throw up. Unfortunately, his last meal had long been digested. He suffered from the dry heaves, which made the pain in the back of his head even worse.

De Falla looked amused. No doubt, he was.

'Now, my friend, the shoe, as you English say, is on the other foot. Though you don't have any footwear.'

He was right. Mix had been stripped of everything. He looked around and saw his hat on a man nearby and beyond that someone wearing his boots. Four men, actually. He must have had a concussion, no slight one. Well, he'd had worse injuries and survived to be better than ever. The chances for living long, though, didn't seem good.

There were bodies everywhere on the ground, none of which was moving or making a sound. He supposed that all but the lightly wounded had been put out of their pain. Not for the sake of mercy but for economy. There was no use wasting food on them.

Someone had pulled the spear out of Stafford's eye.

De Falla said, 'There's still a battle on The River. But there's no doubt who'll win now.'

The Spaniard gestured to two soldiers. They lifted Mix between them and started to march him across the plain, detouring around corpses. When his legs gave way, they dragged him, but de Falla came running. He told them to get a stretcher. Mix didn't need to ask why he was being so well treated, relatively speaking. He was a special prisoner to be saved for special reasons. He was so sick and weak that, at the moment, he didn't even care about the reasons.

They carried him to where the huts began and down a street and out past the huts to a compound. This was very large, though it held only a few prisoners. The log gate was swung open, and he was taken to an enclosure of upright logs set into the ground. Within this was a small hut. He was in a compound within a compound.

The two soldiers set him down inside the hut and checked on the amount of water in a baked-clay pot, his drinking supply. The nightjar was looked into, and one of the soldiers bellowed out a name. A short, thin worried-looking man ran up and got chewed out for not emptying it. Mix thought that he must indeed be special if such details were being taken care of.

Apparently, the previous occupant had not been so highly regarded. The stench was appalling even though the lid was on the thunder mug.

Seven days passed. Mix became better, his strength waxed, though it did not reach its fullness. Occasionally, he was troubled with recurrences of double vision. His only exercise was walking around the hut, around and around. He ate three times a day but not well. He had identified his copia which had been taken off the flagship by his captives, but he was allowed only half the food it gave and none of the cigarettes or liquor. His guards took these for themselves. Though he had smoked only two cigarettes in the past two years, he now yearned fiercely for more.

Daytime wasn't so bad, but late at night he suffered from the cold and the dampness. Most of all he suffered from not being able to talk to anybody. Unlike most of the guards he'd encountered during a dozen periods of incarceration, these refused to say a single word to him. They even seemed to be reserved with their grunts.

On the morning of the eighth day, kramer and his victorious forces returned. From what he could overhear of the guards' conversation, New Albion, Ormondia, and Anglia had been conquered. There would be plenty of loot and women for all, including those who had not participated in the invasion.

Tom thought Kramer was celebrating too soon. He still had New Cornwall and the Huns to deal with. But he supposed that the defeat of their navies had made them pull in their necks for a while.

The other prisoners, about fifty, were hustled from their repair work on the ramparts back into the compound. Sounds of jubilation came from the area around the main gateway, drums beating, flutes shrilling, cheering. Kramer came through first – even at this distance Mix recognized the fat body and the piggish features – on a big chair carried by four men. The crowds shouted their greeting and tried to swarm around him but were pushed back by his bodyguard. After him came his staff and then the first of the returned soldiers, all grinning widely.

The chair was deposited in front of Kramer's 'palace,' a huge log structure on top of a low hill. De Falla came to greet him then, and both made speeches. Mix was too far away to hear what they said.

Some naked prisoners were marched in at spear point and double-stepped to the compound. Among the dirty, bruised, bloodied bunch was Yeshua. He sat down at once with his back to the wall, and his head sank as if he were completely dejected. Tom yelled at him until a man asked him whom he wanted. The man went across the compound and spoke to Yeshua. At first, Tom thought that Yeshua was going to ignore him. He looked at Tom for a moment and then let his head hang again. But after a while he rose, somewhat unsteadily, and walked slowly to the circular enclosure. He looked through the spaces between the logs, his eyes dull. He had been beaten about the face and body.

'Where's Bithniah?' Tom said.

Yeshua looked down again. He said, hollowly, 'She was being raped by many men the last I saw of her. She must have died while they were doing it. She'd stopped screaming by the time I was taken to the boat.'

Mix gestured at some female prisoners.

'What about them?'

'Kramer said he wanted some alive...to burn.'

Mix grunted, and said, 'I was afraid that was why they didn't kill me. Kramer's going to get a special revenge out of me.'

He didn't add, though he was thinking it, that Yeshua would also be in the 'privileged' class. Yeshua must know it, anyway.

He said, 'If we start a ruckus, we might force them to kill some of us. If we're lucky, we'll be among the late unlamented.'

Yeshua raised his head. His eyes were wild and staring.

'If only a man did not have to live again! If he could be dust forever, his sadness and his agonies dissolved into the soil, eaten by the worms as his flesh is eaten! But no, there's no escape! He is forced to live again! And again! And again! God will permit him no release!'

'God?' Tom said.

'It's just a manner of speech. Old habits die hard.'

'It's tough just now,' Tom said, 'but in between the bad times it's not so bad. Hell, I'm sure that someday all this fighting will stop. Most of it, anyway. It's a time of troubles now. We're still getting straightened out, too many people are behaving like they did on Earth. But the setup's different here. You can't hold a man down. You can't tie him to his job and his house because he carries his own food supply with him and it doesn't take long to build a house. You can enslave him for a while, but he'll either escape or kill himself or make his captors kill him, and he's alive again and free and has another chance for the good life.

'Look here! We can make those buggers kill us now so we don't have to go through all the pain Kramer's figuring to give us. The guards aren't here now. Pull back the bar on the gate and let me out. As you can see, I can't reach through to do it myself. Once I'm out, I'll organize the others, and we'll go out fighting.'

Yeshua hesitated, then gripped the big knob at the end of the massive bolt and, straining hard, withdrew it. Mix pushed the heavy gate open and left his prison within a prison.

Though there were no guards within the compound, there were many on the platforms outside the walls and in the towers. These saw Mix leave, but they did not object, which, Tom thought, meant that they knew he had to be released from it soon, anyway. He was just saving them the trouble of opening the gate.

It wouldn't be long before the prisoners would be herded out of the compound.

He called to the others, about sixty, to gather around him.

'Listen, you poor bastards! Kramer's got you marked for torture! He's going to put on a big show, a Roman circus! We're all going to wish soon we were never born, though I guess you know that! So I say we should cheat them! And save ourselves all that pain! Here's what I think we should do!'

His plan seemed wild to them, though mainly because it was unheard of. But it offered escape of a sort which once would not have been regarded as such. It was better than just sitting there like sick sheep waiting to be slain. Their tired eyes took on some life; their exhausted and abused bodies lost their shrunken appearance, swelling up with hope.

Only Yeshua demurred.

'I cannot take a human life.'

Tom said, in an exasperated tone, 'You won't be doing that! Not in the sense we knew on Earth! You'll be giving your man his life! And saving him from torture!'

A man said, 'He doesn't have to take anybody's life. He can

volunteer to be one of those that'll die.'

'Yeah, that's right,' Tom said. 'How about it, Yeshua?'

'No. That would make me a collaborator in murder, hence, a murderer, even if the one murdered was myself. Besides, that would be suicide, and I cannot kill myself. That, too, would be a sin, against...'

He bit his lower lip.

'Look!' Tom said. 'We don't have time to argue. The guards are getting mighty curious now. First thing you know, they'll be storming in here.'

'That is what you want,' Yeshua said.

Angrily, Tom cried out, 'I don't know what you did or where you were when you were on Earth, but whatever it was or whoever you were, you really haven't changed! I've heard you say you've lost your religion, yet you act like you haven't lost a shred of it! You don't believe in God anymore, yet you were just about to spout off about not going against God! Are you crazy, man?'

'I think I've been crazy all my life,' Yeshua said. 'But there are some things I will not do. They are against my principles, even though I no longer believe in The Principle.'

By then the captain of the guards was shouting at the prisoners, demanding to know what they were up to.

'Forget the mad Jew,' a woman said. 'Let's get this over with before they get here.'

'Line up then,' Mix said.

All except Yeshua got into one of two lines in which each person faced another. That was just as well since they were, without him, even-numbered. Opposite Mix was a woman, a brunette whom he vaguely remembered seeing in New Albion. She was pale and trembling but game enough.

He lifted the chamberpot by its rim and said, 'You call it.'

He swung the brown pot up, loosed it, and watched it turn over and over. Sixty-two pairs of eyes were fastened upon it.

'Open end!' The woman called out loudly but shakily.

The container, turning, fell. It landed on its bottom and cracked in two.

'Don't hesitate!' Tom shouted. 'We don't have much time, and you might lose your nerve!'

The woman closed her eyes as Tom stepped up to her and gripped her throat. For a few seconds she held her arms out at right angles to her body. She was attempting to put up no resistance, to make the job easier for him and quicker for her. The will to live was, however, too strong for her. She grabbed his wrists and tried to break his grip. Her eyes opened wide as if she were pleading with him. He squeezed her throat more tightly. She writhed and kicked, driving her knee up between his legs. He bent away though not swiftly enough to avoid getting the knee in the belly.

'Hell, this ain't going to work!' he said.

He released her. Her face was blue by then, and she was gasping. He hit her in the chin, and she dropped onto the ground. Before she could regain consciousness, he was choking her again. It only took a few seconds to still her breath. Wanting to make sure, he held on a little longer.

'You're the lucky one, sister,' he said, and he rose.

The people in his line, which had won the toss or lost it, depending upon the viewpoint, were having the same trouble he'd had. Though the other line had agreed beforehand not to fight against their stranglers, most of them had been unable to keep their promise. Some had torn loose and were slugging it out with their would-be killers. A few were running away, pursued. Some were dead, and some were now trying to choke their chokers.

He looked at the big gate. It was swinging open. Behind it was a horde of guards, all armed with spears.

'Stop it!' he roared. 'It's too late now! Attack the guards!'

Without waiting to see how many had heard him, he ran toward the first of the spearmen. He yelled to give himself courage and to startle the guards into self-defense. But what did they have to fear from an unarmed, naked, and enfeebled man?

The guards nearest him did, however, raise their spears.

Good! He'd hurl himself onto the points, arms out, catching some in his belly and some in his chest.

But the captain bellowed out an order, and they reversed their weapons. The shafts would be used as clubs.

Nevertheless, he leaped, and he saw the butt end of the spear that would knock him senseless.

12

When he awoke, he had two pains in his head, the new one far worse than the old. He also was suffering again from diplopia. He sat up and looked around at the blurred scene. There were bodies of the prisoners here and there. Some had been killed by the others, and some had been beaten to death by the guards. Three of the guards lay on the dirt, one dead, the others bleeding. Apparently, some prisoners had wrested the spears away from the guards and gotten some small revenge before being killed.

Yeshua was standing away from the rest of the prisoners, his eyes closed and his mouth moving. He looked as if he were praying, but Mix doubted that he was.

When he looked back, he saw about twenty spearmen marching through the compound gate. Kramer was leading them. Mix watched the short, fat youth with the dark-brown hair and very pale blue eyes walking toward him. His piggish face looked pleased. Probably, Mix thought, he was happy that

Mix and Yeshua had not been slain.

Kramer stopped a few feet away from Mix. He looked ridiculous, though he must think he made a splendid figure. He wore a crown of oak wood each of the seven points of which sported a round button cut from mussel shells. His upper eyelids were painted blue, an affectation of the males of his land, an affectation which Mix thought was fruity. The upper ends of his black towel-cape were secured around his fat neck with a huge brooch made from copper, an exceedingly rare and expensive metal. On one plump finger was an oak ring in which was set an uncut emerald, also a scarce item. A black towel-kilt was around his paunch, and his knee-length boots were of black fish-leather. In his right hand he held a long shepherd's crook, symbol that he was the protector of his sheep – his people. It also signified that he had been appointed by God for that role.

Behind Kramer were two bloodied and bruised and naked prisoners, whom Mix had not seen before. They were short dark men with Levantine features.

Mix squinted. He was wrong. He did know one of the two. He was Mattithayah, the little man who had mistaken Mix for Yeshua when they had first been Kramer's prisoners.

Kramer pointed at Yeshua and spoke in English.

'Iss zat ze man?'

Mattithayah broke into a storm of unintelligible but recognizable English. Kramer whirled and sent him staggering backward with a blow of his left fist against the jaw. Kramer said something to the other prisoner. This one answered in English as heavily accented as Kramer's, but his native tongue was obviously different.

Then he cried, 'Yeshua! Rabbi! We have looked for you for many years! And now *you* are *here*, too!'

He began to weep, and he opened his arms and walked toward Yeshua. A guard banged the butt of his spear on his back, over the kidney area, and the little man groaned and fell on his knees, his face twisted with pain.

Yeshua had looked once at the two men and had groaned. Now he stood with downcast eyes.

Kramer, scowling and muttering, strode up to Yeshua and seized his long hair. He jerked it, forcing Yeshua to raise his head.

'Madman! Anti-Christ!' he shouted. 'You'll pay for your blasphemies! Yust ass your two crazedt friendss vill pay!'

Yeshua closed his eyes. His lips moved soundlessly. Kramer struck him in the mouth with back of his hand, rocking Yeshua's head. Blood flowed from the right corner of Yeshua's lips.

Kramer screamed, 'Shpeak, you filt! Do you indeedt claim to be Christ?'

Yeshua opened his eyes, and spoke softly.

'I claim only to be a man named Yeshua, just another son of man. If this Christ of yours did exist and if he were here, he would be horrified, driven to madness with despair, at what had happened on Earth to his teachings after he died.'

Kramer, yelling, hit Yeshua alongside the head with his staff. Yeshua fell to his knees and then crumpled forward, his head hitting the earth with a soft thud. Kramer drove the toe of his boot against the fallen man's ribs.

'Renounce your blasphemiess! Recant your Satanic ravingks! You vill excape mush pain in zis worlt if you do, ant you may safe your zoul in the next!'

Yeshua raised his head, but he said nothing until he had regained his breath.

'Do what you will to me, you unclean Gentile.'

Kramer shouted, 'Shut your dirty mous, you inzane monshter!'

Yeshua grunted as Kramer's boot toe drove into his side again, and he moaned for a little while thereafter.

Kramer, his black cloak flapping after him, strode to Mattithayah and his companion.

'Do you shtill maintain zat zis lunatic iss ze Blessedt Zon of Godt?'

The two were pale beneath their dark skins, and their faces looked as if they were made of melting wax. Neither replied to Kramer.

'Answer me, you svine!' he cried.

He began to beat them with the shepherd's staff. They backed away, their hands up to protect themselves, but they were seized by the guards and kept from retreating.

Yeshua struggled to his feet. Loudly, he said, 'He is so savage because he fears that they speak the truth!'

Mix said, 'What truth?'

His double vision was increasing, and he felt as if he should vomit. He was beginning to lose interest in everything but himself. God, if only he could die before he was tied to the stake and the wood set afire!

'I've heard that question before,' Yeshua said.

Mix didn't know for a moment what Yeshua meant. Then illumination flooded in. Yeshua had thought he'd said, 'What *is* truth?'

After Kramer had beaten Mattithayah and his friend into unconsciousness, they were dragged out through the gate by their legs, their heads bumping, their arms trailing along behind their heads. Kramer started to walk toward Yeshua, his staff lifted high as if he intended to give him the same treatment. Mix hoped that he would. Perhaps, in his rage, he'd kill Yeshua now and thus save him from the fire.

The joke would certainly be on Kramer then.

But a sweating panting man ran through the gate, and he cried out Kramer's name. It was thirty seconds, though, before he caught his wind. He was the bearer of ill news.

Apparently, there were two fleets approaching, one from up-River, one from down-River. Both were enormous. The states to the north of Kramer's and the states to the south of the newly conquered territories had been galvanized into allied action against Kramer, and the Huns across from them had joined them. They finally realized that they must band together and attack Kramer before he moved against them.

Kramer turned pale, and he struck the messenger over the head with his staff. The man fell without a sound.

Kramer was in a bad way. Half of his own fleet had been destroyed in its victory, and the number of his soldiers had been considerably reduced. He wouldn't be ready for a long time to launch another attack nor was he well fitted to withstand an invasion from such a huge force.

He was doomed, and he knew it.

Despite Mix's pain and the knowledge of the fire waiting for him, he managed a smile. If Kramer were captured, he would undoubtedly be tortured and then burned alive. It was only just that he should be. Perhaps if Kramer himself felt the awful flames, he might not be so eager to subject others to them when he rose again.

But Mix doubted that.

Kramer shouted orders to his generals and admirals to prepare for the invasion. After they had left, he turned, panting, toward Yeshua. Mix called to him.

'Kramer! If Yeshua is who those two men claim he is, and they've no reason to lie, then what about you? You've tortured and killed for nothing! And you've put your own soul in the gravest jeopardy!'

Kramer reacted as Mix had hoped he would. Screaming, he ran at Mix with the staff raised. Mix saw it come down on him.

Kramer must have pulled his punch. Mix awoke some time later, though not fully. He was upright and tied to a great bamboo stake. Below him was a pile of small bamboo logs and pine needles.

Through the blur, he could see Kramer applying the torch. He hoped that the wind would not blow the smoke away from him. If it rose straight up, then he would die of asphyxiation and would never feel the flames on his feet.

The wood crackled. His luck was not with him. The wind was blowing the smoke away from him. Suddenly, he began coughing. He looked to his right and saw, vaguely, that Yeshua was tied to another stake very near him. Upwind. Good, he thought. Poor old Yeshua will burn, but the smoke from his fire will kill me before I burn.

He began coughing violently. The pains in his head struck him like fists. Vision faded entirely. He fell toward oblivion.

But he heard Yeshua's voice, distorted, far away, like thunder over a distant mountain.

'Father, they *do* know what they're doing!'

J.C. on the
Dude Ranch

Foreword

This story appears for the first time anywhere.

Its genesis lies in an exchange by letter between Bob Bloch and me. I asked him if he'd ever read the novel, Tom Mix Died for Your Sins *by Darryl Ponicsan. He wrote back saying that he had not. And he added, 'I've never read* Jesus Christ on the 101 Ranch, *either.'*

Things like that flow from his lips night and day. He can't help it, and millions are glad that he can't.

But when I read that, I thought. Wow, what a great title for a story! So I wrote him, saying so, and asked him if he intended to write a short story based on that title. If he didn't want to write it, then I'd be happy to do so. He replied that he had no such intention and gave his permission for me to tackle it.

The result is before you. I changed his title because not too many readers nowadays might know about the once very famous 101 Ranch or that Tom Mix once worked there as a cowboy. But, to give Bob circuitous credit for the title and for the final line, I put in a character named Bob Blotch.

This story has a different slant on Jesus from that which appears in the preceding story.

Thanks for the drink, stranger. Name's Soapy Waters. Maybe you read about my grandpa, the famous Texas outlaw, Rough Waters. He always carried a Shakespeare and a Bible in his saddlebag, and he was fond of quoting or maybe misquoting them.

He was the one said, '*All the world's a stage* coach, and it should be robbed.'

That had nothing to do with the morning I was in Big Wash picking up supplies for the XR Dude Ranch. But he did say something I should of paid mind to. 'Once,' he said, 'not knowing the sissy-looking hombre was Wild Bill Hickok, I tried to hold him up. Instead, I got arrested. So *judge not by appearances, lest ye be* jugged.'

If I'd of knowed then what was going to happen when this tall handsome stranger wearing the white ten-gallon hat rode into town under that Arizona sun, I would of quit right then and there. It was *some* mess me and some others got into because we was going by appearances.

The stranger was driving a battered old pickup pulling a trailer with a white horse. The way he started to tie the truck to a hitching post before he remembered he wasn't on a horse told me he was more used to forking a cayuse than driving. Or maybe he just had a lot on his mind. I introduced myself, and close-up I could see he was about thirty-three and had big brown eyes that looked like they seen too much.

J.C. Marison was not only good-looking, even with that long black beard of his'n, the crotch of his levis seemed bigger'n a cow's udder. He was a natural for the XR. He said yes, he was looking for a job. So I told him how to get to McGiddow's Hill and to tell old man Rich I sent him.

'It's not only a dude ranch,' I said, 'it's a working ranch. Some of them women guests like to work the cowboys, too.'

His eyes didn't light up like they should of. Nowadays you can't be too sure, so I said, 'You *do* like women?'

He said they was his favorite kind of people, so I felt maybe I wasn't making a mistake. After he drove off, I banged on the door of Nab's Grocery and Feed until he came down.

'What the hell you doing here so early?' he growled.

'Your sign says any time,' I said.

'Yeah, but we was up to two drinking,' he said. 'I figured you'd be snoring in Swede's bed until noon.'

I didn't tell him I was so loaded I couldn't get my feet up the stairs to her room let alone get anything else up. When I woke up on the pool table, Mary the Swede's mangy old St Bernard was chewing on my boots. That dog's like its owner. It'll eat anything.

When I'd finished loading, it was time for a hair of the dog that bit me. I ambled over to the Last Chance, and somehow by the time I left it was ten. But my hangover was gone.

I see another stranger ride in pushing a big black Cadillac. After he'd parked it in front of the jail and got out I seen he was as big and handsome as J.C. But he wore a black Stetson and a black suit that looked like he was going to an expensive funeral, maybe for a Wall Street banker. His hair was red as my eyeballs was then, and his light blue eyes was what Gramps called 'killer lamps.' The bulge in his crotch was as big as J.C.'s, which was saying something.

After he went into the sheriff's office I hung onto the door handle of my pickup trying to make the peaks of the Superstitious Mountains thirty miles away quit being double. It must of been more than a few minutes before I succeeded. By then the stranger and Sheriff Reverend Bob Blotch come out from the jail. They traded a few words, and then the stranger drove off to the Wild Horse Motel.

Blotch seen me hanging on so the mealymouth strolled over and sneered at me up and down.

'You ain't going to sling me into the calaboose again,' I said. 'I'm suffering from a little liver stroke, but I'll be all right in a minute.'

I was hoping he'd buy my story. The boss expected me to get into trouble Saturday night, but he'd be mad if I didn't show for work Monday morning. Besides, the thought of spending another day behind bars while Blotch read temperance tracts to me was enough to make me even sicker.

To get his mind off me, I said, 'Who's that hombre you was just talking to?'

'It's none of your business,' he said. 'But he's Mr Bub, first name's Bales, come from New York to put the squeeze on your boss. I'll be serving the foreclosure papers on that Abomination of Desolation you call the XR unless Rich comes up with the money. You'll be out of a job soon, you booze-soaked rowdy. *Woe unto them that rise early in the morning that they may follow strong drink. Isaiah, five-eleven.*'

If my Levis wasn't so tight my heart would of been down in my boots. Things had really been going bad for the old man. After his jeep overturned and he was paralyzed from the waist down, bad luck stuck to him tighter'n crabs from a Nogales whorehouse. The dam in the mountains burst and washed away three guest houses. The stable caught fire and burned up ten horses. Rustlers stole a hundred cows and a pedigree bull. Yeah, I know, but rustlers is even more active now than when my grandpa was operating.

Then one of the cowboy studs, Raunchy Sanders, give three guests the clap. Word got around, and we only had half the dudes we usually get.

Blotch quit grinning, and he squinted at me.

'Mr Bub was inquiring about a saddle tramp named J.C. Marison. Said he owed him money and would'like to repay him. Know anybody of that name?'

That sobered me a little. Bub didn't look like he'd chase you unless *you* owed him money. So I said I never heard of Marison. Us debtors have to stick together.

I had to put up with a ten-minute lecture from the sheriff-reverend, but he finally let me go. On the way out I passed the clapboard church Blotch built with the help of God – so he said. Actually it was jail labor done it. There was a big billboard out front of The Church of the Last Days calculated to scare the whiskey out of us sinners. It showed Jesus riding down from the sky on an ass. But it looked more like a jackrabbit than a donkey. The cheapskate Blotch got a drunken vagrant artist to do it instead of ten days in the clinker.

Behind Jesus was a bunch of angels right out of *Revelations*. The lead angel looked mighty like Blotch and he was carrying a rope with a hangman's knot. Running away from the fierce angels was a mob of dissipated-looking people, many carrying fifths of booze, all headed toward a fiery pit. One of the sinners more than resembled me. In the background was the Great Whore of Babylon. The model for her was Swede, another one of Blotch's pet hates. Only, big as her boobs are, they ain't *that* big. I oughta know.

That sign always made me mad, so I floored the accelerator and only took fifteen minutes to get to the ranch. J.C., grinning all over, came out of the boss' house followed by Mary Rich. She was under his spell, I could tell that, so I reminded myself to tell him he wasn't hired to pleasure the boss' daughter. I barreled past them into the living room, where Xavier Rich sat in his wheelchair.

I blurted out the news about Mr Bub, but the boss wasn't as shaken up as I thought he'd be.

He said, 'Things ain't as bad as they look. I think maybe I can float a loan with Mrs Lott. She was in here earlier complaining about the lack of entertainment – you and I know what she means by that – when this good-looking J.C. with the bulge showed up. She fell for him like she was a tree he's axed. I think he can butter her up, if he's got the stamina. She'll loan me the money to keep them fat-ass New York bankers off my neck for a while.'

I thought that was like a drowning man asking for somebody please throw him the anchor, but I didn't say so. Wanda Lott, who us hands referred to as Wants-a-Lot, was a big handsome New Yorker separated from her wealthy husband. She was fifty, though she claimed forty-one. When she come down every spring for two months she always brought along some of her rich hot-pants women friends with her.

'The only trouble with J.C.,' the boss said, 'is his bad manners. He wouldn't take off his hat indoors even when there was women present.'

I was about to tell him Mrs Lott wasn't interested in what his hat covered, but Mary came in then. He dismissed me and I went out to unload the pickup. After lunch, I rode out to help drive a bunch of prime beef on the hoof into the feeding pens. I also kept an eye on J.C. He seemed to know one end of a horse from the other, but when I saw a steer get away from him and run down a wash I wasn't so sure.

So I followed him, one, to check him out, and two, to warn him about Bub. But the steer upped and overed the banks of the wash and took off for the broken rocks and the cactus. No way was even that big white horse of his'n going to get near the critter. Then J.C. did something that made me want to lie down and wait for the DT's to pass. He put away the rope and took off his hat. Something shone in the sun, but it couldn't be what I saw.

It was a halo. Yes, that's what I said. A halo, a ring of light. What? Yes, thank you. Make it a double.

He took that halo in his right hand and flipped it out like it was a Frisbie. It sailed out, widening out as it went, and slipped down over the beast's neck. It stopped dead. J.C. rode up and removed the halo, which then shrank back to normal size, and he put it over his head and the hat over it.

Pretty soon the steer, meek and mild, came trotting back with J.C. behind him. He didn't see me because I ducked back down into the wash.

Then I see the sheriff's jeep on top of McGiddow's Hill, where a road ran on top of it. Blotch was standing by it looking at J.C. through field glasses. I wasn't too surprised he was sneaking around up there. He was always pussyfooting around to catch us in some sort of evildoings. I think he must of thought we was buggering the calves, which none of us had done since we started shaving.

I didn't say nothing to nobody about the halo. What I seen was enough to make even a cowboy think. When the usual barbecue was held that evening, with lots of booze, gorging, singing, and dirty jokes, I helped serve. Mrs Lott kept closer to J.C. than a nursing calf to its mother. Mary Rich was angry about that, I could tell, and her father was mad because she was mad. But neither could do anything about it.

All of a sudden, the boss called me to his chair.

'Goddamn it, Soapy, you didn't bring enough booze! How come? You drink most of it on the way back? Get your ass into town fast and get two more cases each of gin, whiskey, and vodka.'

I walked away hot under the collar even if it was my fault. J.C., who was rid of Wants-a-Lot for a minute 'cause she had to take a piss, stopped me.

'What's the trouble, Soapy?'

I told him, and he said, 'I'll get it.'

Before I could protest, he was gone. But I followed him since Nab wouldn't give him credit unless he had a note from Rich. I was about ten steps behind him when he went into the bunkhouse. But I stopped when I saw through a window what he was doing. He'd started filling three empty gallon jugs with water from the sink faucet. What the hell?, I thought. Pretty soon he filled them and he come out carrying a jug under each arm. I followed him back to the barbecue, and what do you know? He pours the jug water in to the empty bottles, and from one comes gin and from the other vodka!

I ain't lying; I tested them both.

Just as I was going back to the bunkhouse to check out the third jug, I see Mr Bub drive up. Cool as the devil, he introduced himself to the boss, who was about ready to explode when Bub said he thought he'd like to look at what was gonna be *his* property. But Bub didn't see J.C., though he looked around for him. J.C. had disappeared.

Mrs Lott didn't seem to mind. One look at that big handsome dude with the giant swelling, and she just natural gravitated to him. That kept the boss from running Bub's ass off the place, of course, since he couldn't afford to offend her.

I hotfooted it to the bunkhouse and drank some of the stuff in the third jug. It was whiskey, as good as Wild Turkey!

Just as I was going fast out the door before J.C. came back, Sheriff Reverend Blotch grabbed hold of me from the dark and pulled me around the corner. He smelled like he'd crapped in his pants, which, as a fact, he'd done.

'I seen the halo!' he cried. 'And I seen the miracle of the water turning into booze! I know you saw him both times, too! What in shit's going on?'

I said, 'That ain't no kind of language for a preacher. Anyway, you're trespassing on private property.'

Slobbering, he said, 'You dumb, booze-soaked cowboy. If you knew anything about the Bible, you'd be scared shitless. *I* am. Only *I* don't have nothing to fear! But you, Soapy, are among the goats.'

'Now listen,' I said, 'if you think I'm one of them there sodomists, you're crazy. I don't fuck goats at my time of life.'

'You numbskull!' he said. '*The blind shall lead the blind. Matthew,* fifteen-fourteen. But . . . *The eyes of the blind shall be opened. Isaiah,* thirty-five-five. Can't you see who J.C. really is? Don't you know what place this is? You saw the miracles of the halo and the transformation of water into liquor. You shouldn't need a voice from a burning bush to reveal the truth!'

A chill passed over me, and for a moment I thought I was going to fill my britches like he done.

'You mean,' I whispered, 'J.C. is the initials for...?'

'No!' he thundered. 'J.C. ain't Him! He's just pretending to be! J.C.'s the Antichrist! If you read the Bible 'stead of those filthy girl magazines, you'd know that before the true Christ comes, the false one comes! But the faithful will be able to discern between the true and the false!'

'How'd you figure all this out?' I said.

He gasped. 'Surely, you benighted heathen, you've heard of Armageddon? Where the last battle between the evil and the good'll be fought? Where the devil and his henchman, the Antichrist, will be defeated! I always thought Armageddon'd be in Palestine! But I was wrong! This is the place! How do I know? See McGiddow's Hill!'

He spun me around so I could see it, though I knew it was there, the hill named after the prospector who found gold on it in 1885.

'Armageddon,' he bellowed, 'means the Hill of Megiddo! Say 'McGiddow's Hill' fast, and you can hardly tell the difference! And this is the XR ranch! XR's the first two letters in the Greek name for Christ! But the wicked have staked out a claim here first, and Antichrist is J.C. Marison! Get it? J.C., son of Mary! That saddletramp is really the false Messiah posing as the true one! *Now* are you convinced?'

I was convinced he'd been eating loco weed. But I said, 'Yeah? Don't tell me the true one's the stranger in the black hat? Using your reasoning, Bales Bub sounds like Beelzebub. *You* got it backwards. Would Christ pretend to be the devil? No way!'

That stopped him cold. The idea that he might've mistook one for the other and so be one of them hellbent goats woulda knocked the crap outa him if he hadn't already emptied his bowels down his leg. He sobbed like a baby someone snatched his candy from, and he let loose of me. I ran like I just heard there was free drinks at the Last Chance. Knowing he might follow me to the party where he'd raise a ruckus and so piss off the women guests who was figuring on getting laid, I headed away from it.

Blundering around in the dark, I run right into a cholla cactus. You shoulda heard me cussing then. Hell must be a place where nothing but cholla grows, and you can't turn around without getting a hundred of those fishhook needles in your bare ass. Then I heard Blotch yowl when he run into one. I thought I could cuss, but he had professionals like Isaiah and Jeremiah to draw on.

By then I was near a guest house with a light coming through its open window. By the time I got my wind back, I see it was Mrs Lott's. And from the moaning and the carrying-on I knew she'd found herself the entertainment she wanted. I ain't no Peeping Tom, and I always took Gramps' advice about avoiding danger. He was in bed with a whore when Wyatt Earp came looking for him. Instead of fighting or going out of the window, Gramps hid behind one of them thick fancy drapes old-fashioned cathouses had. Later, when he was asked why he didn't shoot it out, he said, *'Discretion is the better part of* velour.'

It wasn't exactly what Bill Shakespeare had his character Falstaff say. But it fit.

So I was gonna tippytoe away, but Blotch saw me in the light. He come astumbling and swearing, but when he heard noise from the window, he forgot about them devil's needles.

'What hellish iniquitous fornications're taking place here?' he choked. 'You trying to tell me Marison is Jesus but he puts up with this shit? You're wrong! He has to be Antichrist!'

It was no use trying to shush him.

'I'll bet my soul it's that wicked serpent himself in there

with a scarlet woman. The devil enjoys fucking. I'll denounce him to the whole world, and the Last Days will've started. He may kill me with his dark powers, but I'll be a martyr and stand on the right hand of God! Glory, hallelujah!'

He did have guts, I'll give him that. He thought he was going to face Satan himself and get blasted on the spot, but he was going through with it. So, since he was taking a look-see, I might as well, too. But only a quick gander. It don't hurt to watch the competition. I ain't no slouch in the saddle myself – when I'm sober – and once a woman tied a blue ribbon on my pecker for first prize. 'Course I was younger then.

Blotch went to the window, and he gasped and shaked like a horse seeing the vet coming at him with a big syringe. The red in his face drained out like watery catsup. I looked over his shoulder, and what I seen I don't ever want to see again.

It was Mrs Lott all right, naked except for spurred boots. Bub was on top of her, naked except for his hat, his ass a blur like he was in a speeded-up porno movie. I never even seen a rattlesnake go so fast. I was flabbergasted. But I couldn't help thinking that he was like J.C. in always keeping his hat on. And wondering if maybe there wasn't some family tie there. Why'd he ask about J.C.? And wasn't the devil, who was a fallen angel, and Jesus cousins of a kind?

You see, I was getting to believe that maybe the reverend had something. Then, when Bub stopped pumping for a moment, leaving half of his dick, about eight inches, out, I believed down to the bottom of my rotten soul. Only a devil could have such a tallywhacker.

From where I stood I could see the upper part of it, and then I see it's ringed by a blue crackling light.

'The devil's halo!' I gasped.

Blotch clutched my hand as if he needed something human, even me, to hang on to. His eyes bulged like the gas in his stomach was going the wrong way. His stink got worse. It was awful and should of warned them someone was watching. But they was too busy to notice. The end of the world could of come then, and they would of thought it was themselves.

Mrs Lott moaned and dug the rowels on her boots into Bub's ass until the blood come. He started up again. When that whopper came out during the strokes the blue ring crackled, snapped, and popped. It was a minute before I caught on that it was real electricity and that every time the charge went in it was giving her a sensation that would of burned out most women. Though with that monster you wouldn't think he needed an auxiliary generator.

She had a hell of a fuse, must of been a hundred-amps rating, and she wasn't going to blow, not in that sense, anyway.

How long it went on, I don't know. Anyway, I wasn't going to interrupt them, specially if he *was* the devil here to stop the second coming. Not *his* but his enemy's.

Blotch, though, finally got up his courage. He yelled, 'Ah, hah, Beelzebub, also named Satan and Lucifer! I've caught you with the Great Whore of Babylon!'

Before I could give him Gramps' advice about such situations, he was through the window and was raving and quoting the Bible left and right though without giving the sources like he usually done. Mrs Lott started screeching, and Bub jumped up and turned toward Blotch. And I like to died.

He didn't have just one monstrous pecker. He had *two*, one above the other. And I seen from its coating he'd been plunging the bottom one into the lower hole at the same time he'd been pistoning the upper.

Now I've heard a lot of strange things about the devil, but I never heard of anything like that.

Even that didn't faze Blotch. He strode right up to him with a bravery that was downright stupid. Bub's red hair beneath his hat was standing up on end as if each hair had a hard on, and those blue eyes was like the open door of a crematorium furnace. I seen in them all of hell I want to know about.

'Thus I expose the ancient evil!' Blotch shouted, and he snatched off Bub's hat.

Mrs Lott's scream drowned out even mine.

That hat had hid two horns. They were broad and flat and curled back close to the head and then rose up into sharp tips.

I think Blotch would of been ripped to shreds by Bub, but the door burst open.

J.C. stepped in, bellowing, 'Hold it, Beylzabub! There's no need harming these Earthpeople!'

Bub cried out, 'So, I got you now, Jayseemarson!'

And he wheeled and pointed his two rigid peters at J.C. like he was going to blast him with them. Which he meant to do, I'm sure, but he's shot so much juice into Mrs Lott he didn't have more'n feeble flashes. They never got halfway to J.C., who otherwise would've been fried if Bub's battery wasn't run down.

J.C. grinned and said, 'I used her as a Delilah to your Samson.'

Then he took off his hat and roped and hog-tied Bub with his halo. Bub struggled to get his arms loose, but he was helpless and knew it.

'You've been chasing me long enough,' J.C. said. 'My orders were to keep you running after me as a diversion while The Project was completed. It's done now, and you'll be going as my prisoner to Quixpot. Anyway, an armistice has just been declared. You would've received the news if your antennae hadn't been tuned only to sex. If the treaty is signed, Earth'll be off-limits from now on.'

Poor old Blotch didn't know what was going on.

Me, though, I seen enough science-fiction movies to guess that these two was opposing secret agents from far-off planets operating on this world. It was easier to believe that than what Blotch believed. As it turned out, before J.C. left – in a UFO, I suppose – he verified the whole thing, though he was cagey about details.

He excused himself then and manhandled Bub up into the hills where he stashed him some place while waiting for the spaceship. And there was a happy ending like they had in the good old grade-B western movies I loved when I was a kid and wish they was still making. It's true J.C. didn't marry the ranch-owner's daughter, which was a shame if he was equipped anything like Bub. As for Mrs Lott, she begged something pitiful to be taken away with Bub. I think she had visions of a whole planetful of humdingers with double-pillared electrical piledrivers ripe for the plucking, or whatever.

She said she'd *give* Rich her whole fortune if she could go along. I never did hear how that came out. But I know Rich got his money and she never came back to the ranch.

Maybe Lott's wife did turn into a pillar of salt. More likely, assault of pillars.

J.C. didn't swear us to silence. He said we could tell everybody the story 'cause nobody was going to believe it. 'Cept maybe some flying-saucer nuts, and who cared about them?

Like Grandpa said, '*Truth will out*, but it's generally got no place to go.'

Blotch just couldn't believe them two was only aliens from other planets. He'd built up a whole world that didn't exist, one in which even if he got killed he was going to be a big-shot sheep and go to heaven while us goats went to hell. He run off without waiting to be introduced to J.C., shaking his head and screaming about speaking in brass tongues and the clash of simples. Something from the Bible, I suppose.

J.C. not leaving until the next night, he took me to the Last Chance for a little talk over drinks. He told me something about his spread out in the stars but not what he was doing here on Earth. I figured I was better off not knowing.

We was on our fifth – glass, not bottle – when all of a sudden the hubbub dies down. I look up and seen what the hush was about, the unthinkable. Blotch was standing inside the doorway, the batwings swinging behind him. It was the first time he ever set foot in a saloon and maybe the last time, though I ain't so sure about that. What followed was sheer pathetic.

He was white as toilet paper and shaking like an outhouse in a hurricane. At first I thought maybe he'd come in for a showdown, was going to call J.C. out into the street. I seen too many Westerns, I guess. But he wasn't wearing guns. Anyway, no matter how screwed-up he was, even with a posse behind him he wasn't going to tackle anybody that wore a halo under his hat and who knows what under his Levis.

Blotch walks up stiff-legged to the bar and planks down a five-dollar bill.

'Drinks for Soapy, Mr Marison, and me.'

That almost knocked me flat. Whoever would of thought the preacher would do such a thing? Aside from his other principles, he was a cheapskate.

Everybody started buzzing then, wondering what'd happened. We downed the redeye, and after Blotch quit choking, he looked with his watery eyes straight into J.C.'s sad eyes. Then, as if the booze'd given him Dutch courage, he speaks.

'You're the son of God!'

J.C. looked grim-faced.

'Smile when you call me that, stranger.'

The Volcano

Foreword

This is one of my fictional-author stories. Just what a 'fictional author' is is explained in the foreword to 'The Phantom of the Sewers.' Suffice it here that this tale was originally bylined by 'Paul Chapin.' The editorial preface below explains just who Chapin was.

Writing as Chapin, I made his private-detective character, Curtius Parry (note the initial letters of the name), a cripple. I imagined that all of Chapin's protagonists would be handicapped in some fashion.

Editorial Preface:

Though no biography of Paul Chapin has yet been published, millions know of the man and his works. The most complete account of him is given in *The League of Frightened Men*, the second volume in the biography of the great detective, Nero Wolfe. We do know that Paul Chapin was born in 1891, that he early showed signs of both brilliance and a Swiftian attitude toward the world, and that he was crippled for life during a hazing incident at Harvard. The critics claim that this event markedly influenced his fictional works, which have been described as hymns to the brute beauty of violence. Chapin's first novel was published in 1929; his best known are *The Iron Heel* (dramatized on Broadway) and *Devil take the Hindmost*. The latter was a best-seller in 1934, perhaps because of the publicity caused by its suppression during a court trial. Its alleged obscenity would seem innocuous today. It was at this time that he became a murder suspect but was proved innocent by Wolfe. Chapin repaid Wolfe by putting him in his next novel under the name of Nestor Whale and killing him off in a particularly gruesome fashion. *The Volcano* is, like all of Chapin's stories, about murder, savagery, and physical and psychic violence. But this tale differs in that it has little of the rhetoric found in his novels, and in that it may be – though we can't be sure – a fantasy.

1

It was easier to believe in ghosts than in a volcano in a Catskills cornfield.

Curtius Parry, private detective, believed in the volcano because the newspapers and the radio stations had no reason to lie. For additional evidence, he had a letter from his friend, the *Globe* reporter, Edward Malone. As he sat in the rear of his limousine traveling over the Greene County blacktop, he was holding in his hand the letter that Malone had sent him two days before.

It was dated April 1, 1935, and it was from Bonnie Havik.

> *Dear Mr Parry,*
>
> *I got to talk a few minutes with Mr Malone without my pa and brothers hearing me. He said he'd send a note from me to you if I could slip it to him. Here it is. I don't have much time, I am writing this down in the basement, they think I'm getting some pear preserves. Please, Mr Parry, help me. The sheriff here is no good, he's dumb as a sheep. They say Wan ran off after my pa and brothers beat him up. I don't think so, I think they did something worse to him. I don't dare tell anybody around here about Wan because everybody'd hate me. Wan is a Mexican. Please do come! I'm so afraid!*

According to Malone's accompanying note, 'Wan' was Juan Tizoc. He'd come up from Mexico a few years before, probably illegally, and had wandered around the country, either begging or working on farms. When last heard of, he'd been a hired hand for the Haviks for three months. He'd slept in a little room in the loft of the barn. Malone had tried to look into it, but its door was padlocked. The sheriff, Huisman, when asked by Malone about Tizoc, had replied that he seemed to have been scared off by the volcano.

Tizoc, Parry thought. That name did not come from Spain. It was indigenous to Mexico, probably Aztec, undoubtedly Nahuatl. Bonnie's description of him had been passed on by Malone. He was short and stocky and had obviously Nahuatl features, a sharp nose with wide nostrils, slightly protruding blocky teeth, and a wide mouth. When he smiled, Bonnie had said, his face lit up like lightning in the sky.

Bonnie was crazy about him. But Tizoc must have been crazy, in the original sense, to have messed around with a white girl in this isolated Catskills community. It was only three years ago, outside a village ten miles away, that a Negro hitchhiker had been murdered because he had ridden in the front seat with the white woman who'd picked him up.

Malone had enclosed a note with Bonnie's note and a preliminary report from the geologists on the scene.

This girl has been, and is being, brutalized by her father and brothers. Her mother also maltreated her, but she, as you know, was killed four days ago by a rock ejected from the volcano. Bonnie has a hideous scar on her face which local gossip says resulted from a red-hot poker wielded by her father. And I saw some bruises on her arms that looked pretty fresh.

On the other hand, some of the yokels say that she might have 'it' coming. They cite the strange phenomena which allegedly took place on the Havik property when Bonnie was eleven. Apparently, spontaneous fires sprang up in the house and the barn, and she was blamed for this. She was beaten and locked up in the basement, and after a year the phenomena ceased. Or so the villagers say.

There are some here who'll tell you, whether or not you ask them, that Bonnie is at 'it' again. It's plain they think that Bonnie is psychically responsible for the volcano, that she has strange powers. And some nonlocal nuts, visitors from Greenwich Village and Los Angeles and other points south of sanity, go along with this theory. It's all nonsense, of course, but be prepared for some wild talk and maybe some wild action.

The geologists' report had been made two days after the field had cracked open and had vomited white-hot lava and white-hot steam. The report was intended for the public but would not be released until the governor had given his permission. Apparently, he did not want to have anything published which would panic downstate New York. Malone had lifted (read: stolen) a copy of it.

The report began in informing the public that the Catskills were not of volcanic origin. The underlying rock was mainly of sedimentary origin, massive beds of sandstone and conglomerates. Under the sandstone where shales.

Yet, unaccountably, the sandstone and the shale were being so heated by some fierce agency that they flowed white-hot and spewed forth from the vent in the cornfield. Pieces of sandstone, heated to a semiliquid, were being hurled outward across the field. Much of the propulsive force seemed to be steam, water of meteoric origin, which exploded beneath the rocks and cannoned them out.

The geologists, after analyzing the gases and the ashes expelled from the cone, had shaken their heads. Based on the analysis of volcanic gases collected at Kilauea, Hawaii, in 1919, the following average composition, or something like it, should have been found: water 70.75 percent, carbon dioxide 14.07 percent, carbon monoxide 0.40 percent, hydrogen 0.33 percent, nitrogen 5.45 percent, argon 0.18 percent, sulfur dioxide 6.40 percent, sulfur trioxide 1.92 percent, sulfur 0.10 percent, and chlorine 0.05 percent.

The composition of the gases from the Havik volcano, by parts per hundredweight, was: oxygen 65, carbon 18, hydrogen 10.5, nitrogen 3.0, calcium 1.5, phosphorous 0.9, potassium 0.4, sulfur 0.3, chlorine 0.15, sodium 0.15, magnesium 0.05, iron 0.006, and other traces of elements 0.004.

Suspended in the hot H_2O ejected, which formed the bulk of the gases, were particles of sodium chloride (table salt) and sodium bicarbonate. There was also much carbon dioxide, and there were particles of charred carbon.

The sandstone lava flowed from the cone at a temperature of 710 degrees C.

Parry read the list three times, frowning until he had put the paper down. Then he smiled and said, 'Ha!'

The chauffeur said, 'What, sir?'

'Nothing, Seton,' Parry said. But he muttered, 'The geologists are so close to it that they don't see it, even if it's elementary. But, surely, it can't be! It just can't!'

2

A few minutes after 1 p.m., the limousine entered Roosville. This looked much like every other isolated agricultural center in southeastern New York. It reminded Parry of the Indiana village in which he had been raised except that it was cleaner and much less squalid. He made some inquiries at the gas station and was directed to Doorn's boardinghouse. Rooms were scarce due to the deluge of visitors attracted by the volcano, but Malone had arranged for Parry to double up with him. Seton was to sleep on a cot in the basement. Mrs Doorn, however, was obviously smitten by the tall, hawkishly handsome stranger from Manhattan. His empty left coat-sleeve, far from embarrassing her, intrigued her. She asked him if he had lost the arm in the war, and she excused her bluntness with the remark that the recent death of her husband was the long-term effect of a wound suffered at St-Mihiel.

'I was wounded, too,' Parry said. 'At Belleau Wood.' He did not add that it was two .45 bullets from a hood's gun which had severed his arm four years ago in a Bowery dive.

A few minutes later, Seton and Parry rode eastward out on the gravel road that met the blacktop in the center of town. It twisted and turned as if it were a snake whose head was caught in a wolf's jaws. It writhed up and down hills thick with a mixture of needle-leaf and broad-leaf trees. It passed along a deep rocky glen, one of the many in the Catskills.

Violence long ago had created the glens, Parry thought. But that was violence which resulted naturally from the geologic structure of the area. The volcano had also been born of violence, but it was unexpected and unnatural. Its presence in the Catskills was as unexplainable as a dinosaur's.

The limousine, rounding a corner of trees, was suddenly on comparatively flat ground. A quarter-mile down the road was the Havik farm: a large two-story wooden building, painted white, and a large red barn. And, behind it, a plume of white steam mixed with dark particles.

The car pulled up at the end of a long line of vehicles parked with the left wheels on the gravel and the right on the soft muddy shoulder. Parry and Seton got out and walked along the cars to the white picket fence enclosing the front yard. Standing there, Parry could see over the heads of the crowd lining the cornfield and past the edge of the barn. In the middle of the broad field was a truncated cone about ten feet high, its sides gnarled and reddish, irresistibly reminding him of a wound which alternately dried up and then bled again, over and over. A geyser of steam spurted from it, and a minute after he had arrived, a glow appeared on the edges of the crater, was reflected by the steam, and then its origin crawled over the black edges. It was white-hot lava, sandstone pushed up from below, oozing out to spread horizontally and to build vertically.

It seemed to him that the ground trembled slightly at irregular intervals as if the thumps of a vast but dying heart were coming through the earth from far away. This must be his imagination, since the scientists had reported an absence of the expected seismic disturbances. Yet – the people in the crowd along the field and in the yard were looking uneasily at each other. There was too much white of eye shown, too much clearing of throat, too much shuffling and backward stepping. Something had gone through the crowd, something that might spook them if the least thing untoward happened.

The door of the county sheriff's car, parked by the gateway, opened, and Sheriff Huisman got out and waddled up to Parry. He was short but very fat, a bubble of fat which smoked a cheap stinking cigar and glared with narrow red eyes in a red face at Parry. Indeed, Parry thought, he was not so much a bubble of fat as a vessel of blood about to burst.

The thin lips in the thick face said, 'You got business here, mister?'

Parry looked at the crowd. Some were obviously reporters or scientists. The majority just as obviously were locals who had no business beyond sightseeing. But the sheriff wasn't going to antagonize voters.

'Not unless you call curiosity a business,' Parry said. There was no need to identify himself as yet, and he could operate better if the Roosville law wasn't watching him.

'Okay, you can go in,' Huisman said. 'But it'll cost you a dollar apiece, if your man's coming in, too.'

'A *dollar*?'

'Yeah. The Haviks been having a tough time, what with their silo burned down and old lady Havik killed only four days ago by a stone from that volcano and people stomping

136

around destroying their privacy and getting in the way. They gotta make it up some way.'

Parry gestured at Seton, who gave the sheriff two dollars, and they went through the gateway. They threaded through the crowd in the barnyard, passed a Pathé news crew, and halted at the edge of the field. This was mainly mud because of the recent heavy rains. Any weeds on it had been burned off by the large and small lava 'bombs' hurled by the volcano. These lay everywhere, numbering perhaps several hundred. When ejected, they had been roughly spherical, but the impact of landing had flattened out the half-liquid rocks. As Seton remarked, these made the field look like a pasture on which stone cows browsed.

The lava had ceased flowing and was slowly turning red as it cooled. Parry turned to look at the back of the barn, which was broken here and there and marked with a number of black spots. A few stones had evidently also struck the back of the house, since the windows were all boarded up except for those protected by the overhang of the porch roof.

A man appeared from around the corner of the barn. Smiling, his hand extended, he strode up to Parry. 'Son of a gun, Cursh!' he said, 'I wasn't really sure you'd come! After all, your client can't pay you anything!'

3

Parry, grinning and shaking his hand, said, 'I donate one case a year to charity. Anyway, I'd pay my client in this case.'

Ed Malone greeted Seton and then said, 'I've found out

some things I didn't have time to report. The locals admit that the volcano is an act of God, but they still think that maybe God wrought it in order to punish the Haviks. They're not much liked around here. They're stand-offish, they seldom attend church, they're drunk night and day, they're slovenly. Above all, the villagers don't like the way the family treats Bonnie, even if, as they say, she is "sorta strange".'

'What about Tizoc?'

'Nobody's seen him. Of course, nobody's really looking for him. Bonnie hasn't said anything to the sheriff because she's afraid he'll spill the beans to her family, and then she'll suffer. She'll be trying to get out today to see you but...'

A sound like several sticks of dynamite exploding whirled them around toward the cone. They cried out with the people around them as they saw a white-hot object soaring toward them. When they turned around again, they saw a hole in the back of the barn and smoke pouring out of it.

The cry of 'Fire!' arose. Parry hurried around with the others to the front of the barn and looked inside. The white-hot rock had landed in a pile of hay by the back wall, and both were blazing. The flames were spreading swiftly toward the stalls, which held three horses. These were screaming and kicking against the stall boards in a frenzy. From near the front of the barn, from the pens, pigs squealed in terror.

During the futile efforts to save the barn, Parry identified the Haviks. The fire had brought all of them out of the house. Henry Havik was a very tall and very thin man of about fifty-seven, bald, broken-nosed, snaggle-toothed, and thick-lipped. The nose was also bulbous and covered with broken veins, the eruptions of whiskey. When he came close to Parry, he breathed alcohol and rotting teeth. The sons, Rodeman and Albert, looked like twenty-year-younger editions of their father. In twenty years, or less, their faces would be broken-veined and their teeth as rotten.

Bonnie had slipped out during the confusion, and though

she should have been concerned about the barn, evidently she was looking for Parry. Seeing Malone, she came toward him, and Malone pointed at Parry. She was just twenty-one but looked older because of some deep lines in her face, the broad scar along the left side of her face, and the loose and tattered gingham dress she wore. Her yellow hair would have been attractive if it had not been so disheveled. In fact, Parry thought, if she were cleaned up and made up and dressed up, she would be pretty. There was, however, something wild and disquieting about the pale blue eyes.

Smoke poured from the barn while men, choking and coughing and swearing, led the horses and drove the pigs out and others manned a bucket brigade. Since the Haviks had no phone, the sheriff had driven off in a hurry to summon the Roosville fire brigade. Parry gestured at Malone and Bonnie followed him, and he led the way to the other side of the house. He would have liked to have stationed Seton as sentinel, but the chauffeur was lost in the seethe of smoke and mob.

Parry said, 'No need for introductions and no time. Tell me about Juan Tizoc, Bonnie. He's the one this is all about, isn't he?'

'You're pretty smart, Mr Parry,' she said. 'Yes, he is. When Juan was first hired by Pa, I didn't pay much attention to him. He was short and dark, Indian-looking, and he had a funny accent. And he was lame, too. He said an American tourist who was speeding hit him when he was a kid, and he couldn't never walk straight again. He was sometimes bitter about that, but when he was with me he was mostly laughing and joking. That was what made me like him so much, at first. There hadn't never been much laughing around here before he came here, let me tell you. I don't know how he did it, since I didn't really see him too much, but he made my days easier. Sorta edged with light even if they wasn't full of it. Ma and Pa kept him humping, he was a hard worker, though he couldn't never seem to satisfy them, and they insulted him a lot, hollered at him, and they was chinchy with the food, too. But he found time for me . . .'

'If he was treated so badly, why didn't he just walk off?'

'He was in love with me,' she said, looking away from him.

'And you?'

She spoke so softly that he could barely hear her.

'I loved him.'

She groaned, and she said, 'And now he's run away, left me!' She paused and then said, 'But I just can't believe he'd leave me!'

'Why not?'

'I'll tell you why! We both knew how we felt about each other even though neither of us'd said a word about it. But we'd looked words enough! I suppose if I'd been a Mexican girl he'd have said something long before, but he knew he might just as well be a nigger as far as Roosville was concerned. And me, I loved him, but I was ashamed of it, too. At the same time, I wondered how any man, even a Mexican, could love me.'

She touched her scar. Parry said, 'Go on.'

'I'd just finished giving the horses their oats when Juan came in to do something or other, I never found out. He looked around, saw no one was there except me, and came straight to me. And I knew what he was going to do and went into his arms and began kissing him. And he was telling me between kisses how much he hated all gringos, especially my family, he wished they'd all burn in hell, except for me, of course, he loved me so much, and then . . .'

Rodeman Havik had passed by the barn door and had seen them. He had called out to his brother and father, and all three had rushed in at Tizoc. He had knocked Rodeman down, but the father and Albert had jumped on him and begun hitting and kicking him. Bonnie's mother had come from the house then and with Rodeman's help had dragged her into the house. There she was shoved into the basement and locked in.

'And that was the last time I saw him,' she said, tears welling. 'Pa said he'd kicked him off the farm, said he told him he'd kill him if he didn't get out of the country. And Pa beat me. He said he ought to kill me, no decent white woman'd let a greaser slobber over her. But I was so ugly I was lucky even a greaser'd look at me.'

'Why does he hate you so much?' Parry said.

'I don't know!' she said, suddenly sobbing. 'But I wish I was brave enough to kill myself!'

'I'll do that for you!' someone bellowed.

4

Henry Havik, his eyes and lips closed down like jackknife blades, soot covering the red of the broken veins of his nose, rushed at his daughter. 'You bitch!' he shouted. 'I told you to stay inside!'

Parry stepped in between Havik and Bonnie, and said, 'If you hit her, I'll have you in jail in ten minutes.'

Havik stopped, but he did not unclench his fists.

'I don't know who you are, you one-armed jackass, but you better step inside! You're interfering with a man and his daughter!'

'She's of age, and she can leave whenever she pleases,' Parry said coolly. He kept his eyes on the farmer while speaking out of the side of his mouth. 'Bonnie! Say the word, and I'll see you into town! And never mind his threats. He can't do a thing to you as long as you have protection. Or witnesses.'

'He wouldn't care where I was!' she said. 'And I'm afraid to go away! I wouldn't know what to do *out there*!'

Parry looked at her with much pity and some disgust. Finally, he said, 'Bonnie, the unknown evil is far better for you than the known evil. You have sense enough to know that. Have the courage, the guts, to do what your good sense tells you you should do.'

'But if I leave here,' she wailed, 'nobody's going to do anything about Juan!'

Havik shouted, 'What?' and he swung at Parry, though it was obvious his primary target was his daughter. Parry blocked Havik's fist with his arm and kicked the man in the knee. At the same time, Malone rammed his fist into Havik's solar plexus. Havik fell gasping for breath and clutching his knee. A moment later, the two sons, closely followed by Sheriff Huisman, came around the corner of the house. Huisman bellowed at everybody to freeze, and everybody except Havik obeyed. He was rolling on the ground in agony.

Huisman listened to all of them talking at once, then he bellowed for, and obtained, quiet. He asked Bonnie to tell him what had happened. After listening to her, he said, 'So you're a private dick, Parry? Well, you don't have no license to practice here.'

'True,' Parry said, 'but that has nothing to do with the situation. I represent Miss Havik – do I not, Bonnie? – and she wishes to leave the premises. She is over twenty-one and so legally free to do so. Mr Havik here attacked us – I have two witnesses to back that statement – and if he doesn't keep quiet, I'll charge him with...'

'This is my property!' Havik said. 'As for you, you dirty knee-kicking Frenchman...'

Parry took Bonnie's elbow and said, 'Let's go. We can send for your clothes later.'

The sons looked at their father. Huisman scowled and bit down on his cigar. Parry knew what he was thinking. He was well aware that the daughter was within her rights. Also, a

New York reporter was watching him closely. What could he do, even if he wished to do anything?

'You'll pay for this, you ungrateful cow,' Havik said. But he did nothing to prevent his daughter from leaving. Trembling, moving only because Parry was pushing and steering her, she walked out of the yard and to the limousine.

5

Parry went to bed at ten o'clock but was too tired to fall asleep at once. The events at the Haviks' had been stimulating enough; those that followed had drained him of even more energy and set his nerves to resonating. He was furious with the sheriff because of the contempt he had openly expressed for Bonnie after hearing her story and his refusal to question the Haviks or search their premises. Plainly, he thought that the beating up of Tizoc had been a worthy, even applaudable, act. And he claimed that there was not enough evidence to warrant an investigation into Tizoc's disappearance. That the sheriff was right about the latter point enraged Parry even more.

After the long session in the back room of the jail, Parry had gotten Bonnie a room at a Mrs Amster's. Then they had shopped at the small dress shop, purchased her clothes, and taken them to her place. She had bathed and put on some makeup – much, she would have considered sinful – and after dressing she had accompanied Seton and Parry to the restaurant. There she had been subjected to openly curious, and some hostile, stares from and much whispering among the patrons. By the time they left, she was in tears.

Afterward, they'd walked around town, and she had told him in detail about her life in the Havik household. Parry was tough, but every once in a while the sufferings and tragedies of humanity refused to be kept at bay. Like the sea pounding a dike, they found a weak spot, and they poured through him. Usually, it was one case, like Bonnie's, representing millions of men, women, and children who were enduring injustice, cruelty, and lack of love, that punched through. And then the others, or his consciousness thereof, roared in after the spearhead.

Parry could not sleep for a long time because he felt as if he were a huge sea shell in which the ocean of suffering was a painful din. Finally, he did drift away, only to be awakened, half-stupefied, by a pounding on the door. He turned on the light and stumbled to the door, noting on the way that Malone, breathing whiskey fumes, had not been roused. The door swung open to reveal his landlady, Mrs Doorn, and Mrs Amster. Immediately, he became wide awake. Before Mrs Amster could stammer out her story, he had guessed what had happened.

A few minutes later, he plunged out the front door into the dimly lit three-in-the-morning night of Roosville. He ran to Huisman's house, which was only a block from the jail. The sheriff wasn't pleased to be pulled out of a beery sleep, but he put on his clothes and went to his car with Parry behind him.

'It's a good thing you didn't go out there by yourself,' he said thickly. 'Old man Havik could've shot your butt off and claimed you was trespassing. As it is, I ain't sure that Bonnie didn't go willingly with her father.'

'Maybe she did,' Parry said, sliding into the front seat. 'There's only one way to find out. If Havik has forced her to come with him, he's guilty of kidnapping. Mrs Amster said only that she woke up in time to see Havik and his sons pushing Bonnie into the car. She hadn't heard a thing before then.'

144

Though Huisman drove as swiftly as the winding gravel road would allow, he did not turn his siren or flashing red lights on. As they turned onto the road to the Havik farm, he turned off his headlights. It was evident, however, that they would not need them. The light from flowing lava and ejected rocks outlined the house brightly.

'That thing looks like it's getting ready to blow!' the sheriff said in a scared voice. 'I ain't never seen it so bright before!'

He and Parry both cried out. A particularly large fragment, a white spot in the eye of night, had risen from the cone and was soaring toward the house. It disappeared behind the roof, and a moment later flames broke out from the area in which it had fallen.

Huisman skidded the car to a stop by the fence with a shrieking of tires, and he and Parry tumbled out. The glare from the cone and from the rooftop flames outlined the house. It also showed them Bonnie, the top of her dress half torn off, her face twisted, running down the porch steps and toward them. She shouted something at them, but the whistling of steam and boomings of ejected rock and the cries of her father and brothers behind her drowned out her words.

Parry shouted at Huisman, 'Havik's got a shotgun!'

Cursing, Huisman stopped and undid the strap over the revolver in his holster. Havik ran out down the steps and into the yard, then halted to point the double-barreled weapon toward Bonnie.

Parry yelled at her to throw herself on the ground. Though she could not have heard him, she sprawled onto the ground heavily. Parry saw by the light of another whirling glowing thing that came from over the house and downward that she had tripped on a small rock, now cooled to a dull red.

Havik's gun boomed twice; pellets tore by Parry.

Huisman had thrown himself down, too, but had clumsily dropped his gun while doing so.

Parry saw where the mortarlike trajectory of the rock would

end, and he cried out. Later, he asked himself why he had tried to warn a man who was trying to kill his own daughter and would undoubtedly have tried to kill him, too. The only answer was that, being human, he was not always, by any means, logical.

There was a thud, and Havik fell, the semiliquid stone bent somewhat around his shattered head, clinging to it. The odor of burning flesh and hair drifted over the yard.

Rodeman and Albert Havik screamed with horror, and they ran to their father. That was all the time the sheriff needed. He recovered his revolver, and, rising, called at the two to drop their rifles. They started to do so but whirled around when several more rocks crashed into the ground just behind them. The sheriff, misinterpreting their actions, fired twice, and that was enough.

6

Curtius Parry had arranged for Bonnie Havik to work as a maid for a Westchester family, and he had talked to a plastic surgeon about the removal of her scar. Having done all he could for her, he was now taking his ease in his apartment on East 45th Street. He had a drink in his hand; Ed Malone, sitting in a huge easy chair near him, held a drink in one hand and a cigarette in the other.

Malone was saying, 'So Tizoc can't be found? So what? At least you saved Bonnie from being murdered, and nothing less than poetic justice got rid of her beastly family for her.'

Parry raised his thick eyebrows and said, 'They're dead, yes, but they're still alive in Bonnie, working their violence in her. It'll be a long time, if ever, before they cease to savage her guts. As for their deaths, *were* they examples of poetic justice? And as for Juan Tizoc, well, if I told you my theory about what actually happened to him, you'd say I was crazy.'

'Tell me anyhow, Cursh,' Malone said. 'I won't laugh at you or call you crazy.'

'I only ask that you keep it to yourself. Very well. The Catskills are not volcanic country, but Mexico is...'

'So?' Malone said after a long silence.

'Consider the theory that some of the townspeople were voicing. They spoke about the spontaneous fires in the Havik house when Bonnie was eleven, and they hinted that Bonnie was somehow responsible for the volcano. But they did not know that in every allegedly authentic case of salamandrism, as it's called, the phenomena always cease when the unhappy child becomes pubescent. So, Bonnie could not be responsible.'

'I'm glad to hear to hear you say that, Cursh,' Malone said. 'I was afraid you were going to base your theory on supernaturalism.'

'*Supernatural* is only a term used to explain the unexplainable. No, Ed, it wasn't Bonnie who heated up the sandstone not too deep in the earth and opened the earth in the cornfield to propel the white-hot stuff out onto the Haviks. It was Tizoc.'

Malone's drink sloshed over his hand, and he said, 'Tizoc?'

'Yes. The Havik men killed him, most bloodily and in a white-hot anger, I'm sure. And they dug a grave in the center of the field and filled it up and smoothed out the dirt over it. They expected that the roots of the corn plants would feed off Tizoc, and the plants themselves would destroy all surface evidences of his grave. This was most appropriate, though the Haviks would not know it, since corn was first domesticated in ancient Mexico. But Mexico is also the land of volcanoes. And a man, even a dead man, expresses himself in the spirit of the land in which he was raised and with the materials and in the method most available.

'The Haviks did not know that Tizoc's hatred was such, his desire for vengeance such, that he burned with these even as a dead man. He burned with hatred, his soul pulsed with violence even if the heart had ceased pulsing. And the sandstone was turned to magma with the violence of his hatred and vengeance...'

'Stop, Cursh!' Malone cried. 'I said I'd not call you crazy, but...'

'Yes, I know,' Parry said. 'But consider this, Ed, and then advance a better theory, if you can. You saw the report the geologists made on the composition and the relative proportions of the gases and the ashes expelled by the volcano. These are not what any volcano so far studied has expelled.'

Parry drank some Scotch and set the glass down.

'The ejected elements, and their relative proportions, are exactly those that compose the human body.'

The Henry Miller
Dawn Patrol

Foreword

This story is not science-fiction, though in its preliminary form it was. But the story didn't work out, so I put it aside and let it ripen – some might say fester – in my unconscious. Eventually, the good old hindbrain, or whatever it is that holds the unconscious, came up with an entirely new concept. And this said that the story should take place in modern times. This also said that the story wouldn't be science-fiction.

In my thinking, however, it could be classed as fantasy. Or perhaps a better label would be the psychology of fantasy.

Whatever the classification of this work, I had a lot of fun writing it. From the mail which the Playboy *editors received, the readers also enjoyed it very much. Some of these were from patients, attendants, and doctors in what are euphemistically called 'nursing homes.'*

Mrs Stoss, head night nurse of the Columbia Nursing Manor, looked into the room. Henry Miller added fake snores to the genuine ones of his three roommates. From under a half-closed lid, he could see the face of The Black Eagle behind and to one side of her jowly head. Over her broad shoulder rose a dark hand with curved thumb and forefinger meeting.

Signal: The Bloody Baroness won't be flying much tonight.

After Stoss and the attendant had left, Henry thought about what The Black Eagle had said before bedtime.

'Listen, Ace. Stoss is out to get your ass in a sling. I don't know what's bugging that fat mama, but she's sure burned about you getting all that dried-up pussy. She don't want nobody happy nohow. She's always bitching about this and that. *This* is you. *That* is the three husbands died on her.

'Whatever she wanted form her men, she didn't get it. Maybe she don't know what it was herself. 'Course, she never mentions fucking. She wouldn't say shit if she had a mouthful. Whatever, Ace, I'm on your side. But if she catches you, can't nobody help you.'

An hour before dawn, he awoke. Piss call. His joy stick was as upright and as hard as that in the Spad XIII he'd flown fifty-nine years ago. He clutched it, moved it to left and right, saw the wings dipping in response.

He climbed out of bed and stood blinking before the dresser. On it were two framed photographs. One was of his daughter, poor wretch. Its glass was cracked, damaged when he'd flung it across the room after she'd refused to smuggle in booze for him.

The other photo was of a man standing by a biplane. He was

a handsome twenty-year-old, a lieutenant of the Army Air Service, himself. The Spad, *The Bitter Pill*, bore a hat-in-the-ring, the 94th Squadron insignia, on its fuselage. The glass shimmered in the faint light, reflecting his days of glory.

Then he'd been half man, half Spad, a centaur of the blue. Flesh welded to wood, fabric, and metal. Now – seventy-nine, bald head, one-eyed, face like a shell-torn battlefield, false teeth, skinny body in sagging pajamas.

But The Lone Eagle was up and ready for another dawn patrol. He limped to the bathroom, favoring the bad knee, and he pissed. His joy stick, which was also, economically, his Vickers machine gun, became as limp as a cigarette in a latrine. Never mind. It'd be functioning when he closed in on the Hun.

After leaving the bathroom, he opened a dresser drawer and removed a leather fur-lined helmet and a pair of flier's goggles. He put these on and taxied to the hall. No enemy craft were in sight. The stench of shit hung in the air, radiated from several hundred obsolete types. They'd crapped in bed, and now some were awake, shrilling for the attendants to clean them up. Nobody was going to do it, though, until after dawn.

Most of the obsoletes were asleep, and they'd be indifferent if they went all day with shit down to their toes. Or, if they were aware of it, they couldn't move, couldn't talk.

Oh, oh! Here came The White Ghost. Around the corner far down the hall, a woman in a wheelchair had appeared. She was up early, looking for a victim. If she kept on her heading, she'd run into the Von Richthofen of the nursing home. Stoss would rave at her like a sergeant reaming out a dumb recruit.

He returned to his hangar to allow The White Ghost to roll on by him. She was ninety-six, but her fuel line wasn't clogged. A real ace, a sky shark, deadly. If she wasn't so damn ugly, he would have challenged her long ago.

Silently, she wheeled on by. She never talked, just cruised day and night, hoping to catch somebody by surprise. As soon as she passed, he banked left and flew down the hall. Though the pace made his undercarriage hurt, and the Hispano-Suiza in his chest thumped, he got to his objective on schedule.

This hangar held only two, Harz and Whittaker. Harz was a snoring lump, big as a Zeppelin Staaken bomber. He could take her any time, but it was the sleek tough fighters he was after. Like Whittaker. A widow – weren't they all? – of unadmitted age but to his keen falcon eye about seventy-four. Except for some of the young nurses, the handsomest craft in the place.

Her framework was splendid, though covered by wrinkled fabric. Her motor cowlings were still shapely, considering the date on which the factory had shipped her out. He classified her as a Fokker D-VIIF, the best.

She'd been sociable enough – until the day he'd zoomed by and dropped a note challenging her. From then on, she was as cool and aloof as the Kaiser invited to dinner by a pig farmer. But she had class. She'd not run squealing to The Baroness.

His motor having quit racing, he glided toward her, then stopped. What the hell! Something was crawling under the sheet over her. A giant cockroach? A water bug? No, it was her hand moving over her cockpit. The sheet was fluttering like fabric ripping from the wing of a Nieuport in a too-long, too-hard dive.

Grinning, he climbed over the bar at the foot of the bed and raised the sheet.

Whittaker moaned, her 185-horsepower, six-cylinder, in-line, water-cooled BMW IIIa purring. Her fingers were playing with her cockpit instrumentation. *Sacré merde!* The hoity-toity Fokker wouldn't answer his challenge, but she wasn't above a jack-off dogfight, a furtive combat with herself.

Under the sheet, in a darkness like the inside of a night cloud, The Lone Eagle glided. Her widespread legs guided him like landing-strip lights. He was ready for sudden action, an air-raid-siren scream, her fists beating at his head like shrapnel from Archie.

He pushed her hand away, felt no start, heard no protest. He nose-dived, the wind screaming through the wind wires and struts, his motor roaring. Then he was zeroed in, firing quick short bursts, what the hell, his tongue was a Vickers machine gun, too.

Now, all caution abandoned, he poured a long, slow stream of fire into her cockpit. The Fokker shuddered and moaned under his blasting. Thank God she wasn't like so many of the Columbia Huns. They weren't too clean; they smelled like the early World War One rotary-engine planes. Castor oil was used then for lubrication, and the poor bastards that breathed it got diarrhea.

Her exhaust pipe was clean and her cockpit was sprayed with some Frenchy-smelling perfume. Tasted like bootleg alky. No time for nostalgia now, though.

Whittaker knew he was present, but she wasn't saying a word to him. Still waters run deep; aces fly high. She'd incorporated him into her fantasy; to her, he wasn't real flesh; he was part of her dreamworld. So what? His Vickers was ready. First, though, a few maneuvers. He crawled on up, grabbed her big round cowlings, chewed on the propeller hubs, then eased the gun into the cockpit. She uttered, softly, lovingly, obscenities and profanities she'd probably not heard until she came to the nursing home.

Now she was tossing him up and down as if he were flying through one air pocket after another, hitting updrafts after each one. Now his Vickers was chattering, eating up the cartridges in the belt, the phosphorus-burning bullets tracing ecstasy across the night sky.

It was too much for the D-VIIF. She gave a loud cry, and her fuel tank ruptured. Shit squirted out over his Vickers and his undercarriage.

Cursing, he zoomed out of the cloud cover, sideslipped from

the bed and raced toward the doorway. The Staaken was up now, yelling but not knowing what was going on. Without her glasses, she was as blind as a doughboy in a smoke screen.

The Baroness' voice rose from somewhere around the corner of the hall. Trapped! No, not The Lone Eagle! He plunged into a hangar tenanted by four pilots long past flight duty. Oh, oh! A visitor! That crazy crone Simmons, the eighty-year-old with eczema, was in bed with poor old Osborn. She was on all fours between his skinny legs. She didn't mind that his feet had been cut off in an accident years ago. All she was interested in was his joy stick. She'd taken out her false teeth and put them on the bed behind her.

The other old vets were snoring away. Simmons raised her face, which looked like a dried-up used rubber, and she snarled gummily at him. Osborn was on his back, desperately trying to gain altitude, but he couldn't get off the runway. A real kiwi. Henry slid under the bed. If The Baroness came in here, she might be so mad at the two above him she'd forget to check his hangar. If Simmons kept her trap shut . . .

Simmons yelled. 'You footless old bastard! My Gawd, I'm sick and tired of sucking limp dicks!'

Henry was so startled he raised his head and banged it against the springs. 'Oh, shit!'

A long silent minute passed. Then the springs began going up and down. Artillery barrage. So Simmons had managed somehow to unjam the old fart's gun. The Lone Eagle should make a run for it. The Baroness would soon be in Whittaker's hangar. He crawled out and stood up. The three oldsters were still sleeping, toothless jaws gaping like baby birds begging for worms. Worms were all they'd get.

Osborn was still on his back. Simmons was standing up, clutching his left thigh with both hands. *Sacrebleu!* His leg was jammed up to the calf up her cockpit. She was bouncing up and down on it like a toy monkey on a stick, a Sopwith Camel caught in an Archie trap. Osborn was being dragged toward the foot of the bed as each bound carried her backward.

She tried to turn as he circled her widely, but her machine movement plunged the stump into her.

He started to take off for Allied territory, then stopped as Simmons screamed. One of her plunges had brought her toes between the false teeth, and they'd closed like a wolf trap. As she fell over the end of the bed, he zoomed out laughing. What next?

The only one in the hall was The White Ghost. Here she came, full throttle, grinning like the skull insignia on the great Nungesser's Nieuport. She'd wait until he began to pass her, then...wham!

She tried to turn as he circled her widely, but her machine didn't have the terrific right torque of a Camel. He got behind her, pushed as fast as his damaged undercarriage allowed, and then let loose. Around the corner, Stoss bellowed like the motors of a Gotha bomber.

Just as he reached the other corner, he heard a scream followed by a crash. He couldn't resist peeking around the corner. The Baroness was on her back. The machine was lying on its side, its pilot sprawled by it. The Black Eagle was laughing too hard to help either of them.

Henry took off for home base, put his flying gear into the dresser drawer, and crawled into bed. The Fokker's shit was all over his fuselage, but he'd just have to endure it until things settled down. Anyway, the shit didn't smell as bad as Stoss' breath.

The old Hispano was thumping as if it had sand in its bearings. He couldn't take too many sorties like this one much longer. One of these days, the motor'd give out and he'd go into the final dive. So what? Was there a better way to die? He wasn't like the other old pilots, too tired, sick, or senile to care about anything. He was going to stay in the combat zone until The Biggest Ace downed him.

Not, however, before he knocked The Bloody Baroness

flaming out of the skies. He hated her as much as she loathed him...to hell with her. He slid back to September 1918. The Big Push. That month, he'd shot down four planes and had busted two Drache observation balloons.

But October first, as he was firing at a Pfalz D-12, that Kraut fighter had come from nowhere behind him. *The Bitter Pill* was in rags, its fabric was burning, his knee was shattered, and boiling radiator water was scalding his legs. He couldn't take to the silk because that asshole, A.E.F. Commander 'Black Jack' Pershing, had forbidden American fliers to carry parachutes.

He'd had to ride the out-of-control ship to the ground while he hoped the fuel tank wouldn't explode. Somehow, he'd managed to sideslip it, putting the fire out, and then he'd leveled out just before he crashed into a small river. The Kraut soldiers who dragged him out thought he was dead. No wonder. His left eye and most of his teeth had been knocked out and he was covered with blood.

It was all downglide from then on. The rest of his life – a crippled carpenter with an ailing wife and four kids. Still, the old joy stick, the trusty Vickers, had functioned splendidly. Though he didn't have as many cartridges in his belts as when he'd flown in the Big One, he had more than some young punks he knew.

His daughter said, 'But, Dad! You're getting worse! The day nurse told me you're losing control of your bowels!'

'Horsepoppy! One of my roommates crapped on the floor – must have thought he was home – and I slipped on it. I didn't take a shower right away, because the night nurse gets uptight if she finds me out of bed after taps.'

She bit her lip, then said, 'Mrs Stoss says you sneak around at night and...uh...bother the old ladies.'

'Any of them complaining?'

'No. But she says most of them are too senile to resist. They don't know what's going on, and those who do are just as bad...'

He chuckled. 'Say it. Just as bad as me.'

The other patients being visited – patients, hell; geriatric prisoners of war – sat on sofas or wheelchairs in the big lounge. They were chattering away like a bunch of French whores or sitting dull-eyed, slack-jawed, drooling, while their relatives tried to get a rise out of them.

By God, a rise could be gotten out of him. Wouldn't they be surprised if they knew just what kind and how many?

'I wish I *had* let you go to the vets' hospital. There aren't any old women there you could take advantage of.'

'You're the one wanted me to come here to Busiris so I wouldn't be so far away from you. So I see you once a month – if I'm lucky.

'And don't give me that crap about sixty miles is a long way to drive. No, I made the right decision, after all, even if it was mainly for your convenience. The vets' hospital is out. If I have to choose between elephants' graveyards...'

'Nurse Stoss says she may have to put you in a room by yourself. Or...uh...restrain you.'

'You mean, strap me down in bed? Or stick me in a straitjacket? Bullshit! You forget I broke out of the toughest prison camp the fucking Krauts had, and I was almost a basket case.'

'Please, Dad, not so loud! And don't use those filthy words! Listen. It won't be easy, but we can work it out if you'll be nice. You could come home...'

'Are you nuts? Your husband hates me! I'd have to sleep on the living-room sofa! That yapping dog drives me crazy!'

'Shh! You're embarrassing me. Mrs Stoss says you're out of control. She thinks –'

'She *thinks!* But she's never *seen* me doing anything! She's crazier than you think I am.'

He waved at The Black Eagle, who was wheeling Mr Zhinsky out of the lounge. The Black Eagle grinned. He knew who'd caused the uproar that morning.

'Who's that colored man?'

'The spade of the Spads. He flew double patrol last night because one of those drunken Zeps they call attendants couldn't make it. He often works double shifts to support his family and put two kids through college. He's one of those lazy niggers your redneck husband's always talking about. He's my buddy, flies wing for me.'

'What're you talking about?'

'Just my senile ramblings.'

She stood up, sniffing, and dabbed at her eyes with a handkerchief. 'If only you could be like the others.'

'You mean, sit around with my mouth open catching flies and let someone wipe my ass for me? Or sing nonsense songs all day and all night until I've driven those who weren't crazy when they came in out of their minds?

'Not me! I'm not giving up! The fucking Kaiser is going to rue the day Wild Hank enlisted. I'm going to keep on racking up my kills.'

'Kills?'

'Just a manner of speaking.'

'Listen, Dad. That nurse says she's treated you with all the compassion and care in the world, and –'

'Compassion? Care? That steely-eyed Hun? The scourge of the skies?'

'Don't talk so crazy! I can't stand it!'

'Maybe we just ought to write to each other. That way, you won't have to listen to your husband bitching about the cost of the gas you use getting here.'

He rose and limped away, not looking at her but saying loudly, 'Next time you come, bring some whiskey! And leave the bullshit at home!'

He passed Mrs Whittaker, who was talking to a visitor. He winked. She turned as red as Von Richtofen's triplane.

Blushing!

So he hadn't been completely a figure in her dreamworld. She had known that he was real flesh. Also, she hadn't told

Stoss the truth about the commotion that morning. The code of the skies was unbroken. Chivalry wasn't dead.

Maybe she was too embarrassed to admit to anyone, even herself, what had happened. Or maybe she thought every woman crapped when she had an orgasm. Maybe her husband had been a kinky shit-eater and she'd believed him when he told her that's how everybody did it. But could anyone be that rotten?

What evil lurked in the hearts of men?

Only God and The Shadow knew.

All quiet on the Western Front. No impending Armistice, though. The Baroness had changed her schedule and now went up on patrol every half-hour. The Black Eagle had warned that she had the red ass for him, was loaded for bear, and was as mad as a wildcat with a tied-off dong in mating season.

'The next time she hears a ruckus, she's heading right for your room. If you're not in it, she's got you. That means a lot of extra legwork for her, and that fat-ass don't like that no way. She hates your guts 'cause you won't lie down and die while you're still living. She isn't getting any ass, but she don't want you to, either. A real bitch in the manger.'

Henry stayed in bed, except for piss call, for five nights. The sixth, Stoss went back to her regular schedule. Henry grinned. The Lone Eagle had outwaited The Bloody Baroness.

The seventh day, he had to get into action. He'd been on furlough too long. His control stick was out of control. His Vickers was throbbing with the pressure of the ammo belts. At 0510, sure that The Baroness was at her HQ, he put on his helmet and goggles.

'Contact!'

'Contact!'

Out of the hangar, down the runway, then soaring into the wild blue yonder, heavy with the fumes of senior-citizen shit.

Target: Mrs Hannover. With that name, she had to be a CL

IIIa, the beautiful escort fighter that looked like a one-seater from a distance. But when an Allied pilot got on its tail, he found himself staring into the red eye of the observer's Parabellum machine gun.

He'd talked to the kid – she was only sixty-five – and he'd found her charming. She did have one functional defect, though. She'd sometimes get a faraway look, as if she were listening to a radio receiver in her head. She quit talking; she didn't even notice when you left.

That was why her children had put her in the nursing home. She was an embarrassment, not to mention that she was rich and they were trying to get her declared incompetent.

At 0513, he came in on a glide path, surveyed the area, found her partner sleeping, and landed in her bed. He was ready to take off, full throttle, if she screamed. Instead, she sighed as if she'd known he was coming, and the dogfight was on.

Not much of a combat though. CL IIIa's *did* fool you.

The only thing that bothered him for a while, aside from the lack of aggressiveness, was that she kept crying out, though softly, 'Jim! Oh, Jim! My God, Jim!' but if she thought he was some other ace, what the hell? You didn't have to be properly identified by the enemy before you downed her.

His long leave had fired him up so that he decided to stay for another tangle. It took only fifteen minutes to reload his Vickers with the Hannover's help, though she still thought he was that jerk, Jim. But just as he was about to shoot again, he felt a stabbing pain in his exhaust pipe. His scream of anguish mingled with her climactic cry, and he barrel-rolled away and out of the bed. It was a crash landing, but he wasn't structurally damaged. The only repairs he needed were to the fabric on his tail and the mid-parts of his wings. They were scraped raw, but he was flight-ready.

The White Ghost was in her machine at the foot of the bed and cackling like The Shadow (a famous World War One ace before he took up crime fighting). The cane she carried concealed under the blanket over her legs, a Hotchkiss cannon if ever he saw one, was thrusting at the Hannover. The White Ghost was trying to goose her, too.

He swore. He'd forgotten the first rule of aerial combat. Always make sure the Boche isn't sneaking up on your tail.

As he rose, he groaned. He was damaged worse than he'd thought. He felt as if a Le Prieur rocket had been shoved up him. Damn The White Ghost!

'*Schweinhund!* I'll rendezvous with you some other time!'

He sped from the hangar as fast as a seventy-nine-year-old Spad could go. Though he needed a breather, he had no time for it. Get back to base before The Baroness intercepted him. The worst of it was that his Vickers hadn't used the second load. It was sticking out from his pajamas like a 7.7mm Lewis in the nose of a Handley Page 0/400 bomber. He was proud that it had an independent life. But he wished at that moment that he could control it.

Puffing, he banked left and shot down the runway and into his hangar. He just had time to take the scene in before his wheels slid out from under him and he ground-looped. A roommate, Tyson, was standing there, his stick hanging out, a puddle of piss on the floor before him. And there was The Bloody Baroness, cursing and on her hands and knees. She must have run in to check on him and slipped on the mess.

Collision course. He slammed onto her back and her nose went down. Thump! She didn't get up or even move. She stayed in the same position, her nose on the ground, her wings and undercarriage under her fuselage, her tail up.

'Aha! Gotcha!'

Why not? He was done for. There was going to be one hell of a court-martial. He'd be grounded, strapped, jailed, confined, incarcerated. No more dawn patrols. Ever.

It was the first time he'd used such an unorthodox tactic. But ramming your Vickers up the enemy's exhaust pipe was a sure way to make a kill, even if the authorities frowned on it.

Though it meant he would go down, too, make the final fall from the big blue, he would add the ace of aces to his list.

He reached under and seized her huge cowlings – they must weigh half a ton apiece – and began the series of maneuvers, Immelmanns, *chandelles, virages,* you name it, that would end in his victory. The only distraction was from Tyson. His usually leaden eyes brightened, and he sneered.

'You filthy buggerer!'

But he walked to his bed and lay down and soon was snoring.

Just before he emptied all of his 7.65mms, she groaned and showed signs of coming to. Then she began panting and moaning. Maybe she was half unconscious, in a fantasy. Like the Fokker and the Hannover, she was only partly in this, to them, disappointing world. Maybe she really didn't know what was going on. Whatever the case, the Vickers was in her exhaust pipe, and that's where she wanted it. She'd wanted it all her life but had been too inhibited to bring it up from the unconscious and tell her husbands that's what she wanted.

It was this that The Black Eagle, whose daughter was a psychology major, had been hinting at.

He didn't care. Psychology-shmychology. Though his Hispano was straining so hard it was about to tear itself loose, he was shooting her down. Let the aftermath be an afterbirth for all he cared, let...

The Black Eagle came in as Henry Miller, the crazy old ace, the last of the fighter pilots of the Big One to engage the Hun, fell off The Baroness. Henry was dead, no mistaking those glazed eyes and that blue-gray color of skin.

Mrs Stoss was on all fours, her big bare ass sticking up, her anus pulsing and dripping. She was muttering something.

Was it 'More! More! Please! Please!'?

Then she was fully awake, and she was screaming as she heaved herself up, and The Black Eagle was laughing hysterically.

The Lone Eagle's smile was broader than his.

The Problem
of the Sore Bridge
– Among Others

Foreword

This is another of my fictional-author stories, originally published in a magazine under the byline of 'Harry Manders.' Manders was the one who was supposed to have narrated the history of his partnership with A.J. Raffles, the famous gentleman burglar. After Raffles' death he became a journalist. When I said 'famous' above, I should perhaps have said once-famous. Any devoted reader of detective and mystery fiction of both the past and present will recognize the names of Harry 'Bunny' Manders and Arthur J. Raffles. In the earlier part of this century Raffles was as well known as Sam Spade and Philip Marlowe and Lew Archer are today. In fact, Raffles was used in English literature as a synonym of a 'gentleman burglar.' It was, I believe, even in the dictionaries, but the dictionaries and encyclopedias in my library, the earliest of which is a 1939 issue, fail to list the word. Too bad.

Sherlock Holmes fans will recognize the story, the title of which is paraphrased by mine. They will also know Inspector Hopkins, though a few of them may not be aware of Inspector Mackenzie. He appeared in the Raffles stories and was the one who finally collared Manders.

I got a big kick out of making the trails of Holmes and Raffles cross, however briefly, and having Raffles solve three crimes which Holmes couldn't.

Editorial Preface:

Harry 'Bunny' Manders was an English writer whose other profession was that of gentleman burglar, circa 1890-1900. Manders' adored senior partner and mentor, Arthur J. Raffles, was a cricket player rated on a par with Lord Peter Wimsey or W. G. Grace. Privately, he was a second-story man, a cracksman, a quick-change artist and confidence man whose only peer was Arsène Lupin. Manders' narratives have appeared in four volumes titled (in America) *The Amateur Cracksman, Raffles, A Thief in the Night,* and *Mr Justice Raffles.* 'Raffles' has become incorporated in the English language (and a number of others) as a term for a gentleman burglar or dashing upper-crust Jimmy Valentine. Mystery story aficionados, of course, are thoroughly acquainted with the incomparable, though tragically flawed, Raffles and his sidekick Manders.

After Raffles' death in the Boer War, Harry Manders gave up crime and became a respectable journalist and author. He married, had children, and died in 1924. His earliest works were agented by E.W. Hornung, Arthur Conan Doyle's brother-in-law. A number of Manders' posthumous works have been agented by Barry Perowne. One of his tales, however, was forbidden by his will to be printed until fifty years after his death. The stipulated time has passed, and now the public may learn how the world was saved without knowing that it was in the gravest peril. It will also discover that the paths of the great Raffles and the great Holmes did cross at least once.

1

The Boer bullet that pierced my thigh in 1900 lamed me for the rest of my life, but I was quite able to cope with its effects. However, at the age of sixty-one, I suddenly find that a killer that has felled far more men than bullets has lodged within me. The doctor, my kinsman, gives me six months at the most, six months which he frankly says will be very painful. He knows of my crimes, of course, and it may be that he thinks that my suffering will be poetic justice. I'm not sure. But I'll swear that this is the meaning of the slight smile which accompanied his declaration of my doom.

Be that as it may, I have little time left. But I have determined to write down that adventure of which Raffles and I once swore we would never breathe a word. It happened; it really happened. But the world would not have believed it then. It would have been convinced that I was a liar or insane.

I am writing this, nevertheless, because fifty years from now the world may have progressed to the stage where such things as I tell of are credible. Man may even have landed on the moon by then, if he has perfected a propeller which works in the ether as well as in the air. Or if he discovers the same sort of drive that brought...well, I anticipate.

I must hope that the world of 1974 will believe this adventure. Then the world will know that, whatever crimes Raffles and I committed, we paid for them a thousandfold by what we did that week in the May of 1895. And, in fact, the world is and always will be immeasurably in our debt. Yes, my dear doctor, my scornful kinsman, who hopes that I will suffer pain as punishment, I long ago paid off my debt. I only wish that you could be alive to read these words. And, who knows, you may live to be a hundred and may read this account of what you owe me. I hope so.

2

I was nodding in my chair in my room at Mount Street when the clanging of the lift gates in the yard startled me. A moment later, a familiar tattoo sounded on my door. I opened it to find, as I expected, A.J. Raffles himself. He slipped in, his bright blue eyes merry, and he removed his Sullivan from his lips to point it at my whiskey and soda.

'Bored, Bunny?'

'Rather,' I replied. 'It's been almost a year since we stirred our stumps. The voyage around the world after the Levy affair was stimulating. But that ended four months ago. And since then...'

'Ennui and bile!' Raffles cried. 'Well, Bunny, that's all over! Tonight we make the blood run hot and cold and burn up all green biliousness!'

'And the swag?' I said.

'Jewels, Bunny! To be exact, star sapphires, or blue corundum, cut *en cabochon*. That is, round with a flat underside. And large, Bunny, vulgarly large, almost the size of a hen's egg, if my informant was not exaggerating. There's a mystery about them, Bunny, a mystery my fence has been whispering with his Cockney speech into my ear for some time. They're dispensed by a Mr James Phillimore of Kensal Rise. But where he gets them, from whom he lifts them, no one knows. My fence has hinted that they may not come from manorial strongboxes or milady's throat but are smuggled from Southeast Asia or South Africa or Brazil, directly from the mine. In any event, we are going to do some reconnoitering tonight, and if the opportunity should arise...'

'Come now, A.J.,' I said bitterly. 'You *have* done all the needed reconnoitering. Be honest! Tonight we suddenly find that the moment is propitious, and we strike? Right?'

I had always been somewhat piqued that Raffles chose to do all the preliminary work, the casing, as the underworld says, himself. For some reason, he did not trust me to scout the layout.

Raffles blew a huge and perfect smoke ring from his Sullivan, and he clapped me on the shoulder. 'You see through me, Bunny! Yes, I've examined the grounds and checked out Mr Phillimore's schedule.'

I was unable to say anything to the most masterful man I have ever met. I meekly donned dark clothes, downed the rest of the whiskey, and left with Raffles. We strolled for some distance, making sure that no policemen were shadowing us, though we had no reason to believe they would be. We then took the last train to Willesden at 11:21. On the way I said, 'Does Phillimore live near old Baird's house?'

I was referring to the money lender killed by Jack Rutter, the details of which case are written in *Wilful Murder*.

'As a matter of fact,' Raffles said, watching me with his keen steel-grey eyes, 'it's the *same* house. Phillimore took it when Baird's estate was finally settled and it became available to renters. It's a curious coincidence, Bunny, but then all coincidences are curious. To man, that is. Nature is indifferent.'

(Yes, I know I stated before that his eyes were blue. And so they were. I've been criticized for saying in one story that his eyes were blue and in another that they were grey. But he has, as any idiot should have guessed, grey-blue eyes which are one color in one light and another in another.)

'That was January, 1895,' Raffles said. 'We are in deep waters, Bunny. My investigations have unearthed no evidence that Mr Phillimore existed before November, 1894. Until he took the lodgings in the East End, no one seems to have heard of or even seen him. He came out of nowhere, rented his third-story lodgings – a terrible place, Bunny – until January. Then he rented the house where bad old Baird gave up the ghost. Since then he's been living a quiet-enough life, excepting the visits he makes once a month to several East End fences. He has a cook and a housekeeper, but these do not live in with him.'

At this late hour, the train went no farther than Willesden Junction. We walked from there toward Kensal Rise. Once more, I was dependent on Raffles to lead me through unfamiliar country. However, this time the moon was up, and the country was not quite as open as it had been the last time I was here. A number of cottages and small villas, some only partially built, occupied the empty fields I had passed through that fateful night. We walked down a footpath between a woods and a field, and we came out on the tarred woodblock road that had been laid only four years before. It now had the curb that had been lacking then, but there was still only one pale lamppost across the road from the house.

Before us rose the corner of a high wall with the moonlight shining on the broken glass on top of the wall. It also outlined the sharp spikes on top of the tall green gate. We slipped on our masks. As before, Raffles reached up and placed champagne corks on the spikes. He then put his covert-coat over the corks. We slipped over quietly, Raffles removed the corks, and we stood by the wall in a bed of laurels. I admit I felt apprehensive, even more so than the last time. Old Baird's ghost seemed to hover about the place. The shadows were thicker than they should have been.

I started toward the gravel path leading to the house, which was unlit. Raffles seized my coattails. 'Quiet!' he said. 'I see somebody – something, anyway – in the bushes at the far end of the garden. Down there, at the angle of the wall.'

I could see nothing, but I trusted Raffles, whose eyesight was as keen as a Red Indian's. We moved slowly alongside the wall, stopping frequently to peer into the darkness of the bushes at the angle of the wall. About twenty yards from it, I saw something shapeless move in the shrubbery. I was all for clearing out then, but Raffles fiercely whispered that we could not permit a competitor to scare us away. After a quick conference, we moved in very slowly but surely, slightly more solid shadows in the shadow of the wall. And in a few very long and perspiration-drenched minutes, the stranger fell with one blow from Raffles' fist upon his jaw.

Raffles dragged the snoring man out from the bushes so we could get a look at him by moonlight. 'What have we here, Bunny?' he said. 'Those long curly locks, that high arching nose, the overly thick eyebrows, and the odor of expensive Parisian perfume? Don't you recognize him?'

I had to confess that I did not.

'What, that is the famous journalist and infamous duelist, Isadora Persano!' he said. 'Now tell me you have never heard of him, or her, as the case may be?'

'Of course!' I said. 'The reporter for the *Daily Telegraph*!'

'No more,' Raffles said. 'He's a free-lancer now. But what the devil is he doing here?'

'Do you suppose,' I said slowly, 'that he, too, is one thing by day and quite another at night?'

'Perhaps,' Raffles said. 'But he may be here in his capacity of journalist. He's also heard things about Mr James Phillimore. The devil take it! If the press is here, you may be sure that the Yard is not far behind!'

Mr Persano's features curiously combined a rugged masculinity with an offensive effeminacy. Yet the latter characteristic was not really his fault. His father, an Italian diplomat, had died before he was born. His English mother had longed for a girl, been bitterly disappointed when her only-born was a boy, and, unhindered by a husband or conscience, had named him Isadora and raised him as a girl. Until he entered a public school, he wore dresses. In school, his long hair and certain feminine actions made him the object of an especially vicious persecution by the boys. It was there that he developed his abilities to defend himself with his fists. When he became an adult, he lived on the continent for several years. During this time, he earned a reputation as a dangerous man to insult. It was said that he had wounded half a dozen men with sword or pistol.

From the little bag in which he carried the tools of the trade, Raffles brought a length of rope and a gag. After tying and gagging Persano, Raffles went through his pockets. The only object that aroused his curiosity was a very large matchbox in an inner pocket of his cloak. Opening this, he brought out something that shone in the moonlight.

'By all that's holy!' he said. 'It's one of the sapphires!'

'Is Persano a rich man?' I said.

'He doesn't have to work for a living, Bunny. And since he hasn't been in the house yet, I assume he got this from a fence. I also assume that he put the sapphire in the matchbox because a pickpocket isn't likely to steal a box of matches. As it was, *I* was about to ignore it!'

'Let's get out of here,' I said. But he crouched staring down at the journalist with an occasional glance at the jewel. This, by the way, was only about a quarter of the size of a hen's egg. Presently, Persano stirred, and he moaned under the gag. Raffles whispered into his ear, and he nodded. Raffles, saying to me, 'Cosh him if he looks like he's going to yell,' undid the gag.

Persano, as requested, kept his voice low. He confessed that he had heard rumors from his underworld contacts about the precious stones. Having tracked down our fence, he had contrived easily enough to buy one of Mr Phillimore's jewels. In fact, he said, it was the first one that Mr Phillimore had brought in to fence. Curious, wondering where the stones came from, since there were no reported thefts of these, he had come here to spy on Phillimore.

'There's a great story here,' he said. 'But just what, I haven't the foggiest. However, I must warn you that...'

His warning was not heeded. Both Raffles and I heard the low voices outside the gate and the scraping of shoes against gravel.

'Don't leave me tied up here, boys,' Persano said. 'I might have a little trouble explaining satisfactorily just what I'm doing here. And then there's the jewel...'

Raffles slipped the stone back into the matchbox and put it into Persano's pocket. If we were to be caught, we would not have the gem on us. He untied the journalist's wrists and ankles and said, 'Good luck!'

A moment later, after throwing our coats over the broken glass, Raffles and I went over the rear rail. We ran crouching into a dense woods about twenty yards back of the house. At the other side at some distance was a newly built house and a newly laid road. A moment later, we saw Persano come over the wall. He ran by, not seeing us, and disappeared down the road, trailing a heavy cloud of perfume.

'We must visit him at his quarters,' said Raffles. He put his hand on my shoulder to warn me, but there was no need. I too had seen the three men come around the corner of the wall. One took a position at the angle of the wall; the other two started toward our woods. We retreated as quietly as possible. Since there was no train available at this late hour, we walked to Maida Vale and took a hansom from there to home. Raffles went to his rooms at the Albany and I to mine on Mount Street.

When we saw the evening papers, we knew that the affair had taken on even more bizarre aspects. But we still had no inkling of the horrifying metamorphosis yet to come.

I doubt if there is a literate person in the West – or in the Orient, for that matter – who has not read about the strange case of Mr James Phillimore. At eight in the morning, a hansom cab from Maida Vale pulled up before the gates of his estate. The housekeeper and the cook and Mr Phillimore were the only occupants of the house. The area outside the walls was being surveilled by eight men from the Metropolitan Police Department. The cab driver rang the electrically operated bell at the gate. Mr Phillimore walked out of the house and down the gravel path to the gate. Here he was observed by the cab driver, a policeman near the gate, and another in a tree. The latter could see clearly the entire front yard and house, and another man in a tree could clearly see the entire back yard and the back of the house.

Mr Phillimore opened the gate but did not step through it. Commenting to the cabbie that it looked like rain, he added that he would return to the house to get his umbrella. The cabbie, the policemen, and the housekeeper saw him reenter the house. The housekeeper was at that moment in the room which occupied the front part of the ground floor of the house. She went into the kitchen as Mr Phillimore entered the house. She did, however, hear his footsteps on the stairs from the hallway which led up to the first floor.

She was the last one to see Mr Phillimore. He did not come back out of the house. After half an hour Mr Mackenzie, the Scotland Yard inspector in charge, decided that Mr Phillimore had somehow become aware that he was under surveillance. Mackenzie gave the signal, and he with three men entered the gate, another four retaining their positions outside. At no time was any part of the area outside the walls unobserved. Nor was the area inside the walls unscrutinized at any time.

The warrant duly shown to the housekeeper, the policemen entered the house and made a thorough search. To their astonishment, they could find no trace of Mr Phillimore. The six-foot-six, twenty-stone* gentleman had utterly disappeared.

For the next two days, the house – and the yard around it – was the subject of the most intense investigation. This established that the house contained no secret tunnels or hideaways. Every cubic inch was accounted for. It was impossible for him not to have left the house; yet he clearly had not done so.

'Another minute's delay, and we would have been cornered,' Raffles said, taking another Sullivan from his silver cigarette case. 'But, Lord, what's going on there, what mysterious forces are working there? Notice that no jewels were found in the house. At least, the police reported none. Now, did Phillimore actually go back to get his umbrella? Of course not. The umbrella was in the stand by the entrance; yet he went right by it and on upstairs. So, he observed the foxes outside the gate and bolted into his briar bush like the good little rabbit he was.'

'And where is the briar bush?' I said.

'Ah! That's the question,' Raffles breathed. 'What kind of a rabbit is it which pulls the briar bush in after it? That is the sort of mystery which has attracted even the Great Detective himself. He was condescended to look into it.'

'Then let us stay away from the whole affair!' I cried. 'We have been singularly fortunate that none of our victims have called in your relative!'

Raffles was a third or fourth cousin to Holmes, though

Two hundred and eighty pounds.

neither had, to my knowledge, even seen the other. I doubt that the sleuth had even gone to Lord's, or anywhere else, to see a cricket match.

'I wouldn't mind matching wits with him,' Raffles said. 'Perhaps he might then change his mind about who's the most dangerous man in London.'

'We have more than enough money,' I said. 'Let's drop the whole business.'

'It was only yesterday that you were complaining of boredom, Bunny,' he said. 'No, I think we should pay a visit to our journalist. He may know something that we, and possibly the police, don't know. However, if you prefer,' he added contemptuously, 'you may stay home.'

That stung me, of course, and I insisted that I accompany him. A few minutes later, we got into a hansom, and Raffles told the driver to take us to Praed Street.

4

Persano's apartment was at the end of two flights of Carrara marble steps and a carved mahogany banister. The porter conducted us to 10-C but left when Raffles tipped him handsomely. Raffles knocked on the door. After receiving no answer within a minute, he picked the lock. A moment later, we were inside a suite of extravagantly furnished rooms. A heavy odor of incense hung in the air.

I entered the bedroom and halted aghast. Persano, clad only in underwear, lay on the floor. The underwear, I regret to say, was the sheer black lace of the *demimondaine*. I suppose that if brassieres had existed at that time he would have been wearing one. I did not pay his dress much attention, however, because of his horrible expression. His face was cast into a mask of unutterable terror.

Near the tips of his outstretched fingers lay the large matchbox. It was open, and in it writhed *something*.

I drew back, but Raffles, after one soughing of intaken breath, felt the man's forehead and pulse and looked into the rigid eyes.

'Stark staring mad,' he said. 'Frozen with the horror that comes from the deepest of abysses.'

Emboldened by his example, I drew near the box. Its contents looked somewhat like a worm, a thick tubular worm, with a dozen slim tentacles projecting from one end. This could be presumed to be its head, since the area just above the roots of the tentacles was ringed with small pale-blue eyes. These had pupils like a cat's. There was no nose or nasal openings or mouth.

'God!' I said shuddering. 'What is it?'

'Only God knows,' Raffles said. He lifted Persano's right hand and looked at the tips of the fingers. 'Note the fleck of blood on each,' he said. 'They look as if pins have been stuck into them.'

He bent over closer to the thing in the box and said, 'The tips of the tentacles bear needlelike points, Bunny. Perhaps Persano is not so much paralyzed from horror as from venom.'

'Don't get any closer, for Heaven's sake!' I said.

'Look, Bunny!' he said. 'Doesn't that thing have a tiny shining object in one of its tentacles?'

Despite my nausea, I got down by him and looked straight at the monster. 'It seems to be a very thin and slightly curving piece of glass,' I said. 'What of it?'

Even as I spoke, the end of the tentacle which held the object opened, and the object disappeared within it.

'That *glass*,' Raffles said, 'is what's left of the *sapphire*. It's eaten it. That piece seems to have been the last of it.'

'Eaten a sapphire?' I said, stunned. 'Hard metal, blue corundum?'

'I think, Bunny,' he said slowly, 'the sapphire may only have looked like a sapphire. Perhaps it was not aluminum oxide but something hard enough to fool an expert. The interior may have been filled with something softer than the shell. Perhaps the shell held an embryo.'

'What?' I said.

'I mean, Bunny, is it inconceivable, but nevertheless true, that that thing might have *hatched* from the jewel?'

5

We left hurriedly a moment later. Raffles had decided against taking the monster – for which I was very grateful – because he wanted the police to have all the clues available.

'There's something very wrong here, Bunny,' he said. 'Very sinister.' He lit a Sullivan and added in a drawl, 'Very *alien*!'

'You mean un-British?' I said.

'I mean. . . un-Earthly.'

A little later, we got out of the cab at St James' Park and walked across it to the Albany. In Raffles' room, smoking cigars and drinking Scotch whiskey and soda, we discussed the significance of all we had seen but could come to no explanation, reasonable or otherwise. The next morning, reading the *Times*, the *Pall Mall Gazette*, and the *Daily Telegraph*, we learned how narrowly we had escaped. According to the papers, Inspectors Hopkins and Mackenzie and the private detective Holmes had entered Persano's rooms two minutes after we had left. Persano had died while on the way to the hospital.

'Not a word about the worm in the box,' Raffles said. 'The police are keeping it a secret. No doubt, they fear to alarm the public.'

There would be, in fact, no official reference to the creature. Nor was it until 1922 that Dr Watson made a passing reference to it in a published adventure of his colleague. I do not know what happened to the thing, but I suppose that it must have been placed in a jar of alcohol. There it must have quickly perished. No doubt the jar is collecting dust on some shelf in the backroom of some police museum. Whatever happened to it, it must have been disposed of. Otherwise, the world would not be what it is today.

'Strike me, there's only one thing to do, Bunny!' Raffles said, after he'd put the last paper down. 'We must get into Phillimore's house and look for ourselves!'

I did not protest. I was more afraid of his scorn than of the police. However, we did not launch our little expedition that evening. Raffles went out to do some reconnoitering on his own, both among the East End fences and around the house in Kensal Rise. The evening of the second day, he appeared at my rooms. I had not been idle, however. I had gathered a supply of more corks for the gatetop spikes by drinking a number of bottles of champagne.

'The police guard has been withdrawn from the estate itself,' he said. 'I didn't see any men in the woods nearby. So, we break into the late Mr Phillimore's house tonight. If he is late, that is,' he added enigmatically.

As the midnight chimes struck, we went over the gate once more. A minute later, Raffles was taking out the pane from the glass door. This he did with his diamond, a pot of treacle, and a sheet of brown paper, as he had done the night we broke in and found our would-be blackmailer dead with his head crushed by a poker.

He inserted his hand through the opening, turned the key in the lock, and drew the bolt at the bottom of the door open. This had been shot by a policeman who had then left by the kitchen door, or so we presumed. We went through the door, closed it behind us, and made sure that all the drapes of the front room were pulled tight. Then Raffles, as he did that evil night long ago, lit a match and with it a gas light. The flaring illumination showed us a room little changed. Apparently, Mr Phillimore had not been interested in redecorating. We went out into the hallway and upstairs, where three doors opened onto the first floor hallway.

The first door led to the bedroom. It contained a huge canopied bed, a midcentury monster Baird had bought secondhand in some East End shop, a cheap maple tallboy, a rocking chair, a thunder mug, and two large overstuffed leather armchairs.

'There was only one armchair the last time we were here,' Raffles said.

The second room was unchanged, being as empty as the first time we'd seen it. The room at the rear was the bathroom, also unchanged.

We went downstairs and through the hallway to the kitchen, and then we descended into the coal cellar. This also contained a small wine pantry. As I expected, we had found nothing. After all, the men from the Yard were thorough, and what they might have missed, Holmes would have found. I was about to suggest to Raffles that we should admit failure and leave before somebody saw the lights in the house. But a sound from upstairs stopped me.

Raffles had heard it, too. Those ears missed little. He held up a hand for silence, though none was needed. He said, a moment later, 'Softly, Bunny! It may be a policeman. But I think it is probably our quarry!'

We stole up the wooden steps, which insisted on creaking

under our weight. Thence we crept into the kitchen and from there into the hallway and then into the front room. Seeing nobody, we went up the steps to the first floor once more and gingerly opened the door of each room and looked within.

While we were poking our heads into the bathroom, we heard a noise again. It came from somewhere in the front of the house, though whether it was upstairs or down we could not tell.

Raffles beckoned to me, and I followed, also on tiptoe, down the hall. He stopped at the door of the middle room, looked within, then led me to the door of the bedroom. On looking in (remember, we had not turned out the gaslights yet), he started. And he said, 'Lord! One of the armchairs! It's gone!'

'But-but...who'd want to take a chair?' I said.

'Who, indeed!' he said, and ran down the steps with no attempt to keep quiet. I gathered my wits enough to order my feet to get moving. Just as I reached the door, I heard Raffles outside shouting, 'There he goes!' I ran out onto the little tiled veranda. Raffles was halfway down the gravel path, and a dim figure was plunging through the open gate. Whoever he was, he had had a key to the gate.

I remember thinking, irrelevantly, how cool the air had become in the short time we'd been in the house. Actually, it was not such an irrelevant thought since the advent of the cold air had caused a heavy mist. It hung over the road and coiled through the woods. And, of course, it helped the man we were chasing.

Raffles was as keen as a bill-collector chasing a debtor, and he kept his eyes on the vague figure until it plunged into a grove. When I came out its other side, breathing hard, I found Raffles standing on the edge of a narrow but rather deeply sunk brook. Nearby, half shrouded by the mist, was a short and narrow footbridge. Down the path that started from its other end was another of the half-built houses.

'He didn't cross that bridge,' Raffles said. 'I'd have heard him. If he went through the brook, he'd have done some splashing, and I'd have heard it. But he didn't have time to double back. Let's cross the bridge and see if he's left any footprints in the mud.'

We walked Indian file across the very narrow bridge. It bent a little under our weight, giving us an uneasy feeling. Raffles said, 'The contractor must be using as cheap materials as he can get away with. I hope he's putting better stuff into the houses. Otherwise, the first strong wind will blow them away.'

'It does seem rather fragile,' I said. 'The builder must be a fly-by-night. But nobody builds anything as they used to do.'

Raffles crouched down at the other end of the bridge, lit a match, and examined the ground on both sides of the path. 'There are any number of prints,' he said disgustedly. 'They undoubtedly are those of the workmen, though the prints of the man we want could be among them. But I doubt it. They're all made by heavy workingmen's boots.'

He sent me down the steep muddy bank to look for prints on the south side of the bridge. He went along the bank north of the bridge. Our matches flared and died while we called out the results of our inspections to each other. The only tracks we saw were ours. We scrambled back up the bank and walked a little way onto the bridge. Side by side, we leaned over the excessively thin railing to stare down into the brook. Raffles lit a Sullivan, and the pleasant odor drove me to light one up too.

'There's something uncanny here, Bunny. Don't you feel it?'

I was about to reply when he put his hand on my shoulder. Softly, he said, 'Did you hear a groan?'

'No,' I replied, the hairs on the back of my neck rising like the dead from the grave.

Suddenly, he stamped the heel of his boot hard upon the plank. And then I heard a very low moan.

Before I could say anything to him, he was over the railing. He landed with a squish of mud on the bank. A match flared under the bridge, and for the first time I comprehended how thin the wood of the bridge was. I could see the flame through the planks.

Raffles yelled with horror. The match went out. I shouted, 'What is it?' Suddenly, I was falling. I grabbed at the railing, felt it *dwindle* out of my grip, struck the cold water of the brook, felt the planks beneath me, felt them sliding away, and shouted once more. Raffles, who had been knocked down and buried for a minute by the collapsed bridge, rose unsteadily. Another match flared, and he cursed. I said, somewhat stupidly, 'Where's the bridge?'

'Taken flight,' he groaned. 'Like the chair!'

He leaped past me and scrambled up the bank. At its top he stood for a minute, staring into the moonlight and the darkness beyond. I crawled shivering out of the brook, rose even more unsteadily, and clawed up the greasy cold mud of the steep bank. A minute later, breathing harshly, and feeling dizzy with unreality, I was standing by Raffles. He was breathing almost as hard as I.

'What *is* it?' I said.

'*What* is it, Bunny?' he said slowly. 'It's something that can change its shape to resemble almost anything. As of now, however, it is not what it is but *where* it is that we must determine. We must find it and kill it, even if it should take the shape of a beautiful woman or a child.'

'What are you talking about?' I cried.

'Bunny, as God is my witness, when I lit that match under the bridge, I saw one brown eye staring at me. It was embedded in a part of the planking that was thicker than the rest. And it was not far from what looked like a pair of lips and one malformed ear. Apparently, it had not had time to complete its transformation. Or, more likely, it retained organs of sight and hearing so that it would know what was happening in its neighborhood. If it sealed off all its organs of detection, it would not have the slightest idea when it would be safe to change shape again.'

'Are you insane?' I said.

'Not unless you share my insanity, since you saw the same things I did. Bunny, that thing can somehow alter its flesh and bones. It has such control over its cells, its organs, its bones – which somehow can switch from rigidity to extreme flexibility – that it can look like other human beings. It can also metamorphose to look like objects. Such as the armchair in the bedroom, which looked exactly like the original. No wonder that Hopkins and Mackenzie and even the redoubtable Holmes failed to find Mr James Phillimore. Perhaps they may even have sat on him while resting from the search. It's too bad that they did not rip into the chair with a knife in their quest for the jewels. I think that they would have been more than surprised.

'I wonder who the original Phillimore was? There is no record of anybody who could have been the model. But perhaps it based itself on somebody with a different name but took the name of James Phillimore from a tombstone or a newspaper account of an American. Whatever it did on that account, it was also the bridge that you and I crossed. A rather sensitive bridge, a sore bridge, which could not keep from groaning a little when our hard boots pained it.'

I could not believe him. Yet I could *not* not believe him.

6

Raffles predicted that the thing would be running or walking to Maida Vale. 'And there it will take a cab to the nearest station and be on its way into the labyrinth of London. The devil of it is that we won't know what, or whom, to look for. It could be in the shape of a woman, or a small horse, for all I know. Or maybe a tree, though that's not a very mobile refuge.

'You know,' he continued after some thought, 'there must be definite limitations on what it can do. It has demonstrated that it can stretch its mass out to almost paper-thin length. But it is, after all, subject to the same physical laws we are subject to as far as its mass goes. It has only so much substance, and so it can get only so big. And I imagine that it can compress itself only so much. So, when I said that it might be the shape of a child, I could have been wrong. It can probably extend itself considerably but cannot contract much.'

As it turned out, Raffles was right. But he was also wrong. The thing had means for becoming smaller, though at a price.

'Where could it have come from, A.J.?'

'That's a mystery that might better be laid in the lap of Holmes,' he said. 'Or perhaps in the hands of the astronomers. I would guess that the thing is not autochthonous. I would say that it arrived here recently, perhaps from Mars, perhaps from a more distant planet, during the month of October, 1894. Do you remember, Bunny, when all the papers were ablaze with accounts of the large falling star that fell into the Straits of Dover, not five miles from Dover itself? Could it have been some sort of ship which could carry a passenger through the ether? From some heavenly body where life exists, intelligent life, though not life as we Terrestrials know it? Could it perhaps have crashed, its propulsive power having failed it? Hence, the friction of its too-swift descent burned away part of the hull? Or were the flames merely the outward expression of its propulsion, which might be huge rockets?'

Even now, as I write this in 1924, I marvel at Raffles' superb imagination and deductive powers. That was 1895, three years before Mr Wells' *War of the Worlds* was published. It was true that Mr Verne had been writing his wonderful tales of scientific inventions and extraordinary voyages for many years.

But in none of them had he proposed life on other planets or the possibility of infiltration or invasion by alien sapients from far-off planets. The concept was, to me, absolutely staggering. Yet Raffles plucked it from what to others would be a complex of complete irrelevancies. And I was supposed to be the writer of fiction in this partnership!

'I connect the events of the falling star and Mr Phillimore because it was not too long after the star fell that Mr Phillimore suddenly appeared from nowhere. In January of this year Mr Phillimore sold his first jewel to a fence. Since then, once a month, Mr Phillimore has sold a jewel, four in all. These look like star sapphires. But we may suppose that they are not such because of our experience with the monsterlet in Persano's matchbox. Those pseudo jewels, Bunny, are eggs!'

'Surely you do not mean that?' I said.

'My cousin has a maxim which has been rather widely quoted. He says that, after you've eliminated the impossible, whatever remains, however improbable, is the truth. Yes, Bunny, the race to which Mr Phillimore belongs lays eggs. These are, in their initial form, anyway, something resembling star sapphires. The star shape inside them may be the first outlines of the embryo. I would guess that shortly before hatching the embryo becomes opaque. The material inside, the yolk, is absorbed or eaten by the embryo. Then the shell is broken and the fragments are eaten by the little beast.

'And then, sometime after hatching, a short time, I'd say, the beastie must become mobile, it wriggles away, it takes refuge in a hole, a mouse hole, perhaps. And there it feeds upon cockroaches, mice, and, when it gets larger, rats. And then, Bunny? Dogs? Babies? And then?'

'Stop,' I cried. 'It's too horrible to contemplate!'

'Nothing is too horrible to contemplate, Bunny, if one can do something about the thing contemplated. In any event, if I am right, and I pray that I am, only one egg has so far hatched. This was the first one laid, the one that Persano somehow obtained. Within thirty days, another egg will hatch. And this time the thing might get away. We must track down all the eggs and destroy them. But first we must catch the thing that is laying the eggs.

'That won't be easy. It has an amazing intelligence and adaptability. Or, at least, it has amazing mimetic abilities. In one month it learned to speak English perfectly and to become well acquainted with British customs. That is no easy feat, Bunny. There are thousands of Frenchmen and Americans who have been here for some time who have not yet comprehended the British language, temperament, or customs. And these are human beings, though there are, of course, some Englishmen who are uncertain about this.'

'Really, A.J.!' I said. 'We're not all that snobbish!'

'Aren't we? It takes one to know one, my dear colleague, and I am unashamedly snobbish. After all, if one is an Englishman, it's no crime to be a snob, is it? Somebody has to be superior, and we know who that someone is, don't we?'

'You were speaking of the thing,' I said testily.

'Yes. It must be in a panic. It knows it's been found out, and it must think that by now the entire human race will be howling for its blood. At least, I hope so. If it truly knows us, it will realize that we would be extremely reluctant to report it to the authorities. We would not want to be certified. Nor does it know that we cannot stand an investigation into our own lives.

'But it will, I hope, be ignorant of this and so will be trying to escape the country. To do so, it will take the closest and fastest means of transportation, and to do that it must buy a ticket to a definite destination. That destination, I guess, will be Dover. But perhaps not.'

At the Maida Vale cab station, Raffles made inquiries of various drivers. We were lucky. One driver had observed another pick up a woman who might be the person – or thing – we were chasing. Encouraged by Raffles' pound note, the cabbie described her. She was a giantess, he said, she seemed to be about fifty years old, and, for some reason, she looked familiar. To his knowledge, he had never seen her before.

Raffles had him describe her face feature by feature. He said, 'Thank you,' and turned away with a wink at me. When we were alone, I asked him to explain the wink.

'She – it – had familiar features because they were Phillimore's own, though somewhat feminized,' Raffles said. 'We are on the right track.'

On the way into London in our own cab, I said, 'I don't understand how the thing gets rid of its clothes when it changes shape. And where did it get its woman's clothes and the purse? And its money to buy the ticket?'

'Its clothes must be part of its body. It must have superb control; it's a sentient chameleon, a superchameleon.'

'But its money?' I said. 'I understand that it has been selling its eggs in order to support itself. Also, I assume, to disseminate its young. But from where did the thing, when it became a woman, get the money with which to buy a ticket? And was the purse a part of its body before the metamorphosis? If it was, then it must be able to detach parts of its body.'

'I rather imagine it has caches of money here and there,' Raffles said.

We got out of the cab near St James's Park, walked to Raffles' rooms at the Albany, quickly ate a breakfast brought in by the porter, donned false beards and plain-glass spectacles and fresh clothes, and then packed a Gladstone bag and rolled up a traveling rug. Raffles also put on a finger a very large ring. This concealed in its hollow interior a spring-operated knife, tiny but very sharp. Raffles had purchased it after his escape from the Camorra deathtrap (described in *The Last Laugh*). He said that if he had had such a device then, he might have been able to cut himself loose instead of depending upon someone else to rescue him from Count Corbucci's devilish automatic executioner. And now a hunch told him to wear the ring during this particular exploit.

We boarded a hansom a few minutes later and soon were on the Charing Cross platform waiting for the train to Dover. And then we were off, comfortably ensconced in a private compartment, smoking cigars and sipping brandy from a flask carried by Raffles.

'I am leaving deduction and induction behind in favor of intuition, Bunny,' Raffles said. 'Though I could be wrong, intuition tells me that the thing is on the train ahead of us, headed for Dover.'

'There are others who think as you do,' I said, looking through the glass of the door. 'But it must be inference, not intuition, that brings them here.' Raffles glanced up in time to see the handsome aquiline features of his cousin and the beefy but genial features of his cousin's medical colleague go by. A moment later, Mackenzie's craggy features followed.

'Somehow,' Raffles said, 'that human bloodhound, my cousin, has sniffed out the thing's trail. Has he guessed any of the truth? If he has, he'll keep it to himself. The hardheads of the Yard would believe that he'd gone insane, if he imparted even a fraction of the reality behind the case.'

7

Just before the train arrived at the Dover station, Raffles straightened up and snapped his fingers, a vulgar gesture I'd never known him to make before.

'Today's the day!' he cried. 'Or it should be! Bunny, it's a matter of unofficial record that Phillimore came into the East

End every thirty-first day to sell a jewel. Does this suggest that it lays an egg every thirty days? If so, then it lays another *today!* Does it do it as easily as the barnyard hen? Or does it experience some pain, some weakness, some tribulation and trouble analogous to that of human women? Is the passage of the egg a minor event, yet one which renders the layer prostrate for an hour or two? Can one lay a large and hard star sapphire with only a trivial difficulty, with only a pleased cackle?'

On getting off the train, he immediately began questioning porters and other train and station personnel. He was fortunate enough to discover a man who'd been on the train on which we suspected the thing had been. Yes, he had noticed something disturbing. A woman had occupied a compartment by herself, a very large woman, a Mrs Brownstone. But when the train had pulled into the station, a huge man had left her compartment. She was nowhere to be seen. He had, however, been too busy to do anything about it even if there had been anything to do.

Raffles spoke to me afterward. 'Could it have taken a hotel room so it could have the privacy needed to lay its egg?'

We ran out of the station and hired a cab to take us to the nearest hotel. As we pulled away, I saw Holmes and Watson talking to the very man we'd just been talking to.

The first hotel we visited was the Lord Warden, which was near the railway station and had a fine view of the harbor. We had no luck there, nor at the Burlington, which was on Liverpool Street, nor the Dover Castle, on Clearence Place. But at the King's Head, also on Clearence Place, we found that he – it – had recently been there. The desk clerk informed us that a man answering our description had checked in. He had left exactly five minutes ago. He had looked pale and shaky, as though he'd had too much to drink the night before.

As we left the hotel, Holmes, Watson, and Mackenzie entered. Holmes gave us a glance that poked chills through me. I was sure that he must have noted us in the train, at the station, and now at this hotel. Possibly, the clerks in the other hotels had told him that he had been preceded by two men asking questions about the same man.

Raffles hailed another cab and ordered the driver to take us along the waterfront, starting near Promenade Pier. As we rattled along, he said, 'I may be wrong, Bunny, but I feel that Mr Phillimore is going home.'

'To Mars?' I said, startled. 'Or whatever his home planet may be?'

'I rather think that his destination is no farther than the vessel that brought him here. It may still be under the waves, lying at the bottom of the straits, which is nowhere deeper than twenty-five fathoms. Since it must be airtight, it could be like Mr Campbell's and Ash's all-electric submarine. Mr Phillimore could be heading toward it, intending to hide out for some time. To lie low, literally, while affairs cool off in England.'

'And how would he endure the pressure and the cold of twenty-five fathoms of sea water while on his way down to the vessel?' I said.

'Perhaps he turns into a fish,' Raffles said irritatedly.

I pointed out of the window. 'Could that be he?'

'It might well be *it*,' he replied. He shouted for the cabbie to slow down. The very tall, broad-shouldered, and huge-paunched man with the great rough face and the nose like a red pickle looked like the man described by the agent and the clerk. Moreover, he carried the purplish Gladstone bag which they had also described.

Our hansom swerved toward him; he looked at us; he turned pale; he began running. How had he recognized us? I do not know. We were still wearing the beards and spectacles, and he had seen us only briefly by moonlight and matchlight when we were wearing black masks. Perhaps he had a keen sense of odor, though how he could have picked up our scent from among the tar, spices, sweating men and horses, and the rotting garbage floating on the water, I do not know.

Whatever his means of detection, he recognized us. And the chase was on.

It did not last long on land. He ran down a pier for private craft, untied a rowboat, leaped into it, and began rowing as if he were training for the Henley Royal Regatta. I stood for a moment on the edge of the pier; I was stunned and horrified. His left foot was in contact with the Gladstone bag, and it was melting, flowing *into* his foot. In sixty seconds, it had disappeared except for a velvet bag it contained. This, I surmised, held the egg that the thing had laid in the hotel room.

A minute later, we were rowing after him in another boat while its owner shouted and shook an impotent fist at us. Presently, other shouts joined us. Looking back, I saw Mackenzie, Watson, and Holmes standing by the owner. But they did not talk long to him. They ran back to their cab and raced away.

Raffles said, 'They'll be boarding a police boat, a steam-driven paddlewheeler or screwship. But I doubt that it can catch up with *that*, if there's a good wind and a fair head start.'

That was Phillimore's destination, a small single-masted sailing ship riding at anchor about fifty yards out. Raffles said that she was a cutter. It was about thirty-five feet long, was fore-and-aft rigged, and carried a jib, forestaysail, and mainsail – according to Raffles. I thanked him for the information, since I knew nothing and cared as much about anything that moves on water. Give me a good solid horse on good solid ground any time.

Phillimore was a good rower, as he should have been with that great body. But we gained slowly on him. By the time he was boarding the cutter *Alicia*, we were only a few yards behind him. He was just going over the railing when the bow of our boat crashed into the stern of his. Raffles and I went head over heels, oars flying. But we were up and swarming up the rope ladder within a few seconds. Raffles was first, and I fully expected him to be knocked in the head with a belaying pin or whatever it is that sailors use to knock people in the head. Later, he confessed that he expected to have his skull crushed in, too. But Phillimore was too busy recruiting a crew to bother with us at that moment.

When I say he was recruiting, I mean that he was splitting himself into three sailors. At that moment, he lay on the foredeck and was melting, clothes and all.

We should have charged him then and seized him while he was helpless. But we were too horrified. I, in fact, became nauseated, and I vomited over the railing. While I was engaged in this, Raffles got control of himself. He advanced swiftly toward the three-lobed monstrosity on the deck. He had gotten only a few feet, however, when a voice rang out.

'Put up yore dooks, you swells! Reach for the blue!'

Raffles froze. I raised my head and saw through teary eyes an old grizzled salt. He must have come from the cabin on the poopdeck, or whatever they call it, because he had not been visible when we came aboard. He was aiming a huge Colt revolver at us.

Meanwhile, the schizophrenic transformation was completed. Three little sailors, none higher than my waist, stood before us. They were identically featured, and they looked exactly like the old salt except for their size. They had beards and wore white-and-blue-striped stocking caps, large earrings in the left ear, red-and-black-striped jerseys, blue calf-length baggy pants, and they were barefooted. They began scurrying around, up came the anchor, the sails were set, and we were moving at a slant past the great Promenade Pier.

The old sailor had taken over the wheel after giving one of the midgets his pistol. Meanwhile, behind us, a small steamer, its smokestack belching black, tried vainly to catch up with us.

After about ten minutes, one of the tiny sailors took over the wheel. The old salt and one of his duplicates herded us into the cabin. The little fellow held the gun on us while the old sailor tied our wrists behind us and our legs to the upright pole of a bunk with a rope.

'You filthy traitor!' I snarled at the old sailor. 'You are betraying the entire human race! Where is your common humanity?'

The old tar cackled and rubbed his gray wirelike whiskers.

'Me humanity? It's where the lords in Parliament and the fat bankers and the church-going factory owners of Manchester keep theirs, me fine young gentleman! In me pocket! Money talks louder than common humanity any day, as any of your landed lords or great cotton spinners will admit when they're drunk in the privacies of their mansion! What did common humanity ever do for me but give me parents the galloping consumption and make me sisters into drunken whores?'

I said nothing more. There was no reasoning with such a beastly wretch. He looked us over to make sure we were secure, and he and the tiny sailor left. Raffles said, 'As long as Phillimore remains – like Gaul – in three parts, we have a chance. Surely, each of the trio's brain must have only a third of the intelligence of the original Phillimore I hope. And this little knife concealed in my ring will be the key to our liberty. I hope.'

Fifteen minutes later, he had released himself and me. We went into the tiny galley, which was next to the cabin and part of the same structure. There we each took a large butcher knife and a large iron cooking pan. And when, after a long wait, one of the midgets came down into the cabin, Raffles hit him alongside the head with a pan before he could yell out. To my horror, Raffles then squeezed the thin throat between his two hands, and he did not let loose until the thing was dead.

'No time for niceties, Bunny,' he said, grinning ghastlily as he extracted the jewel-egg from the corpse's pocket. 'Phillimore's a type of Boojum. If he succeeds in spawning many young, mankind will disappear softly and quietly, one by one. If it becomes necessary to blow up this ship and us with it, I'll not hesitate a moment. Still, we've reduced its forces by one-third. Now let's see if we can't make it one hundred percent.'

He put the egg in his own pocket. A moment later, cautiously, we stuck our heads from the structure and looked out. We were in the forepart, facing the foredeck, and thus the old salt at the wheel couldn't see us. The other two midgets were working in the rigging at the orders of the steersman. I suppose that the thing actually knew little of sailsmanship and had to be instructed.

'Look at that, dead ahead,' Raffles said. 'This is a bright clear day, Bunny. Yet there's a patch of mist there that has no business being there. And we're sailing directly into it.'

One of the midgets was holding a device which looked much like Raffles' silver cigarette case except that it had two rotatable knobs on it and a long thick wire sticking up from its top. Later, Raffles said that he thought that it was a machine which somehow sent vibrations through the ether to the spaceship on the bottom of the straits. These vibrations, coded, of course, signaled the automatic machinery on the ship to extend a tube to the surface. And an artificial fog was expelled from the tube.

His explanation was unbelievable, but it was the only one extant. Of course, at that time neither of us had heard of wireless, although some scientists knew of Hertz's experiments with oscillations. And Marconi was to patent the wireless telegraph the following year. But Phillimore's wireless must have been far advanced over anything we have in 1924.

'As soon as we're in the mist, we attack,' Raffles said.

A few minutes later, wreaths of grey fell about us, and our faces felt cold and wet. We could barely see the two midgets working furiously to let down the sails. We crept out onto the deck and looked around the cabin's corner at the wheel. The old tar was no longer in sight. Nor was there any reason for him to be at the wheel. The ship was almost stopped. It obviously must be over the space vessel resting on the mud twenty fathoms below.

Raffles went back into the cabin after telling me to keep an eye on the two midgets. A few minutes later, just as I was beginning to feel panicky about his long absence, he popped out of the cabin.

'The old man was opening the petcocks,' he said. 'This ship will sink soon with all that water pouring in.'

'Where is he?' I said.

'I hit him over the head with the pan,' Raffles said. 'I suppose he's drowning now.'

At that moment, the two little sailors called out for the old sailor and third member of the trio to come running. They were lowering the cutter's boat and apparently thought there wasn't much time before the ship went down. We ran out at them through the fog just as the boat struck the water. They squawked like chickens suddenly seeing a fox, and they leaped down into the boat. They didn't have far to go since the cutter's deck was now only about two feet above the waves. We jumped down into the boat and sprawled on our faces. Just as we scrambled up, the cutter rolled over, fortunately away from us, and bottom up. The lines attached to the davit had been loosed, and so our boat was not dragged down some minutes later when the ship sank.

A huge round form, like the back of a Brobdingnagian turtle, broke water beside us. Our boat rocked, and water shipped in, soaking us. Even as we advanced on the two tiny men, who jabbed at us with their knives, a port opened in the side of the great metal craft. Its lower part was below the surface of the sea and suddenly water rushed into it, carrying our boat along with it. The ship was swallowing our boat and us along with it.

Then the port had closed behind us, but we were in a metallic and well-lit chamber. While the fight raged, with Raffles and me swinging our pans and thrusting our knives at the very agile and speedy midgets, the water was pumped out.

As we were to find out, the vessel was sinking back to the mud of the bottom.

The two midgets finally leaped from the boat onto a metal platform. One pressed a stud in the wall, and another port opened. We jumped after them, because we knew that if they got away and got their hands on their weapons, and these might be fearsome indeed, we'd be lost. Raffles knocked one off the platform with a swipe of the pan, and I slashed at the other with my knife.

The thing below the platform cried out in a strange language, and the other one jumped down beside him. He sprawled on top of his fellow, and within a few seconds they were melting together.

It was an act of sheer desperation. If they had had more than one-third of their normal intelligence, they probably would have taken a better course of action. Fusion took time, and this time we did not stand there paralyzed with horror. We leaped down and caught the thing halfway between its shape as two men and its normal, or natural, shape. Even so, tentacles with the poisoned claws on their ends sprouted, and the blue eyes began to form. It looked like a giant version of the thing in Persano's matchbox. But it was only two-thirds as large as it would have been if we'd not slain the detached part of it on the cutter. Its tentacles also were not as long as they would have been, but even so we could not get past them to its body. We danced around just outside their reach, cutting the tips with knives or batting them with the pans. The thing was bleeding, and two of its claws had been knocked off, but it was keeping us off while completing its metamorphosis. Once the thing was able to get to its feet, or I should say, its pseudopods, we'd be at an awful disadvantage.

Raffles yelled at me and ran toward the boat. I looked at him stupidly, and he said, 'Help me, Bunny!'

I ran to him, and he said, 'Slide the boat onto the thing, Bunny!'

'It's too heavy!' I yelled, but I grabbed the side while he pushed on its stern; and somehow, though I felt my intestines would spurt out, we slid it over the watery floor. We did not go very fast, and the thing, seeing its peril, started to stand up. Raffles stopped pushing and threw his frying pan at it. It struck the thing at its head end, and down it went. It lay there a moment as if stunned, which I suppose it was.

Raffles came around to the side opposite mine, and when we were almost upon the thing, but still out of reach of its vigorously waving tentacles, we lifted the bow of the boat. We didn't raise it very far, since it was very heavy. But when we let it fall, it crushed six of the tentacles beneath it. We had planned to drop it squarely on the middle of the thing's loathsome body, but the tentacles kept us from getting any closer.

Nevertheless, it was partially immobilized. We jumped into the boat and, using its sides as a bulwark, slashed at the tips of the tentacles that were still free. As the ends came over the side, we cut them off or smashed them with the pans. Then we climbed out, while it was screaming through the openings at the ends of the tentacles, and we stabbed it again and again. Greenish blood flowed from its wounds until the tentacles suddenly ceased writhing. The eyes became lightless; the greenish ichor turned black-red and congealed. A sickening odor, that of its death, rose from the wounds.

8

It took several days to study the controls on the panel in the vessel's bridge. Each was marked with a strange writing which we would never be able to decipher. But Raffles, the ever redoubtable Raffles, discovered the control that would move the vessel from the bottom to the surface, and he found out how to open the port to the outside. That was all we needed to know.

Meantime, we ate and drank from the ship's stores which had been laid in to feed the old tar. The other food looked nauseating, and even if it had been attractive, we'd not have dared to try it. Three days later, after rowing the boat out onto the sea – the mist was gone – we watched the vessel, its port still open, sink back under the waters. And it is still there on the bottom, for all I know.

We decided against telling the authorities about the thing and its ship. We had no desire to spend time in prison, no matter how patriotic we were. We might have been pardoned because of our great services. But then again we might, according to Raffles, be shut up for life because the authorities would want to keep the whole affair a secret.

Raffles also said that the vessel probably contained devices which, in Great Britain's hands, would ensure her supremacy. But she was already the most powerful nation on Earth, and who knew what Pandora's box we'd be opening? We did not know, of course, that in twenty-three years the Great War would slaughter the majority of our best young men and would start our nation toward second-classdom.

Once ashore, we took passage back to London. There we launched the month's campaign that resulted in stealing and destroying every one of the sapphire-eggs. One had hatched, and the thing had taken refuge inside the walls, but Raffles burned the house down, though not until after rousing its human occupants. It broke our hearts to steal jewels worth in the neighborhood of a million pounds and then destroy them. But we did it, and so the world was saved.

Did Holmes guess some of the truth? Little escaped those

gray hawk's eyes and the keen gray brain behind them. I suspect that he knew far more than he told even Watson. That is why Watson, in writing *The Problem of Thor Bridge*, stated that there were three cases in which Holmes had completely failed.

There was the case of James Phillimore, who returned into his house to get an umbrella and was never seen again. There was the case of Isadora Persano, who was found stark mad, staring at a worm in a match box, a worm unknown to science. And there was the case of the cutter *Alicia*, which sailed on a bright spring morning into a small patch of mist and never emerged, neither she nor her crew ever being seen again.

Brass and Gold
(*or* Horse and Zeppelin in Beverly Hills)

Foreword

This is one of The Beverly Hills Trilogy, the other two being 'Down in the Black Gang' and 'Riders of the Purple Wage.' All were written while I lived in Beverly Hills, and all take place there. I lived for the first and I hope the last time in my life in an apartment building while in B.H. My cat and I got a little crazier each day, a little unhappier. One day, when I opened the lid of a mailbox and a hand came out and took the letter I was about to drop in, I knew I had to get out. It was either that or go amok.

So we moved to a small house on South Holt in Los Angeles, not far from Beverly Hills but far enough – I thought. Then a flash flood barreled down Burton Way and around the corner and down into my garage, which was set halfway below the street level. Over half of my collection of books and magazines, still in packing boxes, was destroyed. All my Oz books, my Tarzans and Doc Savages and many other valuable pulps, many of my science-fiction books and magazines, including Science Wonder and Air Wonder, stuff I'd been collecting since 1929, a lot of my manuscripts, and so on.

So we moved to the biggest house I'd ever owned deeper in the city. I did sort of dislike leaving the huge fir tree and the giant raven which sat on top of it, but I wasn't far enough from the maleficent influence of B.H.

I was somewhat happy in the big house on South Burnside, and when I got laid off with thousands of others by the aerospace industry a month before the first landing on the moon, I became very happy. I decided to take the plunge, become a full-time writer. I didn't have to travel more than a few feet on foot to go to work. No more ninety-mile roundtrips each day on the freeway. And I was never going to work for anybody else again. If things *got so bad I couldn't make a living at writing, I'd take up bank robbing.*

I don't live now in the land of earthquakes and mudslides. I live in a land of cyclones, violent electrical storms, and ice-age winters. I like it. But the strange thing is that when I go to the L.A. area for a visit, I now like it. I don't even get uneasy when I walk through Beverly Hills, though I do make a wide detour around the street-corner mailboxes.

A man named Brass lived in Beverly Hills in its slum area south of the tracks along Santa Monica Boulevard. Brass was surrounded by Golds, Goldsteins, Goldbergs, Goldfarbs, and by Silvers, Silversteins, Silverbergs, and Silverfarbs.

'I give up! I surrender!' he would yell out of his apartment window when the gold of the full moon had turned green with smog. He would take another swallow from the fifth of Old Turkey, smack his lips, and lean out of the window again.

'Carry me off in your Brinks to your bank, and lock me up in the vault! Melt me down! Make rings and bracelets from me! But you will find that there is more to me than a potential profit in money! Brass is good for more than herding horses or boozing it up!'

Brass was, if you believed the neighbors, a drunken goy poet from Utah. He was supposed to have been a sheepman before being driven from the land by the cattle barons. This rumor infuriated Brass, who was born of a long line of horse raisers. He was also maddened by the other rumor, which said that he was a cowboy.

Where he came from, he could ride for a day and not see a cow, he would shout out the window. But no one seemed to hear him. At night the neighbors were holding noisy parties which shut out all outside sounds or they were attending parties elsewhere.

In the daytime the men were at their offices and the wives were leaning out of their windows and shouting at their neighbors across the way. Between the buildings were complexes of clotheslines on which hung hundred-dollar bills drying in the smog-green and dollar-green sun.

'It isn't like it was in the old country, the Bronx,' Mrs Gold cried to her neighbor. 'There it was people that counted the money, not money that counted the people!'

'For God's sakes, shut up!' Brass roared out of his window. 'I'm a poet! I can't write poetry while all this talk of money, which I don't have, anyway, is making the welkin ring!'

Mrs Samantha Gold saw his mouth moving in the gold of his beard. She smiled and waved. Time was when she wasn't so friendly. The day she looked out of her third-story window into the second-story window of the apartment building next door and saw a bearded man with long hair, wearing a hat, and reading a tall thick book, she thought he was a Talmudic scholar or a rabbi or both.

It is a well-known fact that no Talmudic scholars or rabbis live north of Olympic Boulevard in Beverly Hills. It is not good for them, they can't pay the high rents, and they cause embarrassing pauses in conversations. If caught in town on any day but Saturday, they are scourged back to Olympic and southwards with credit cards, which have sharp cutting edges.

Mrs Gold called the city police the first time she saw Brass. But the investigating officer reported that Brass had no car. He could not be persecuted with overtime parking tickets or a summons for running red lights. The officer would, however, watch Brass closely. There was always the chance he would jaywalk.

The report ended up on the desk of the Gentile mayor. In a speech to the Chamber of Commerce, he revealed that there were people in the city who paid less than $400 a month rent. Some were not paying over $150 a month.

'I'm all for the depressed and underprivileged, as you well know!' the mayor thundered. 'But that kind of people must get out! They're ruining the image of Beverly Hills!'

Wild applause.

Mrs Samantha Gold talked to the cop and found out that Brass was not a rabbi. He wasn't even Jewish.

'Time was when you could identify a person by the way he looked,' she said. 'Everything's mixed up now. Even the young businessmen sometimes look like hippies.'

She added, when the cop eyed her, 'But well-dressed hippies with expensive clothes. And clean.'

'That's right,' he said. 'Take me. Irish Catholic, and yet my name's Oliver Francis Cromwell.'

Cromwell was not eyeing her because of her near-subversive remarks. She was just over thirty, and, if she would lose fifteen pounds, she could have worked as a double for Sophia Loren.

Mrs Gold, two months before, had looked more like Sophie Tucker or Sidney Greenstreet. She was of the Conservative faith, but, where others were addicted to whiskey or cigarettes or heroin, she lusted after pork on rye with mushroom gravy. Her husband locked her in the bedroom and slipped her a restricted but well-balanced and Mosaically correct breakfast through a small door originally installed for the dog. At noon the maid pushed through another tray. At evening her husband let her out of the bedroom but supervised her while she cooked.

Nevertheless, she sometimes succeeded in her smuggling. Once, her husband unexpectedly came home at noon, and she had to put the sandwich and gravy in a plastic container and lower it outside the window on a string.

Brass, the golden poet, hungry because he had spent his month's money on rent and Old Turkey, took the sandwich and gravy and ate them.

Mrs Gold's husband, searching for hidden food, discovered the string, but he could prove nothing. The next day, Mrs Gold found that she had lost enough weight to squeeze through the dog door. She went to Brass' apartment to thank him for having saved her and also to demand the sandwich back. And they fell in love.

Samantha Gold read much because she had little else to do. She knew, or thought she knew, why she was in love with

Brass. He resembled her father when he was young, though Brass was much taller. There were other reasons, of course. He was a poet. And she was even more thrilled because he was a cowboy, though he soon set her straight on that.

There were obstacles to their romance. He was a Gentile, and he drank heavily. Mrs Gold told him that his alcoholism was, however, no big problem for her. Her father hit the bottle more than was good for him.

Brass said, 'My drinking is no problem for me, either, except when I'm broke.'

'You sure don't look like a Gentile,' Samantha said, sitting on a chair and looking at him with the huge Loren-type eyes.

'Madame, I am *not* a Gentile,' he said. 'I'm a Mormon. You're the Gentile, since all non-Mormons are Gentiles. Actually, I'm a jack Mormon, so, in a sense, you're right. I've fallen from grace, which also happens to be the name of my ex-wife. It's a statistical fact that the rate of alcoholism among Mormons is even lower than among devout Jews. But when a Mormon does drink, he dives deeper into the golden sea of alcohol – to quote Bacchylides – than anyone else, never emerging with the pearl of great price, of course.

'It's a case of overcompensation, I suppose. But I am a poet. Therefore, it is an aesthetic, and perhaps a theological, obligation for me to drink. I'll thank you to leave me now. I feel a poem coming on.'

'Robert Graves says that every true poet worships at the feet of the Goddess,' she said. 'Is that what you mean by theological?'

She looked and felt at that moment like an Athena, although not as slim as she would have liked it, and she knew it. He knew it, too, because he got down on his knees, put his hands on her knees, and looked up at her while he recited an extemporaneous sonnet. She liked the poem, and she loved the feel of his hands on her knees, which had been untouched by male hands for months. But she didn't like the odor of booze, even though it was very expensive booze. However, when she was offered a ham sandwich, she decided she could tolerate Old Turkey.

Between bites, she said, 'I would've thought you'd go to Haight-Ashbury or West Venice or Mount Shasta. This is a strange place for a practically penniless poet.'

'This is a strange place for anybody,' he said. He was still glowing with the sparks of his poetry and the comets ejected by his gonads. 'I wanted to go someplace nobody else would think of going to, a really alien place for a poet. So I'm here.'

His grandfather had left him a small sum which was parceled out in monthly lumps by lawyers. His grandfather had deplored Brass' fall from grace, but he had admired him because he refused to kiss any man's boots, manured or clean. And Brass was, at least, 'a bum with honor,' and 'a beard with a stiff neck.' This last phrase delighted Brass.

'Let's not talk of money. Let's talk of love,' he said, getting on his knees again. He looked up past her breasts – like an astronaut staring past the enormous circle of Earth – at the long and lovely Mediterranean face behind the sandwich.

'Not talk of money?' she said. 'This is Beverly Hills. My husband says that money comes first here and love just naturally tags along. Like a shark follows a boat for garbage.'

Brass winced. His poetry dealt with beauty.

Samantha finished that sandwich and looked at the refrigerator. Brass sighed and got to his feet and clumped across the bare floor on his high-heeled boots. While she watched him prepare another sandwich, she told him folk tales of Beverly Hills.

There was Mrs Miteymaus, who labored for twenty hours before giving birth to a thousand-dollar bill. The Internal Revenue Service agent, clad in mask, gown, and gloves, assisted the obstetrician and deducted 90 percent before the umbilical cord was clipped. Mrs Miteymaus decided to ship the baby off to an orphanage and claim a deduction for charity.

The baby was eventually adopted by a bank and thereafter yielded 8.1 percent interest. News of this reached Mrs Miteymaus through a malicious friend (the adjective was redundant, Samantha admitted), causing Mrs Miteymaus such grief that she swore never again to have sexual intercourse, even with her husband.

Brass asked her if the tale was true that Beverly Hills was the only city in the world with so many cops they had to be pulled off the streets during rush hours to keep them from hindering the flow of traffic.

Samantha replied that that folk tale was true.

Uninhibited by her third sandwich, she told him of her personal life and some of its sorrows. Once, she thought she was losing her husband's love because she was getting too fat. But now that she had slimmed down, relatively speaking, she still was getting no loving from him. Irving was stepping out on her with a shicksa who drank.

'The world is one fester of hate and betrayal and grief,' he said. 'Even when I used to stand night watch on the lone prairie, with only the horses and me and the moon, the wind brought sounds and smells of hate and betrayal and grief and of a rotting world from hundreds of miles away.

'I could hear sobbing and screaming and smell gasoline and dead robins. Then I'd put my nose down into my horse's mane and breathe deeply. It was good honest beautiful horse sweat. Few smells are lovelier, I can tell you.'

Mrs Gold put her ham sandwich aside so it would not interfere and bent over and stuck her nose against his chest. The woolen plaid shirt still radiated faint odors of horse.

'One more washing in detergents with enzymes, and it'll be gone forever,' he said. 'I'll hate that day.'

He kissed the back of her neck. She shuddered as if she were a mare into whose flanks spurs had been pressed, and she ate no more of ham that day.

They continued to meet in the morning and sometimes in

the afternoon. But the day came when she could no longer slide out on her back through the dog door. She went to the window after a struggle to free herself and signaled Brass. He was sitting at his window with nothing on but his ten-gallon Stetson. He was polishing his boots and composing a poem to the Bitch Goddess. He was also wondering if he should take an oath of chastity for a week or two. The divine spark was cooling off. The Muse liked her worshippers to be horny, but She did not want them to expend all their fire and seed on lesser beings, in this case, Samantha Gold.

Neither had a telephone available, so she was restricted to waving at him. She did not call out because her neighbors would then have known what was going on – as if they didn't already know.

Finally, having found a conjunction of words which would rhyme with 'equine,' he opened his eyes. After some mystification, he understood her. The maid had gone to the grocery store and he could come in because the maid usually forgot to lock the door. He dressed and put food and booze in a sack and went over to her apartment. She explained why she couldn't leave, and after he had quit rolling on the floor and laughing – and smashed the sandwich while doing so – he took the key to her bedroom out of the dresser drawer in Irving's bedroom.

Her bedroom was as elegantly middle-class as he had expected. The huge framed photograph of a World War I Zeppelin in flight was something he had not expected. Beside it was a photograph of a young man with a handlebar moustache. He wore the uniform of a German naval officer, circa 1918.

'My father,' Samantha said.

'Your father was an airship?'

'You've been drinking again. No, he was a *leutnant* on a Zeppelin.'

Brass was intrigued, but he was also impatient to get away

before the maid returned. And the consciousness that she was wearing nothing under a thin dress was making him forget his primary fidelity to the Goddess.

Later, while they were resting in his darkened room, he said, 'All right, I'll meet your father, though I don't know why he'd be glad to know me.'

'He's a poet, too, in a way,' she said. 'He's a lovely old man even if a little odd. I think he's in love with his dirigibles. That's all he wants to talk about, except when he happens to think about the governor. Then he raves and rants and calls him Abdul von Schicklgruber, the Plutocrats' Pet. I don't pay any attention to politics; if you can't make it big in the movies, try something else, I always say. Anyway, Zeppelins are his love. He dreams of them, builds models of them, reads books on them. And I dream of Zeppelins, too, after I've visited him. Every Sunday night, those big things sail through my dreams.'

'I dreamed of my horse the other night,' Brass said. 'She's dead now, hit by a truck two days before I came to Beverly Hills. She had big dark eyes, like yours. Liquid, full of love, and a hunger in them for something I couldn't ever figure out. Mostly, a horse just wants hay and carrots and water and rest and sugar lumps now and then. But when I looked into those eyes, I knew that tiny brain behind them had its dreams, too. Or maybe they were mirrors for my dreams.'

She sat up and said, 'Your horse's eyes remind you of mine?'

'That's a compliment,' he said. He did not dare tell her the rest of the dream. 'When I woke I thought I smelled her sweat, but it wasn't hers.'

'Mine?' she said, and she went to the refrigerator.

'You better lay off,' he said, 'or you won't be able to get back through the front door, let alone the dog door.'

She was bending over. He could visualize the beautiful dark tail of the mare swishing back and forth.

Sunday, she told Brass that she had convinced Irving that he had forgotten to lock the bedroom door. She had had to lie because the maid had told him that his wife had left the bedroom. Usually, Irving accompanied her on Sundays on her visits to her father. He did so not because he liked her father or her company but because he wanted to make sure she ate nothing forbidden. But today he had had to attend to business that had suddenly come up.

'Some business, that shicksa he's seeing,' she said. 'But I'm getting my revenge.'

She walked out. A few minutes later, Brass followed. He met her on the porch of her father's house in the most depressed area of Beverly Hills. The house cost a mere $50,000 and would have brought $12,000 in Peoria, Illinois, after effective heating had been installed.

They found Mr Goldbeater in the backyard working on a model of his last ship, which had gone down in flames in a raid over England. It was his *tour de force* model. Thirty feet long, it had four gondolas with gasoline motors that worked and a control gondola in which a small man could fit if he didn't mind a prenatal position. A big black *formée* cross, American flag, California state flag, and Star of David were painted on the sides.

Brass did not comment; he had seen stranger conjunctions.

The old man looked surprised, but he smiled and pumped Brass' hand vigorously. They went into the house, which was crowded with smaller models of Zeppelins and dirigibles. The old man insisted on pouring a drink six fingers high, and Brass was not reluctant to accept.

'Here's to the return of horses,' Mr Goldbeater said. 'And to the downfall of Abdul von Schicklgruber.'

'Here's to the comeback of gasbags,' Brass said, and they drank.

Samantha surprised both by filling a glass with bourbon.

'Here's to the triumph of true love,' she said, and she drank.

'The waters of Kentucky bring out what lies dearest to our hearts,' Mr Goldbeater said.

He looked at his daughter and at Brass.

'How long have you been laying Samantha?'

'Papa!'

'Not long enough,' Brass said, holding his glass for a refill.

'A fine figure of a woman,' Mr Goldbeater said. 'And a big heart, if a weak mind. Too good for that *schlemiel* Irving. And you're a fine broth of a lad.'

He drank again and then said, 'Irving runs around with a shicksa that drinks daiquiris.'

He shuddered.

Samantha sat down and held out her glass for a refill. She hated alcohol, but it was the only anaesthetic handy.

'Papa, how long have you known?'

'When you walked in. It was bound to happen, unless you became so fat eating forbidden fruit – if you don't mind my calling pork on rye that – that a man wouldn't want to have anything to do with you.'

Brass looked at the portrait of Samantha's mother. He knew then where she had gotten her magnificent breasts and why a man who loved Zeppelins would have asked her mother to marry him.

When he left, Brass was reeling in body and mind. Around him was a cloud, and through it poked the huge nose of a black Zeppelin high over London. This was the recurring dream of old man Goldbeater.

In Brass' apartment, Samantha confessed that that was her recurring dream, too.

'There's this black curly cloud miles up, and there's the city sprawled out on its back below. And then, suddenly, there's a drone of motors, and this tremendous round-nosed and very long thing slides out of the clouds. It's great and powerful and also sinister, so sneaky and evil, and it penetrates the air so irresistibly. And it horrifies me, yet attracts me.'

He looked down at her and said, '*Feuer Ein!*'

'Fire one!' she said a moment later, breathing hard. 'I didn't know you knew German?'

'I've seen a lot of movies about submarine warfare,' he said when he had regained his breath. 'I don't know what the krauts said when they ordered bombs dropped. *Lässen fallen die Bomben, Dreckkopf?*'

'I have to go home,' she said dreamily. 'Or I'll fall asleep, and Irving will come home, and then you'll see the bombs drop. Right on me.'

'I must have had too much bourbon at your father's,' he said. 'Otherwise, why would I be asking you to stay here and let Irving find out about us? So he divorces you? Don't you love me?'

'You keep telling me that money isn't all,' she said. 'And I keep telling you that love isn't all, either. I'm secure with Irving. He isn't ever going to divorce me unless I get very nasty. He thinks it'd give him a bad name with the wives of his business friends, which means his friends would give him a bad name. He'd find a way to cut me off without a cent. And you . . .'

'So what do we do, just continue our affair?'

'Until it comes to a natural end.'

'All endings, from the viewpoint of the person being ended, are unnatural,' he said.

That phrase possessed him; a poem started to come on. He did not even see or hear Samantha leave the room.

After his poem on the finality of things was cast in its final form, Brass began to think of Samantha again. But he had little time to think and less to act. The absentee landlord, a coy Gentile, sold the apartment building. Two days later, the crane and its giant steel ball and the bulldozer arrived. The tenants threatened to sue, and the landlord, on vacation in Hawaii, said, 'Sue me.' He pointed out that he had sent the tenants letters six months ago telling them why and when they must leave. If they had not received them, they should blame the postal service, which was deteriorating along with everything else.

The big ball struck thunder and quake and plaster through the building, and the pieces of ceiling falling on him awoke Brass. He dressed hastily and packed without folding anything. He had decided, as soon as he opened his eyes, that he was not going to force the authorities to carry him out after all. Buildings were almost as insubstantial as love; nothing lasted forever. A six-story high-rent apartment building would be erected here; other men and women would fall in love while living in it and would make their decisions to run away or stay. And then that building, too, would be torn down.

But it wasn't easy to demolish love, which, after all, was more like an animal, a living creature, than a construction of inorganic material. He would make one more attempt. If he failed, he would at least have given Beverly Hills another item of folklore.

It took him most of the morning to rent a horse in Griffith Park, rent a car and trailer, and transport the beast to the heart of downtown Beverly Hills, the corner of Wilshire Boulevard and Beverly Drive.

There he mounted his white horse and, repressing the desire to cry, 'Hi-Yo, Silver, Awa-a-ay!', he urged the horse into a gallop eastward on Wilshire. Inaudible music of Rossini's *Lone Ranger Overture*. Audible shrill of police whistles, blare and bleep of car horns, scream of brakes, caw of curses flying by like ravens.

Before reaching Doheny, he turned south on one of those streets named after trees, the sparks flying from the iron shoes of his charger and the cigars dropping from the mouths of the Rolls-Royce salesmen in the agency near the corner. There were, as usual, no parking spaces available, so he rode down the strip of grass between curb and sidewalk, slid to a halt, jumped off, tied the panting beast to a bush, and ran upstairs to the third floor past the astonished manager, who had just opened the front door.

He beat on the door of the Golds' apartment, got no answer, and shoved the door in with a kick followed by his shoulder. The maid was gone, but Samantha's faint cries reached him. He ran down the hall and turned the corner.

Samantha was stuck in the dog door.

She looked up at him and said, 'I tried to signal you, but you've kept your blinds down. Then I asked the maid to get you, and she told me Irving paid her wages, not me. But she did give me a special-delivery letter from my father.

'Father took off in his model, his mini-Zeppelin he called it in the letter. He left this morning, headed for Sacramento. He said he was going to bomb that *schweinhund* in the governor's mansion. And he wished you and me good luck.'

Samantha started to cry. Brass tried to pull her out of the opening, but he stopped when she began to groan with pain.

'I thought you would've lost weight since you stopped seeing me,' he said.

'Irving decided to let me eat all the pork on rye and mushroom gravy that I wanted. That way, I wouldn't be able to sneak out. He found out that the best jailor is the prisoner himself. Herself, in this case.

'But then I heard that your building was going to be torn down, and I got my father's letter. I knew that I had to do something brave and worthwhile, too. So I tried to get out so I could run off with you. With you I could have my sandwiches and love, too. So you drink too much and our floors are bare. So what?'

Brass kicked the door until his feet hurt and then he battered it with chairs until he had shattered a dozen. But Irving, knowing the flimsiness and sleaziness of modern construction, had had the door built to order.

A siren wailed decrescendo outside.

'I wanted to carry you off on my horse,' Brass said. 'For a few blocks, anyway. Then we would transfer to my rental Mustang and take off for the mountains.'

'You go on,' she said. 'But don't wait for me. I just now saw why I'm stuck. I made my choice, even if I tried to cancel it. I knew that if I refused to eat so much I could get out easily. But I couldn't. So you go. I made my choice. Besides, truth to tell, I'm afraid of horses.'

He got down on his knees and kissed her. Her breath had a not unpleasant odor of pork on rye and kosher pickles.

He stood up. 'Good-bye.'

'Good-bye,' she said.

He walked down the front steps of the building. A policeman, looking at his hat and silver-buckled belt and boots, said, 'This horse belong to you, Buck?'

It lay on the sidewalk, breathing its last in bloodied foam. Ridden hard, it had been overloaded with a mixture of carbon monoxide, nitric acid, ozone, acetone, formaldehyde, and vaporized lead.

'No horse of mine, officer,' Brass said politely. 'You ought to call the fire department. There's a woman in three oh eight trying to get born.'

The policeman misunderstood him and called for an ambulance. Brass did not enlighten him. He walked away. Two deaths behind him and what lay ahead?

On Wilshire, he stopped to watch a parade of several hundred young men and women. They were well dressed, well fed, well schooled, and obviously the sons and daughters of those they were marching against. The carried placards:

WORSHIPPERS OF MAMMON, REPENT!
BEVERLY HILLS SUCKS!
UP YOUR LOVE OF MONEY!
REMEMBER SODOM AND GOMORRAH!

There were some older people in the parade, including some rabbis, ministers, and priests. Today was not a holy day, and so they might be scourged out of the city, but it would be by billies and mace, not credit cards. Police sirens were whooping in the distance; forces were hastening in response to the calls of alarmed citizens.

Brass waved his hat and cheered and thought about joining them. But he had just gotten out of one kind of prison, and he did not, at that moment, feel up to enduring another. He needed to breathe some comparatively fresh air in the pines and to make more songs for the Goddess. Everyone served in his own way.

In the car, pointed for the mountains, he turned the radio on. A UFO had been sighted heading for the state capital. The National Guard jets were scrambling. Their trails froze while the sun sparked on the mysterious slow-moving vehicle.

The Jungle Rot Kid
on the Nod

Foreword

I've written a number of Tarzan pastiches and also a biography of the lord of the jungle, known in England as the very cosmopolitan and cultured nobleman, Lord Greystoke. (Yes, Virginia, there is a real Tarzan.)

Edgar Rice Burroughs wrote highly fictionalized books about Tarzan, and it is his name that leaps to the mind when Tarzan is mentioned. (Unless you're one of those people who know Tarzan only through the movies, and if you are you don't know the real Tarzan.) I became hooked on Burroughs' Tarzan books when I was very young and haven't quite overcome this addiction yet.

But in recent years I've read and admired (though I'll never get hooked on them) the works of another Burroughs, first name William. His stories, if you can call them stories, are composed in a wild absurdist style and put together with some very unconventional techniques. I especially recommend his Nova Express.*

Almost all his works contain large elements of homosexuality, drug addiction, violence, sadism, masochism, paranoia, an aversion to and contempt for women, and an emphasis on the more nauseating aspects of this world (and other worlds, too).

The mixture of these sounds very unattractive, but his vaulting imagination and wild metaphors make his unique works mentally stimulating.

Unfortunately, even the most erudite reader is often puzzled by many of the references. They're too subjective. Many of these can be understood by reading William Burroughs' autobiography, Junkie. *A reader shouldn't have to go to this to comprehend*

*Now available from Granada Paperbacks.

William's fiction. Nevertheless, even if the reader fails to grasp these references, he or she may find that his fiction is well worth reading and, in fact, mentally stimulating.

And so, one day, while rereading Nova Express, *I thought: What if it had been William Burroughs, not Edgar Rice Burroughs, who had written the Tarzan books?*

I was sure that there would be no market for such a double pastiche if I wrote it. The so-called obscenity and pornography in it would not keep it from being published. This was 1968. Henry Miller and William Burroughs were being published, and my own 'Riders of the Purple Wage' had appeared in Harlan Ellison's Dangerous Visions *the year before. But the pastiche would not be accepted by any science-fiction magazine. For some reason I didn't think of sending it to* Playboy *magazine. However, I doubt they would have taken it. The editors might have enjoyed it but would have thought it unsuitable for the majority of their readers.*

Despite the lack of a sale, I wrote it because it seemed as if it would be fun doing so, and it was, and I wanted to find out if I could emulate William Burroughs' style. It took three hours for the first writing. Two days later I went back to it and did the second and final draft in an hour.

Well, it did sell and almost immediately. But to a very strange publication. I mean by strange that it was the very last place I would have thought it would be sold to.

Roger Lovin, an editor for the American Art Agency publications, all porno, was also a science-fiction fan. He'd heard about the pastiche, asked to see it, read it, and arranged that it should be printed in Broadside. *This was, according to Norman Spinrad, a very raunchy girlie magazine, godawful. But he laughed and added, 'And it's the best of the American Art Agency's line, their class production.'*

Lovin didn't care. He wanted to ensure that the pastiche was in print. So it came out in Broadside *in the midst of huge naked breasts and stockings with garter belts filled by some pretty-faced but too-mammalian women. The other featured fillers were*

'French Girls For Sale' *and* 'My Love Affair With 60 Starlets,' *both nonfiction. All but 0.01 percent of the readers must have been very puzzled by my story, if they bothered to read it at all.*

I'm looking through that issue now. The photos of the women and the prose of the nonfiction items seem rather inhibited and innocuous. Almost innocent. Standards have changed much in eleven years.

Two years later, Charles Platt got the 'Kid' reprinted in New Worlds Science Fiction, *an English magazine devoted to 'new wave' experimental writing. Quite a leap.*

In 1971 Norman Spinrad put together an anthology titled The New Tomorrows, *a work which contained some of the best examples of the 'new' type of science-fiction. He included 'The Jungle Rot Kid On The Nod' and wrote a preface to it which credited my pioneering efforts in the field of science-fiction.*

A few years ago I tried to write a pastiche in which Edgar Rice wrote Nova Express. *It didn't work, so I threw it away. There's a lesson in this failure somewhere, though I don't know what it is. Perhaps it is that you shouldn't push things too far. But you have to try. Otherwise, you get no place at all.*

If William Burroughs instead of Edgar Rice Burroughs had written the Tarzan novels...

Tapes cut and respliced at random by Brachiate Bruce, the old mainliner chimp, the Kid's asshole buddy, cool blue in the orgone box

from the speech in Parliament of Lord Greystoke alias The Jungle Rot Kid, a full house, SRO, the Kid really packing them in.

–Capitalistic pricks! Don't send me no more foreign aid! You corrupting my simple black folks, they driving around the old plantation way down on the Zambezi River in air-conditioned Cadillacs, shooting horse, flapping ubangi at me... Bwana him not in the cole cole ground but him sure as shit gonna be soon. Them M-16s, tanks, mortars, flamethrowers coming up the jungle trail, ole Mao Charley promised us!

Lords, Ladies, Third Sex! I tole you about apeomorphine but you dont lissen! You got too much invested in the Mafia and General Motors, I say you gotta kick the money habit too. Get them green things offen your back...nothing to lose but your chains that is stocks, bonds, castles, Rollses, whores, soft toilet paper, connection with The Man...it a long way to the jungle but it worth it, build up your muscle and character cut/

...you call me here at my own expense to degrade humiliate me strip me of loincloth and ancient honored title! You hate me cause you hung up on civilization and I never been hooked.

You over a barrel with smog freeways TV oily beaches taxes inflation frozen dinners time-clocks carcinogens neckties all that shit. Call me noble savage... me tell you how it is where its at with my personal tarzanic *purusharta*... involves kissing off *dharma* and *artha* and getting a fix on *moksha* through *kama*...

Old Lord Bromley-Rimmer who wear a merkin on his bald head and got pecker and balls look like dried-up grapes on top a huge hairy cut-in fold-out thing it disgust you to see it, he grip young Lord Materfutter's crotch and say – Dearie what kinda gibberish that, Swahili, what?

Young Lord Materfutter say – Bajove, some kinda African cricket doncha know what?

...them fuckin Ayrabs run off with my Jane again... inter-solar communist venusian bankers plot... so it back to the jungle again, hit the arboreal trail, through the middle tearass, dig Numa the lion, the lost civilizations kick, tell my troubles to Sam Tantor alias The Long Dong Kid. Old Sam always writing amendments to the protocols of the elders of mars, dipping his trunk in the blood of innocent bystanders, writing amendments in the sand with blood and no one could read what he had written there selah

Me, I'm only fuckin free man in the world... live in state of anarchy, up trees... every kid and lotsa grownups (so-called) dream of the Big Tree Fix, of swinging on vines, freedom, live by the knife and unwritten code of the jungle...

Ole Morphodite Lord Bromley-Rimmer say – Dearie, that Anarchy, that one a them new African nations what?

The Jungle Rot Kid bellowing in the House of Lords like he calling ole Sam Tantor to come running help him outta his mess, he really laying it on them blueblood pricks.

...I got *satyagraha* in the ole original Sanskrit sense of course up the ass, you fat fruits. I quit. So long. Back to the Dark Continent... them sheiks of the desert run off with Jane again... blood will flow...

Fadeout. Lord Materfutter's face phantom of erection wheezing paregoric breath. – Dig that leopardskin jockstrap what price glory what? cut/

This here extracted from John Clayton's diary which he write in French God only know why... *Sacre bleu! Nom d'un con!* Alice she dead, who gonna blow me now? The kid screaming his head off, he sure don't look like black-haired gray-eyed fine-chiseled featured scion of noble British family which come over with Willie the Bastard and his squarehead-frog goons on the Anglo-Saxon Lark. No more milk for him no more ass for me, carry me back to old Norfolk / / double cut

The Gorilla Thing fumbling at the lock on the door of old log cabin which John Clayton built hisself. Eyes stabbing through the window. Red as two diamonds in a catamite's ass. John Clayton, he rush out with a big axe, gonna chop me some anthropoid wood.

Big hairy paws strong as hold of pusher on old junkie whirl Clayton around. Stinking breath. Must smoke banana peels. *Whoo! Whoo!* Gorilla Express dingdonging up black tunnel of my rectum. Piles burst like rotten tomatoes, sighing softly. Death come. And come. And come. Blazing bloody orgasms. Not a bad way to go...but you cant touch my inviolate white soul...too late to make a deal with the Gorilla Thing? Give him my title, Jaguar, moated castle, ole faithful family retainer he go down on you, opera box... *ma tante de pisse*...who take care of the baby, carry on family name? *Vive la bougerie!* cut/

Twenty years later give take a couple, the Jungle Rot Kid trail the killer of Big Ape Mama what snatch him from cradle and raise him as her own with discipline security warm memory of hairy teats hot unpasteurized milk...the Kid swinging big on vines from tree to tree, fastern hot baboonshit through a tin horn. Ant hordes blitzkrieg him like agenbite of intwat, red insect-things which is exteriorized thoughts of the Monster Ant-Mother of the Crab Nebula in secret war to take over this small planet, this Peoria Earth.

Monkey on his back, Nkima, eat the red insect-things, wipe out trillions with flanking bowel movement, Ant-Mother close up galactic shop for the day...

The Kid drop his noose around the black-assed motherkiller and haul him up by the neck into the tree in front of God and local citizens which is called go-mangani in ape vernacular.

–You gone too far this time the Kid say as he core out the motherkillers asshole with fathers old hunting knife and bugger him old Turkish custom while the motherkiller rockin and rollin in death agony.

Heavy metal Congo jissom ejaculate catherinewheeling all over local gomangani, they say – Looka that!

Old junkie witch doctor coughing his lungs out in sick gray African morning, shuffling through silver dust of old kraal.

–You say my son's dead, kilt by the Kid?

Jungle drums beat like aged wino's temples morning after. Get Whitey!

The Kid sometimes known as Genocide John really liquidate them dumbshit gomangani. Sure is a shame to waste all that black gash the Kid say but it the code of the jungle. Noblesse obleege.

The locals say – We dont haffa put up with this shit and they split. The Kid dont have no fun nomore and this chimp ass might hairy not to mention chimp habit of crapping when having orgasm. Then along come Jane alias Baltimore Blondie, she on the lam from Rudolph Rassendale type snarling – You marry me Jane else I foreclose on your father's ass.

The Kid rescue Jane and they make the domestic scene big, go to Europe on The Civilized Caper but the Kid find out fast that the code of the jungle conflict with local ordinances. The fuzz say you cant go around putting a full-nelson on them criminals and breakin their necks even if they did assault you they got civil rights too. The Kid's picture hang on post office and police station walls everywhere, he known as Archetype Archie and by the Paris fuzz as *La Magnifique Merde* – 50,000 francs dead or alive. With the heat moving in, the Kid and Baltimore Blondie cut out for the tree house.

Along come La sometime known as Sacrifice Sal elsewhere as Disembowelment Daisy. She queen of Opar, ruler of hairy little men-things of the hidden colony of ancient Atlantis, the Kid always dig the lost cities kick. So the Kid split with Jane for awhile to ball La.

–Along come them fuckin Ayrabs again and abduct Jane, gangbang her...she aint been worth a shit since...cost me all the jewels and golden ingots I heisted offa Opar to get rid of her clap, syph, yaws, crabs, pyorrhea, double-barreled dysentery, busted rectum, split urethra, torn nostrils, pierced eardrums, bruised kidneys, nymphomania, old hashish habit, and things too disgusting to mention...

Along come The Rumble To End All Rumbles 1914 style, and them fuckin Huns abduct Jane...they got preying-mantis eyes with insect lust. Black anti-orgone Horbigerian Weltanschauung, they take orders from green venusians who telepath through von Hindenburg.

–*Ja Wohl!* bark Leutnant Herrlipp von Dreckfinger at his Kolonel, Bombastus von Arschangst. –Ve use die Baltimore snatch to trap der gottverdammerungt Jungle Rot Kid, dot pseudo-Aryan *Oberaffenmensch*, unt ve kill him unt den all Afrika iss ours! Drei cheers for Der Kaiser unt die Krupp Familie!

The Kid balling La again but he drop her like old junkie drop pants for a shot of horse, he track down the Hun, it the code of the jungle.

Cool blue orgone bubbles sift down from evening sky, the sinking sun a bloody kotex which spread stinking scarlet gashworms over the big dungball of Earth. Night move in like fuzz with Black Maria. Mysterious sounds of tropical wilds...Numa roar, wild boars grunt like they constipated, parrots with sick pukegreen feathers and yellow eyes like old goofball bum Panama 1910 cry *Rache!*

Hun blood flow, kraut necks crack like cinnamon sticks, the Kid put his foot on dead ass of slain Teuton and give the victory cry of the bull ape, it even scare the shit outta Numa King of the Beasts fadeout

The Kid and his mate live in the old tree house now...surohc lakcaj fo mhtyhr ot ffo kcaj* chimps, Numa roar, Sheeta the panther cough like an old junkie. Jane alias The Baltimore Bitch nag, squawk, whine about them mosquitoes tsetse flies ant-things hyenas and them uppity gomangani moved into the neighborhood, they'll turn a decent jungle into slums in three days, I aint prejudiced ya unnerstand some a my best friends are Waziris, whynt ya ever take me out to dinner, Nairobi only a thousand miles away, they really swingin there for chrissakes and cut/

...trees chopped down for the saw mills, animals kilt off, rivers stiff stinking with dugout-sized tapewormy turds, broken gin bottles, contraceptive jelly and all them disgusting things snatches use, detergents, cigarette filters...and the great apes shipped off to USA zoos, they send telegram: SOUTHERN CALIFORNIA CLIMATE AND WELFARE PROGRAM SIMPLY FABULOUS STOP NO TROUBLE GETTING A FIX STOP CLOSE TO TIAJUANA STOP WHAT PRICE FREEDOM INDIVIDUALITY EXISTENTIAL PHILOSOPHY CRAP STOP

...Opar a tourist trap, La running the native-art made-in-Japan concession and you cant turn around without rubbing sparks off black asses.

The African drag really got the Kid down now...Jane's voice and the jungle noises glimmering off like a comet leaving Earth forever for the cold interstellar abysms...

The Kid never move a muscle staring at his big toe, thinking of nothing – wouldn't you? – not even La's diamond-studded snatch, he off the woman kick, off the everything kick, fulla horse, on the nod, lower spine ten degrees below absolute zero

*Old Brachiate Bruce splice in tape backward here.

like he got a direct connection with The Liquid Hydrogen Man at Cape Kennedy...

The Kid ride with a one-way ticket on the Hegelian Express thesis antithesis synthesis, sucking in them cool blue orgone bubbles and sucking off the Eternal Absolute...

The Voice of
the Sonar
in My
Vermiform Appendix

Foreword

This work is one of my 'polytropical paramyths,' a half-serious neologism I invented. In simple English, 'many-turning alongside-of-myth.' This high-sounding label stands for short stories which are closer to the films of the Marx Brothers and The Three Stooges than anything else I can think of. They're the absurdist yet meaningful kind of fiction that I love to read and sometimes write.

'Sonar' exemplifies one of my earliest beliefs and passions. That is, that you may find The Truth only in yourself, yet, paradoxically, you may also find it outside yourself. There are codes all around us and in us, codes which, if cracked, would Reveal all.

It may take a cracked person to crack them. Which is only fair.

Whiteness blinked within Barnes. The whiteness was like a traffic signal light from which the red plastic lens had fallen.

It was his resonance again. There was too much whiteness around him. The laboratory walls and ceiling were fishbelly white. The floor was penguin-breast pseudo-marble. The two doctors wore white.

But Miss Mbama, the technician, though she, too, wore white, was black. This was why Barnes kept turning his revolvable chair to stay zeroed in on her. Then the bursts of whiteness in his brain were reduced in brightness and frequency.

Miss Mbama (née Kurtz) was a tall well-built young woman with a towering bush of *au naturel* hair and West African Bush Negro features modified by some alpine bush Bavarian ancestors. She was good-looking and should have been used to stares. But his embarrassed her. Her expression told that she was thinking of asking him why he rotated like a weathercock with her as the wind. But he had decided not to answer her. He was tired of explaining that he could not explain.

Electrodes were taped to his scalp, over his heart, and over his appendix. (He wore only pajama pants.) Wires ran from the electrodes to the instruments on the far side of the room. The cathode ray tubes flashed squiggles, dots, sine waves, square waves, and complex Lissajous figures.

One instrument was emitting: ping! ping! Like the sounds the supersubmarine in the old *Journey to the Bottom of the Sea* TV show emitted as it cruised fifty miles under the surface in search of the giant sentient roaring radish.

There was a submarine of sorts inside him – shades of

Fantastic Voyage and the saving teardrop! – a tiny vessel which carried a sonar transceiver.

From another instrument issued a woman's voice speaking a language which had baffled the greatest linguists of the world.

Doctor Neinstein leaned over Barnes. His white jacket cut off Barnes' view of Mbama, and the whiteness resonated blindingly inside Barnes. Between flashes, he could, however, see quite clearly.

'I hate to cut it out,' Doctor Neinstein said. 'I loathe the very idea. You can see how upset I am. I always am happiest when cutting. But we're losing a priceless opportunity, a unique chance, to study it. However, the welfare of the patient comes first, or so they taught us in medical school.'

A reporter, also dressed in white (he wanted to be the twenty-first-century Mark Twain), stepped up to Barnes. He thrust a microphone between doctor and patient.

'A few final comments, Mr Barnes. How's it feel to be the only man in the world to have an appendix and then lose it?'

Barnes snarled, 'That isn't my only claim to fame, Scoop. Shove off.'

'Thank you, Mr Barnes. For those who've just tuned in, this is Doctor Neinstein's laboratory in the John Hopkins Medico-psychic Annex, donated by the philanthropist recluse, Heward Howes, after Doctor Neinstein performed an operation on him. The nature of the operation is still unknown. But it is common knowledge that Heward Howes now eats only newspapers, that his bathroom is in a bank vault, and that the government is concerned about the flood of counterfeit hundred-dollar bills whose source is apparently Las Vegas. But enough of this idle chatter, folks.

'Our subject today is Mr Barnes, the most famous patient of the twenty-first century – so far. For the benefit of those who, through some incredible bad luck, have missed the case of Mr Barnes, he is the only person in the world who still has genes responsible for growing an appendix. As you know, genetic control has eliminated the useless and often dangerously diseased appendix from the entire human population for fifty years. But due to a purely mechanical oversight...'

'...and a drunken lab assistant,' Barnes said.

'...he was born with the genes...'

'Stand back, journalistic dog!' Doctor Neinstein snarled.

'Quack! Butcher! You're interfering with the freedom of the press!'

Doctor Neinstein nodded at his distinguished colleague, Doctor Grosstete, who pulled a lever projecting from the floor behind a dressing screen in the far corner. Scoop's yell rose from the trapdoor like the mercury in a thermometer in the mouth of a malarial patient.

'Hmm. G in *altissimo*,' Doctor Grosstete said. 'Scoop was in the wrong profession, but then I guess he knows that now.'

There was a faint splash and then the bellowings of hungermad crocodiles.

Doctor Grosstete shook his head. 'Opera's loss. But in the ecology of things...'

'Nothing must interfere with the march of medical science,' Doctor Neinstein said. For once, the mournful lines of his face were winched up into a smile. But the strain was too great, and the fissures catenaried again. He bent over Barnes and applied a stethoscope to the bare skin of the right lower quadrant of the abdomen.

'You must have a theory by now explaining why a woman's voice is coming from the sonar,' Barnes said.

Neinstein jerked the thumb of his free hand at the screen which showed a sequence of what looked like hieroglyphs.

'Observe the video representation of the voice. I'd say there is a very small ancient Egyptian female riding inside that device. Or on top of it. We'll not know until we cut it out. It refuses to obey our commands to return. Doubtless, some circuit has malfunctioned.'

'It refuses?' Barnes said.

'Forgive the pathetic fallacy.'

Barnes' eyebrows rose. Here was a physician who read more than medical literature. Or was the phrase an echo of a humanities course which the good doctor had had to endure?

'Of course, linguistics is not my profession. So you must not pay any attention to my theory.'

Here was a medical doctor who admitted he was not omniscient.

'What about the white flashes I get? Those are in your proper province. I'd say they reflect my idiosyncratic resonances, so to speak.'

'Tut, tut, Mr Barnes. You're a layman. No theories, please.'

'But all these phenomena are inside me! I'm originating them! Who is better qualified to theorize than I?'

Neinstein hummed an unrecognizable and discordant tune, causing Grosstete, the opera buff, to shudder. He tapped his foot, did a little shuffle-off-to-Buffalo without releasing the stethoscope, looked at his wristwatch, and listened to the sounds coming up from the tiny prowling U-boat.

Barnes said, 'You'll have to abandon your original theory that I was insane. You're all hearing the voice and seeing it on the crt. Even if no one so far has seen the flashes in my head. Unless you think the voice is a mass illusion? Or is the correct term a hallucination?'

Doctor Grosstete said, 'Listen! I could have sworn she was reciting from *Aida! Never fading, endless love!* But no! She's not speaking Italian. And I don't understand a single word.'

Mbama went by on Barnes' left, and he followed her with his eyes as far as he could. The pulses of white faded reluctantly like the noise of popcorn in a cooling pan.

'Miss Mbama does look remarkably like Queen Nefertiti, except for her skin color, of course,' Barnes said.

'Aida was Ethiopian, not Egyptian,' Doctor Grosstete said. 'Please remember that, if you don't want to be embarrassed in a musical group. Both Egyptians and Ethiopians are

Caucasians, by the way. Or largely so.'

'Get your program here,' Barnes said. 'You can't tell your race without a program.'

'I was only trying to help,' Grosstete said. He walked away, looking like Doctor Cyclops with a bellyache.

Two men entered the laboratory. Both wore white. One was red; one, yellow. Doctors Big Bear and Chew. The red linguist said, 'How!' He attached a tiny recorder to Barnes' abdomen. The yellow linguist asked Neinstein for a thousand pardons, but would he please stand out of the way?

Big Bear's dark broad big-nosed face hung before Barnes. He saw him as an afterimage for several seconds. He was standing on the edge of a great plain with tall yellow-brown grass and half-naked men wearing feathers and riding painted ponies in the distance, and nearby was a herd of great dark-furred dark-eyed round-humped bison. The voice in his ears had become a man's, chanting in a language which was a mixture of fricatives and sadness.

The scene vanished. The woman's voice returned.

Big Bear had left to talk to Doctor Neinstein, who was looking very indignant. Chew stood before Barnes, who saw a landscape as if he were looking out of the window of a jet taking off. Pagodas, rice fields, kites flying over green hills, a drunken poet walking along the edge of a blue brook.

Why was it he got pictures from red and yellow but not from black and white? Black was the absence of color, and white was a mixture of all colors. This meant that, in reality, blacks were uncolored people and whites (of the lighter variety) were the colored folks. Except that whites were not white, they were pink or brown. Some were, anyway. And blacks were not black, they were brown.

Not that that had anything to do with his getting pulses of white from his resonance, his inner tuning fork, unexplainedly aberrating now. He also, now he thought about it, must get pulses of black in between the white when he looked at Miss

Mbama. But he did not see these. Black was a signal, but just not there, just as, in an electronic circuit, a pulse could mean yes or 1, and a nonpulse could mean no or zero. Or vice versa, depending on the code you used.

Barnes told Chew what he had been thinking. Chew told Barnes to pick up his feet and hang on to the chair. He whirled Barnes around many times in the revolving chair while the wires wrapped themselves around Barnes and the chair. Then Chew rotated him swiftly to his original position with the wires hanging loose. The pulses of different colors and flashes of landscapes scared Barnes. He seemed to have flown from the laboratory into an alien kaleidoscopic world.

The voice was a high-pitched gabble until the chair stopped whirling.

He described everything to Chew.

'Perhaps there is something to your theory of resonances,' Chew said. 'It's quasimystical, but that doesn't mean it can't describe certain phenomena, or be used to describe them, anyway. If a man had a way to determine what truly sets him to vibrating, what wave lengths he is tuned to, down under all the inhibitions and wounds, then he would have no trouble being happy.

'But you did not have this superresonance until you got sick. So what good is it to you or to anybody?'

'I'm like a TV antenna. Turn me in a particular direction, and I get a particular frequency. But I may only pick up a fuzzy image and audio, or a ghost. Turn me another direction, and I receive a strong frequency. Strong to me; weak to you.'

Barnes swiveled on the chair to point directly at Mbama.

'How about a date tonight, Mbama?' he said. Her name was a murmur of immemorial elms, of drowsy bees, or something from Tennyson. At the same time, the woman's voice from the sonar became even drippier with honey and with the suggestion of silk sliding over silk. And the hieroglyphs on the cathode ray tubes bent and shot little arrows at each other.

'Thanks for the invitation,' she said. 'You're a nice guy, but my boyfriend wouldn't like it. Besides, you aren't going anyplace for a week or more, remember? You'll be in bed.'

'If you and your friend should ever split...'

'I don't believe in mixed dating.'

'Pull your feet up again,' Doctor Neinstein said. 'Close your eyes. If some linguist can whirl you around, I certainly can. But I'll take the experiment further than he did.'

Barnes drew his legs up and closed his eyes. He opened them a minute later because he felt the chair turning. But no one was standing close enough to have turned the chair.

Mbama was obeying Neinstein's signals. She was walking only a few feet from him in a circle around him. And he and the chair were rotating to track her.

Neinstein made a strangling sound.

'Telekinesis,' Chew said.

'Walk back this way,' Barnes said to Mbama. He closed his eyes again. The chair turned.

'I don't even have to see her,' Barnes said, opening his eyes. Mbama stopped walking. The chair overtracked, then returned so that Barnes' nose pointed along a line that bisected her.

'I have to go to lunch,' Mbama said. She walked through the door. Barnes rose, stripped off the electrodes, and followed her, picking up his pajama top as he went out.

Neinstein shouted, 'Where do you think you're going? You're scheduled for surgery shortly after lunch. Our lunch, not yours. Don't you dare eat anything. Do you want another enema, maybe an upper colonic? Your appendix may burst at any moment. Just because you don't feel any pain, don't think...! Where *are you* going?'

Barnes did not answer. The pinging and the voice of the woman were coming, not from the machines, which had been disconnected, but from inside him. They contended in his ears. But the white pulses were gone.

An hour later, Miss Mbama returned. She looked frightened. Barnes staggered in after her and collapsed into the chair. Doctor Neinstein ordered him to go to the emergency room immediately.

'No, just give me first aid here,' Barnes said. 'I hurt a lot of places, but the worst is in my appendix. And he didn't even touch me there.'

'Who's he?' Neinstein said, applying alcohol to the cut on Barnes' temple.

'Miss Mbama's boyfriend, who's no boy but a man and a big one. Ouch! It didn't do any good to try to explain that I couldn't help following her. That I was, literally, swept off my feet. That I'm a human radar sending out pulses and getting back strange images. And when I started to talk about psychophysical resonances, he hit me in the mouth. I think I got some loose teeth.'

Neinstein touched Barnes' abdomen, and Barnes winced.

'Oh, by the way, I got plenty of referents for you linguists,' he said. 'I'm seeing what the voice is talking about, if it is a voice. Miss Mbama's boyfriend jarred something besides my teeth loose. I got a neural connection I didn't have before.'

'Sometimes kicking a malfunctioning TV set helps,' Grosstete said.

Chew and Big Bear stuck electrodes on Barnes' body and adjusted the dials of several instruments. Peaks, valleys, ditches, arrows, skyrockets shot across the faces of the tubes and then rearranged themselves into the outlines of Egyptian-type hieroglyphs.

Barnes described the words that coincided with the images.

'It's like an archaeologist with scuba gear swimming through the halls of a palace, or, perhaps, a tomb in sunken Atlantis. The beam of light he's shining on the murals picks out the hieroglyphs one by one. They swim out of darkness and then back into it. They're figures, abstract or stylized birds and bees and animal-men, and there are strange figures which seem to be purely alphabetical mingled with these.'

Big Bear and Chew agreed that the so-called voice was actually a series of highly modulated sonar signals. They were registering the differing depths and ridges on the wall of his vermiform appendix as the tiny bloodmarine cruised up and down.

Hours went by. The linguists sweated over sound and visual referent. Everybody had coffee and sandwiches, except Barnes, who had nothing, and Doctor Grosstete, who drank grain alcohol. Neinstein talked on the phone three times, twice to postpone the operation and once to tell an angry editor he did not know where his reporter was.

Suddenly, Big Bear shouted, 'Eureka!'

Then, 'Champollion!'

Then, 'Ventris!'

He held up a long piece of paper covered with phonetic symbols, codes for the hieroglyphs, and some exclamation marks.

'There's the hieroglyphs for *this* and for a copula, and there's one for the definite article and that one, that means *secret*, every time so far. Let's see. THIS IS THE SECRET OF THE...UNIVERSE? COSMOS? THE GREAT BEGETTER? THIS IS THE WORD THAT EXPLAINS ALL. READ, O READER, LITTLE MAN, THIS IS THE WORD...'

'Don't be afraid, man! Say the word!' Chew said.

'That's all there is!' Barnes said, and he groaned. 'There's only a gap, a crack...a corruption. The word is gone. The infection has eaten it up!'

He bent over, clutching at his abdomen.

'We must operate!' Neinstein said.

'McBurney's incision or the right rectus?' Doctor Grosstete said.

'Both! This the The Last Appendectomy! We'll make it a

double show! Are all the guests in the amphitheater? Are the TV crews ready? Let us cut, Doctor Grosstete!'

Two hours later, Barnes awoke. He was in a bed in the laboratory. Mbama and two nurses were standing by.

The voice and the pingings were gone. The pulses and the visions were fled. Mbama walked by, and she was only a good-looking black girl.

Neinstein staightened up from the microscope. 'The sonar is only a machine. There is no Egyptian queen riding in it. Or on it.'

Grosstete said, 'The tissue slides reveal many microscopic indentations and alto reliefs on the inner walls of the appendix. But nothing that looks like hieroglyphs. Of course, decay has set in so deeply . . .'

Barnes groaned and mumbled, 'I've been carrying the secret of the universe. The key to it, anyway. All knowledge was inside me all my life. If we'd been one day sooner, we would know All.'

'We shouldn't have eliminated the appendix from man!' Doctor Grosstete shouted. 'God was trying to tell us something!'

'Tut, tut, Doctor! You're getting emotional!' Doctor Neinstein said, and he drank a glass of urine from the specimens on Miss Mbama's table. 'Bah! Too much sugar in that coffee, Mbama! Yes, Doctor, no medical man should get upset over anything connected with his ancient and honorable profession – with the possible exception of unpaid bills. Let us use Occam's razor.'

Grosstete felt his cheek. 'What?'

'It was coincidence that the irregularities on Barnes' appendix reflected the sonar pulses in such a manner that the hieroglyphs and a woman's voice seemed to be reproduced. A highly improbable – but not absolutely impossible – coincidence.'

Barnes said, 'You don't think that, in the past, appendixes

became diseased to indicate that the messages were ripe? And that if only doctors had known enough to look, they would have seen...?'

'Tut, tut, my dear sir, don't say it. See The Word? The anesthesia has not worn off yet. After all, life is not a science-fiction story with everything exhaustively, and exhaustingly, explained at the end. Even we medical men have our little mysteries.'

'Then I was just plain sick, and that was all there was to it?'

'Occam's razor, my dear sir. Cut until you have only the simplest explanation left, the bare bone, as it were. Excellent, that! Old Occam had to have been a physician to invent that beautiful philosophical tool.'

Barnes looked at Miss Mbama as she walked away, swaying. 'We have two kidneys. Why only one appendix?'

Monolog

Foreword

Here's a short horror tale about a strange birth. It appeared in 1973 in an anthology titled Demon Kind, *the stories of which were about children with very strange talents and inclinations. The title of the book gave me an idea for a short story to be titled* Demon Kine. *Maybe I'll write it someday.*

'She's sick of me being sick.

'And I am sick. This thing is growing in me, eating me away. I can't tell her, but she can see it. She looks at its hump, at least, I think it's a hump. I can't look down and see if it is or not. But it's there. I see her looking at it.

'No pain yet. When does cancer start hurting? And I won't be able to yell. I can tell her, but the words won't come out right. And if I try to yell, something happens. My throat closes up. But when the pain hits...

'How can I be anything but sick? She doesn't like me when I'm healthy. I grew and grew and was big and strong. I went to school. I got good grades, very good. I was a great football player and trackman. Well, pretty good, anyway. But mother didn't like that.

' "Child, you're growing too fast, too big. Where's my baby boy? The little one I nursed with my own breasts. The little one I held in my arms until he went to sleep. The little one who sat on my lap while I sang to him until his little head nodded and he slept the sleep of angels. So sweet, so adorable, so soft-skinned, curly-headed, so sweet and lovable. Where is he?"

'Well, Mother, I look out the window and see the same thing every day except for the coming and going of the seasons. The leaves grow out, Mother, they begin as soft buds, tender to the fingers. But the full-grown leaf is the purpose of the bud, Mother. It can't stay a bud forever. If it does, it dies. And the leaf comes out, and it does its work, and then summer comes and goes, is gone, and fall comes, and the leaf is its most beautiful when it dies. And then it falls, and it decays and it

252

makes the soil more fertile. Or provides food and a home or a blanket for insects. Or for whatever.

'Does the tree hate the leaf because it isn't a bud forever? No, it doesn't, Mother. So why do you hate me? Yes, you do, though you haven't got the guts to admit it. You've hated me ever since I left you. But I had to leave you because I had to go to school, Mother. I couldn't be a baby forever, and I had to go to kindergarten, finally, even if you did manage to delay that for a year. And then I knew, in the way that children know, mainly because adults are such lousy liars, that you were beginning to hate me. But it wasn't until I started first grade that I knew for sure. Your hatred got so terrible, it blazed behind your smile, your kisses, your voice. Always getting harder and harder, your voice, until it broke. It was too brittle to stay in one piece.

'And it's, I mean, it was only when I was completely a baby, when I turned my back on growing up because – because I knew you loved me only then – it was only then that you loved me. But I couldn't stay a baby all the time, even to be loved by you. There was a world outside, and I wanted to be the equal of the boys and girls I was going to school with. To do that, Mother, I had to grow along with them. There was no other way to do it.

'So I grew, and as I got bigger, Mother, you got smaller. In the physical sense, of course. Relatively speaking, of course. In one very large sense, you have never gotten any smaller than you were the day you bore me. No smaller, no change in you or me. Not in one sense. Our relationship, the fact that you are my mother and I'm your baby boy, that hasn't changed. That has stayed as it was that day, even though it wouldn't look like it to outsiders and often not to me.

'But everything does change, Mother. Including that relationship. Even if a thing refuses to grow, it becomes bent, turned in, curved too too much, like a boar's tusk or a ram's horn. It turns and it drives into the flesh and then into the same bone from which it grew. The tusk, the horn come home, Mother, come home to die and perhaps, to kill.

'But I'm not dying, Mother. Yes, I am, in one large sense. But not in another equally large sense. Does that make sense, Mother? And where are you, Mother? Ah, I see you now. You've just come out of church. Where, no doubt, as you look at Mother and Son, you pray – somewhere deep inside you – that you and I, too, shall be changeless wood or stone and the babe in your arms never grow larger. You pray that both of us will be motionless and unchanging like wood or stone.

'I'm one way, Mother, you already have your wish. I am motionless as wood or stone, except for being able to blink my eyes and try to talk now and then. That's why you prop me up here by the window so I can see the street, its unchanging changing, and see you as you go to the store or to prayer.

'Outside, motionless and unchanging. Inside, something happened almost a year ago, but I couldn't tell you about it. And if I had, what could I have said except call the doctor, Mother?

'Things don't ever stop changing. Things go on and on, Mother, things deep down. Like trolls working away in the dark bowels of the mountain. In the mountain of my brain. No, of my soul. Of my body, also, Mother. What is the difference between my soul and my body? I don't know. One may be the other. I do know that, when one grows, the other grows. Sometimes.

'And something in me grows and grows, Mother. I lie here, a living tomb, a coffin of myself. I waste away. I've heard you say so yourself. My arms and legs are thinning away. My eyes grow larger as my face sinks away. The bones are beginning to look out through the flesh. I've heard you say so yourself, Mother. Not in a hushed voice to a doctor in the next room. To my face as you smile.

'But my belly grows and grows, and you've said so yourself. It's a tumor, a cancer eating my body as you, my beloved mother who doesn't love me, have eaten up my soul. It's only begun to hurt lately. I've tried to tell you it does, tried to tell you it hurts me sometimes.

'When it's very late at night, and you are not snoring, and the traffic noises have died, I hear it grow, Mother. It makes little noises. It stirs, it rustles, it munches. The cancer is munching away at me, Mother.

' "Good!" you say!

'You don't say? But you do say it with everything but words. If you watch this thing grow and don't call a doctor in, then it'll be too late when you do have to call him in, when you can't put it off any longer, can't blind and deafen yourself to what's going on in the unchangeable me. Too late.

'But you'll be glad, won't you, Mother? Glad because the big, dirty, whiskery, tobacco-smelling, beer-smelling unchangeable that shouldn't have changed, but did change, has died. Yet, Mother, I'm not dirty, I don't smell like cigarettes or beer. Not any more. I can't smoke unless you hold the cigarette for me, which you won't do. And I can't drink beer unless you give it to me, which you won't. So I've gone through the withdrawal pains, Mother, without a word of complaint. Though sometimes, when you looked into my eyes, you must have known. But you didn't look long, did you, Mother? Those are bloodshot old man's eyes, not the clear blue-white eyes of a baby.

'I'm not dirty or whiskery any more, though, am I? You bathe me every day. You don't neglect me in that way. And you shave me every day, too, and run your fingers over my face, and you smile. You remember when it was even softer, don't you?

'You don't smile long, though. You can close your eyes and imagine I'm the baby boy, but you have to open your eyes, and then you hate me.

'I hear the door slam downstairs, Mother. And now I hear the steps creak. You'll be coming up and asking me how I am. Knowing I can't speak except to babble like a baby. My words, so clear in my mind, come out all mixed up, chopped up, like a big salad bowl of unintelligibility. The babbling of an infant. But disgusting, because an infant babbles because he's learning to talk, and he will talk. But I babble because I've forgotten, and I will never remember.

'And now I hear the hallboards creaking under your feet. I hear you humming the lullaby you say you used to sing to me when I was a baby. I think I hear it. The door is closed, and you don't hum loudly. Perhaps I've heard it so often that I hear it even when it's not audible.

'And now, now, Mother, it moved, it moved! It's eaten so much of me away that it's slid into the eaten-away place! It's moved, Mother!

'And now, and now, this must be the end. Oh, God, I said I wanted to die! I've said it so many years. Since I started to school. I've said it. If my mother doesn't love me, I'll die. I wished I could die. And now I am dying, and I'm scared.

'Scared to death! That's a good one! It's getting dark, dark. I'm sliding away, too, like that thing that's sliding from one place to another in me. The cargo of death shifting in the hold as the ship starts to turn over . . . what am I talking about? I'm slipping down, down. This is really it? Death? Slipping down, down! Getting smaller, smaller?

'At least . . . but I was wrong. I was going to say it doesn't hurt. But it's beginning to hurt. It's eating away. Clawing, too. Getting bigger. Or nearer. I'm getting closer, not it. But that's crazy. When two things approach, both get closer. It hurts. I'm glad I can't see. I'm glad it's dark. It's bad enough to hear it, but to see it . . .

'No. I hear Mother. She's coming down the hall. Now she's at the door. And I can't talk, I can't say what I always wanted to say. Would she listen if I could say it? No. Would she understand if she did listen? Oh, Mother, don't let me die. Or if you do, please tell me, tell me . . .

'There you are, Mother. Mother! You were trying to

scream. But you couldn't. It froze in your throat, like it does in mine. You fell. Here I come, Mother. Down off the bed. Weak but able. Don't lie on the floor, Mother. Staring. Rigid. I'm the one that had the stroke.

'No, I didn't have the stroke, not this *I*. Mother! Here I come! My other self! I'm getting out all the way! I got out, Mother! I broke open when I clawed my way out, Mother. I was about to die in there, Mother! Darkness and pressure and wetness, Mother! There I was sliding together, hurting inside and outside. Oh, the terrible pain, Mother! And the fear, the fear, doubled-up, couldn't get out, my stomach ready to explode... What? What am I talking about? Mother! It's all sliding together, and I'm sliding away at the same time!

'I didn't mean to scare you, Mommy. Ain't my fault I'm all bloody! Mommy! You kin put your loveycums in the tub now! Fwever, muvver. Fwever!

'Your baby boy's back! Your little loveydumcum's here, muvver. Wash the bad old blood off me, muvver!

'Blood! I can't help cwying, muvver!

'There's a dead man on my beddy-bye, muvver, and things hanging out of him!'

The Leaser
of Two Evils

Foreword

Every now and then, a word, a phrase, a picture or image will flash into my mind. I'll write them down with the hope that some day I can use them. There are some of these fragments that quickly grow to wholes, and I soon write stories based on them. Others may stay in the notebook for years before something pops up out of the unconscious and says, 'Here's what's been growing in the darkness. Take it and use your conscious and make a story out of it.'

Of such was 'The Henry Miller Dawn Patrol' and of such is 'The Leaser of Two Evils.' Both had been just titles that I'd thought of, for no reason that I can determine, and both had been sitting in the darkness in my mind for at least twelve years, brooding, pacing the cell, feeling the walls and floors for a way to get to the light.

Suddenly, they broke loose from their cell with a hell of a yell, like the young monk in the limerick, and they said, 'Let's get to work!'

And we did. But though we had the go-ahead, we had to work very hard to get the two stories in just the right shape.

On the other hand, some of these germinating ideas grew suddenly, full-blown, and all I had to do was to sit down at the machine and write. Well, that's almost all I had to do.

There are still many ideas and titles that have been waiting in the notebook even longer and nothing has happened and perhaps never will.

I am still waiting for something to result from the title, A Flock of Ducts. *And nothing has yet come from* The Erodynamics Engineer. *Or* Dwellers in the Pup Tense. *Or* Rule 42. *This last, you'll remember, is to found in* Alice in Wonderland. *Rule*

42 states that all persons more than a mile high must leave the courtroom. And then there's the germ of a story titled Two Blue Einsteins. *Though I've striven with that a dozen times in the past fifteen years, I've been able to do nothing with it.*

But we'll see.

Detective-Lieutenant John Healey had had a bad day. That morning he'd raided a massage parlor and had caught in a compromising position a prominent politician, William 'Big' Pockets. It was difficult to say who was the most embarrassed, Pockets or the vice squad. The city council had been notified before the bust so that this very situation could be avoided. But Pockets had just returned from a vacation and so had not gotten the word.

For a dangerous minute, Healey had considered arresting him. Discretion had won over his outrage, but he'd hurt. Later, he'd raided an adult bookstore which had displayed his sister's complete works. He was certain his men didn't know she'd written these, but twice he turned suddenly and caught them grinning at him.

That evening he'd attended the first meeting of a citizens' decency league, which he'd help found, though in an unofficial capacity. The first item on the agenda was the title of the new organization. A woman had proposed the Association for Suppression of Sin. That seemed like a good idea until Healey had written out the initials.

Red-faced, choking, he had pointed this out, and half the people had laughed themselves silly and half had booed. After the uproar subsided, the man suggested the Society for Preventing Evil and Rotten Morality. That was voted down during a terrible tumult. The third moron had proposed the League against Undesirable Sexual Transgressions, as if there could be any desirable. During the howls that followed, Healey caught on. The Warriors Against the Suppressors had sent saboteurs to make a mockery of the good people.

263

Then a fourth person almost had his proposed title spelled out, Committee of Christian...before Healey shouted him down. Afterward, though, he couldn't help wondering what the final word was. When he got home, he'd go through the K section of the dictionary.

As chairperson, Healey had ordered the infiltrators ejected. This was done with much screaming about freedom of speech, as if those filth-mongerers had the right to pollute the moral atmosphere. But T.W.A.T.S. had agents throughout the auditorium, and the meeting ended in fistfights. One citizen had an attack of nervous diarrhea, though not fatal, and the cops had to be called.

Healey burst into his own house as if he was raiding it with the authority of a search warrant. He strode into the back bedroom, yanked open the closet doors, and began ripping the dresses, skirts, and gowns from the hangers and the wigs from the boxes. That helped his red mood cool off a little, but he wasn't so angry he followed his original intention of scissoring them. What good would it do? His sister would just buy more clothes with her ill-gotten money.

The rest of the evening was torture. He tried to watch TV, but the networks were still de-emphasizing violence and stressing bra-less jigglers, their idea of sexual stimulation, and they were right. He shut the set off and paced back and forth. He couldn't even drink to raise his spirits. He abhorred all strong liquor, not to mention the weak. Nor could he take a tranquilizer, though he badly needed one. No drugs except those prescribed by a doctor would pass his lips, and he wasn't going to tell a pill-pusher why he needed them.

But the temptation to knock himself out with a strong sedative was almost overpowering. That would show the bitch. If he slept, she would, too. On the other hand, when most of the drug wore off, she might wake up and still be uninhibited enough by it to do something crazy. Like dancing in the street with only her wig, bra, panties, and high heels on. He shuddered and went to bed. His last thought was that at least he wouldn't dream.

He woke in the morning with the stereo blaring that detested rock. His mouth tasted as if it had been used for an ashtray. Which he hoped to God was all that it had been used for. His brain was a size-9 foot jammed into a size-6 shoe. Stale tobacco fumes hobnobbed with whiskey stink. His eyes were rotten onions. And, 'Oh, my God!', his anus was sore and dribbling stickiness.

Quivering, his stomach twisting like a snake trying to bite its own tail, he shot out of bed and into the shower. Ten minutes later, physically clean but mentally still filthed, he went into the front room. It was a shambles, dirty glasses, an empty fifth, a forest-fire aftermath of butts and ashes. He'd have to clean up before the cleaning woman got here. After turning off the stereo, he ran back to the back bedroom. Horrified, he gazed at the rumpled sheets, spotted with what looked like poltergeist crap but wasn't.

The kitchen table held her typewriter and carbons from a manuscript. At least she'd done some writing before the orgy. When it came to work, all Healeys were conscientious. Though in her case, the world'd be better off if she neglected it.

Unable to eat breakfast, he read part of her new novel. *Prude and Prejudice* by Jane Austen-Healey. It was her usual filth, its only redeeming quality being, not social significance, but its potentiality for making money. Whatever her vices, a disdain for money was not among them. Thank God, at least she wasn't a Communist.

The novel took place in the near-future, which made it science-fiction, another black mark against it. The women's-lib movement had resulted in an accelerating number of young impotents. One of these, a shamus named John – the bitch named all her protagonists John – had gone to a penitorium.

This was run by a mad scientist, Herr Doktor Sigmund Arschtoll, who'd invented a quick method of transplanting male genitals. John Jemencule had been given a penis guaranteed to rise, but he'd found that occurred only when he was in church and singing hymns.

The scientist had offered a refund or a new cock. John had taken the latter, only to discover that it only inflated during the singing of the national anthem. Arschtoll couldn't understand what had gone wrong. So he offered John, who was a detective – all Jane's heroes were dicks, the bitch – the job of tracking down the culprit. John had accepted, though not before getting another organ.

The moment he stepped into the men's room across the hall, he discovered that it was of the gay persuasion.

'Zee vhat I mean?' Arschtoll said. 'De manufacturer'ss schlipped in a bad bunch on me. Prooff it, andt I'll giff you four grandt and trow in an Iron Cross.'

'First, give me another pri – pri – pri –, uh, male member,' John Jemencule said. 'They can't all be bad, can they?'

'De only way to findt out iss to be scientific. Dat is ekshperiment. Here. Try dis vone.'

It was too late to start the new case that day. Jemencule went home to watch the Erotic Box Office channel on TV. By the time he'd seen three shows, he was wondering what was wrong with his fourth organ. He found out when he switched to a straight channel, which was showing a musical version of *The Sheep-man.*

John Healey threw the carbons on the floor. No use destroying them; Jane hid the top copy. This couldn't go on. Like it or not, he must see a psychiatrist. He wasn't mentally ill, but he'd do anything to get rid of Jane, anything that was moral, that is.

Doctor Irving Mundwoetig, *Cut-Rates for Oral and Anal Fixations, Multiple Personalities a Specialty,* looked across his mahogany banana-shaped desk at Healey.

'It's no disgrace. You'd be surprised how many policemen have sneaked in. Take off that ridiculous fake moustache and those dark glasses and tell me what troubles you.'

Healey gulped and then blurted, 'I'm a schizo!'

'Aren't we all? Well, begin at the beginning. You don't mind if I drink and smoke? It makes me more relaxed.'

John reared up from his chair. 'I hate those filthy habits! *All* filthy habits!'

'You don't shit?'

'I'm leaving. I have to put up with dirty talk from my fellow officers, but I don't have to from you.'

'Most rigid,' the doctor murmured. 'Very well. No you-know-what from now on. So, sit down.'

Haltingly, blushing, squirming, Healey told him of the terrible events of the past four years.

'This case could make me famous, a best-seller author,' the doctor murmured.

'What?'

'Nothing. Did anything traumatic occur just before the emergence of your sister?'

'I woke up one morning and found the spare bedroom closet full of women's clothes. And a douche bag in the extra bathroom, for pity's sake!'

'At least she's clean. What I meant was, did anything traumatic happen before then?'

'Nothing.'

'You've repressed the incident, since *you yourself* purchased the feminine articles.'

'Not me!' Healey shouted. 'She did it! Don't you dare say I'm the same person as that cu – cu –...uh...woman!'

Sighing, Mundwoetig poured out a triple bourbon.

'Okay. When you were twelve, you went for a hike in the woods near your home. You took your female German shepherd along. A *police* dog, note. Your twin sister, Jane, insisted on following you. You forced her to leave, but she

refused to go without Princess. Neither was ever seen again.
You think some sick man killed the dog, raped your sister,
murdered her, then buried both someplace.'

'I think he raped Princess, too.'

The doctor's eyebrows rose. 'Oh? Why?'

'You know how those perverts are.'

'Anyway, you felt great guilt. Your child's mind determined
then that you'd be a cop, avenge your sister by ridding the
world of perversion. Since then you've led a very puritanical
life. You've never even had intercourse with a woman.'

'With anyone.'

'Curious you should say that. However, you have been
having intercourse in your persona as Jane Austen-Healey,
porno writer and, to use your own phrase, general all-around
slut.'

'I can't take it anymore! I've thought of committing suicide,
that'd show the bitch, but it wouldn't look good on my record.
On the other hand, maybe I'd be doing her a service. Like
putting a sick cur out of its misery.'

'How do you know she's not having fun fu-. . . uh, isn't well-
adjusted?'

'Would you call a woman well adjusted who maliciously and
vindictively forces her own brother to get bug – bug – bug –
sod – sod – sod –. . . degrades him?'

'You say she usually takes over when you're asleep? But
lately you've been blanking out in the evening, always at
home? Are you aware that sometimes the new persona absorbs
the old. . .? Do you feel faint, Mr Healey?'

'It must be the smoke.'

'If you can't stand the smoke of speculation, you'll never be
able to endure the heat of the fire of fact. Hmm! Not a bad
phrase. I'll put it in my. . . never mind. But it does need
polishing. Anyway, I'll just drink if the smoke really gets you
down. Now, what we have to do is find out *why* Jane has
appeared. We might get a clue to that by observing *how* she

behaves. This is a mystery, and you're a detective. If you applied the same type of reasoning in this case as you do in your police work, then...'

'You want me to arrest myself and then read my rights to myself?'

'That *would* be a bizarre turn! The readers...uh, I meant to say we've done all we can this session. Besides, the bottle is empty. I'll see you tomorrow.'

Swaying, the doctor rose.

Healey groaned and said, 'Oh, God, Doc, what if she took over while I was on duty? I'd be disgraced. The department would drum me out if I was caught arresting a public comfort-station queen while I was in drag.'

'It could be worse. If you were caught going...'

'Don't you dare say it! Doc, you think we got enough time?'

'I certainly hope so. There's not enough material yet. I mean... Hey! I just thought of something! It's a wonder you didn't long before now. Why don't you correspond with her? You might establish a beautiful relationship. You must admit there's a wide communication gap between you two.'

Dear Jane:

He erased the words. He wasn't a hypocrite. He wouldn't address as *Dear* anyone he hated, unless that person owed him money.

But the omission might make her furious.

Dearest Jane,

Please. Could we correspond? Maybe we could work something out, get to like each other. Then I'd give you more of my prime time if you'd quit boozing and whoring around and would write respectable novels. You could take over right after my supper and maybe then you could get to bed early and without sinning and I could get some rest. And I wouldn't wake up feeling like I'd been raped all night. Though God knows, with you it's not rape.

He tore the sheet up. No use pi – pi – angering her.

But the longer he sat up trying to mentally compose a friendly letter, the angrier he got. Why should he demean himself? Besides, he couldn't trust her to limit herself to the agreed-upon timesharing. Let a bitch get her nose in, and she'd take over the whole kennel.

Jane:

I give up. You got me by the ~~balls short hairs~~ neck. But I just can't take it any more. There's only one way out for me. And for you. Unless you agree to reform 100 percent. Believe me, if you don't, I'm going to shoot myself in the head. It'll be a suicide-homicide case, though the police won't know it. But, though I'm desperate, I am open to reason. If you can tell me how we can work this out, and it's moral, I'll do it.

Brother!

You think I like it any better than you do? You don't know how disgusted I am to be incarcerated in the body of such a repulsive uptight bluenose. Or the nausea I have to overcome each night when I find myself in your clumsy hairy ugly body. I should have boobs and a cunt and be properly fucked. And I yearn to have a baby. It's your goddamn fault I can't.

I wish I could peel you like I do my panties and drop you in the garbage. But I can't. So, remember that two can play at this game. If you don't quit bugging me, I'll take poison. I've written a letter by you in which you confess to being a closet alcoholic, smoker, drug addict, porno writer, and queen. Don't think about killing yourself before I can put it on the table for the police to read. A dear friend will mail his copy to the D.A. if the police don't get the first one. Your fingerprints will be all over the sheets, and it's no trouble for me to forge your signature.

Your fuzz brothers and the decency league will piss on your grave. Have a good day.

John groaned. The bitch wasn't easily scared. She had his great courage.

Jane had completed her latest offering of dirt. John read the carbons from the point at which he'd left off.

Jemencule, Arschtoll's undercover agent, had gone to work for the maker of artificial penises. (Burning with indignation, Healey skimmed through the many pages of sexual scenes obligatory in hardcore porno. But he read carefully the descriptions of how the organs were made.)

The owner, Professor Castor Fouteur, another mad scientist, used a fairly simple recipe to prepare his wonder pricks. He dumped tons of bull pizzles into a vat, added some chemicals, turned on a low heat, and thus made a vast pot of liquid protein. Add a dash of Spanish fly, stir well, and run off into molds, where the cooling stuff formed huge phalli lacking only the nerves. These were handstitched in separate rooms.

The rooms were air-conditioned; music of the workers' choice was piped in; there were four ten-minute sex breaks. Morale, though not morals, was high.

After a hundred pages, during which Jemencule's sleuthing was often interrupted by sexbook boilerplate orgies in which he unfortunately couldn't participate, he figured out what was wrong with the product. The chemicals in the vat had accidentally sensitized the protein to certain types of sound. When the phalli were subjected to the genre of music played in each room, conditioned reflexes, a kind of imprinting, were installed in them. This explained why the penises only became erect under certain circumstances.

It wasn't the gays or the sheep that had made Jemencule's organs stand at attention. It was the Muzak in the men's room and the film score.

But, unscrupulous bastard that he was, he decided to keep the secret to himself until he could sell it for a huge sum to a syndicate. Before leaving the factory, he concealed six organs in his clothing. Not only would he need them as samples for analysis, he could use them himself. All he had to do to ensure potency was to affix one suited to the type of his date, musically speaking. If she loved rock, he'd play that in his pad. If she was a classical buff, Beethoven's Fifth would guarantee a tremendous fu – fu –...uh...coitus. And what a climax!

But a surprise doorcheck exposed him manifold. Fouteur tortured him – all Jane's Johns were tortured, the vindictive so-and-so – until he confessed. The professor couldn't permit the spy to go free, and he was temporarily short of protein supply anyway. Screaming, Jemencule was added to the basic recipe of bull's pizzles.

'What your sister symbolizes there,' Mundwoetig said, 'is that you're a big prick. But she, in a literary sense, turns you into a bunch of little pricks. Hence, you become harmless and, in fact, comic. Not to be taken seriously.'

'Horse poppies!'

'What's meat to the unconscious is poison to the conscious. Hmm. Like that phrase. This is going to be a cornerstone classic.'

The doctor poured out a large glass from a gallon-sized decanter.

'My analyst and I really got someplace last session. I'm off the hard stuff now, a giant step forward in my therapy. However, back to work. We're at the stage where I can give you some clues, but you'll have to work out their significance yourself. Otherwise, you'll refuse to believe it.

'Jemencule becomes soup before being made into many practically independent phalli. That is, they're more organisms than organs.

'Neverhard, in *Sensuality and Sensibility*, is pressed flat as a shadow by a triphammer and then buried in a bed of pansies.

'Heisslippen, the time traveler in *Man's Fouled Park*, accidentally becomes part of a dinosaur egg.

'Petard, in *Enema*, is eaten by a giant Venus flytrap.

'Does all this suggest anything to you? No? All right. Is Jane unconsciously encoding messages to you? And to herself of course? You don't think so. Well, try this one on for size. Pizzle, in *Prude and Prejudice*, equates with puzzle. Solve the puzzle, and you've got a pizzle. Does that grab you?'

'You're nuts.'

'Would I spend all my time talking to funny-farm candidates if I wasn't? Just joking. But sit down! It's time for a long hard penetration of your defense mechanisms. You act as if your sister is an entirely separate entity from you. Originally, she was. But now she's not a person who was born by your mother. Like Athena sprung full-grown from Zeus' head, Jane was conceived full-blown – maybe I should retract that phrase and say completely adult – in your own mind.

'She's an artificial personality *you've* made. Thus, she can behave as you unconsciously wish you could. Yet you need not be guilty about her mode of life because she's an independent person.

'On the other hand, you do feel guilt because of what happened to her. Which was really what? Here's something you've been dodging whenever I bring it up. You say Jane took Princess back with her so Jane'd have both a companion and a guardian in the woods. But . . .'

'You're even more perverted than my sister is! I don't have to let you bury me in your filth! I won't listen to it!'

Mundwoetig, shouting, staggered after Healey as he ran down the hall. But the detective couldn't understand the words because of the finger jammed into each ear. Which made Mundwoetig wonder, fleetingly, if he'd overlooked an aural fixation in his patient.

Healey, plunging into the crowd in the lobby, could hear well enough to know that the doctor had quit shouting. And he could hear him suddenly stop yelling and start whistling at him. Fighting the urge to turn back, he kept running.

So many suicides took place in bedrooms because they were where the fu – fu – fu – conceptions occured. A bedroom was the beginning, the alpha, and so should be the end, the omega. And since he was born naked, he'd go out naked. Almost, anyway. He just hadn't been able to take off his shorts. A man had to preserve at least a minimum decency.

His finger curled around the trigger of the .38, the muzzle of which was close to his temple.

'Good-bye, Jane. I'm really sorry about the whole thing, though God knows I didn't do anything to start it. I just can't stand this any more. I've spread newspapers around so the blood won't mess up the carpet. Here goes!'

A loud voice, a woman's but recognizable as that of the child he'd known so well but so briefly, spoke.

'Oh no, you don't! You're not going to kill me twice. I managed to eavesdrop today, for the first time ever. I understood what your analyst was saying, even if you didn't, you dumbhead. So I've been bulldozing my way through the barriers because I knew that if I didn't we'd die.

'I don't particularly care for the way I'm going to use to save us. But it's the lesser of two evils.

'So...I'm pulling the switch, you dogfucker!'

The doctor, approaching the front porch of Healey's house, could hear the barking.

'Too late, too late,' he muttered as he swung open the unlocked front door. 'Oh, well. Win a few, lose a lot. Maybe it's for the best. Or am I rationalizing?'

Healey bounded awkwardly toward him, his tongue hanging out. Mundwoetig patted him on the head, which encouraged him to rear up and lick the doctor's face.

'Sit, Princess!'

The Phantom
of the Sewers

Foreword

Now and then, here and there, I write a 'fictional-author story.' This is a tale supposedly written by an author who is a character in fiction. An example would be David Copperfield or Anna Karenina. No stories by them have as yet appeared in print, but I wouldn't be surprised if they don't show up someday in a magazine or a book.

The first that I wrote under a fictional-author byline was the novel Venus on the Half-Shell *by 'Kilgore Trout.' Breathes there a person who doesn't know of Kilgore Trout? Plenty, I've found out. But millions are well acquainted with this sadsack science-fiction author who appears in Kurt Vonnegut's* God Bless You, Mr Rosewater,* Slaughterhouse-Five,* *and* Breakfast of Champions.* *And many, a few years ago, were astonished to see this novel appear on the bookstands. Here they had thought all along that Trout was only a fictional character, yet here was a novel by Trout with a bibliography of Trout's works, a short biography, and a photograph on the back cover of a scroungy-looking long-bearded much-shafted science-fiction author.*

That was I under all that hair, which was actually pieces of a wig glued onto my face.

A lot of readers were fooled into believing that Trout really lived. Others weren't, and these wrote letters, hordes of them, to poor Mr Vonnegut asking if he was the real author of the Trout book. My apologies to him.

However, the novel was written as the supreme way of honoring my then-favorite science-fiction writer. It was offered as the highest tribute I could pay.

---

* Now available from Granada Paperbacks.

Incidentally, I discovered that by being another person, that is, Kilgore Trout, I could break the writer's block I'd been suffering under or with. So, every time a block hove up on the horizon, I'd shift into the persona of a fictional author and the block would disappear. Since it was not I, Philip José Farmer, who was writing but a fictional author, who wasn't loaded down with a writer's block, then I could write. And after the story by the fictional author was finished, the block didn't come back. Not for a long time, anyway.

A neat trick, this fooling yourself, even if I do say so myself. Who's better qualified to say so?

There was a writer character in Venus on the Half-Shell, *a Jonathan Swift Somers III. So I wrote a story by him and then another and hope to write more. These were done for fun; no writer's block existed then. But I'd like to point out that Somers III is the son of another Jonathan Swift Somers, the very bad and oft-frustrated poet whose epitaph appears in Edgar Lee Masters'* Spoon River Anthology. *It's a case of wheels within wheels within wheels.*

There are three fictional-author stories in this collection. The one you are about to read is one of them. Originally, this appeared in a magazine as 'It's the Queen of Darkness, Pal' by 'Rod Keen.' Rod Keen was the creation of Richard Brautigan, and he appeared very briefly in Brautigan's The Abortion: An Historical Romance 1966. *Keen was a sewer worker who handed in a manuscript to the curator of a very peculiar library on a hill in San Francisco. His sole comment was that it was a science-fiction tale.*

I recommend this wild book to all; it's one of my favourites.

I think that Brautigan, in giving this sewer worker the name of Rod Keen, was obliquely presenting his opinion of the works of a very well known and rich writer of San Francisco who has the brass-bound audacity to call his stuff 'poetry.' I share this opinion, and so I've given the antihero in this tale a somewhat similar name. And made him a very bad poet.

The ending lines of 'The Phantom of the Sewer' are not quite what they were in the original version.

Also, just as I wrote Venus *with a slight Vonnegutian flavor, so I wrote this story with a slight Brautiganian flavor.*

It's been fun being Trout, Keen, John H. Watson, M.D., Bunny Manders, Paul Chapin, Leo Queequeg Tincrowdor, and Somers III. Not to mention Lord Greystoke, otherwise known as Tarzan, and Maxwell Grant, the author of The Shadow *stories. I hope to have more fun in the future.*

1

All day long, Red McCune worked the city like a galley slave. Ben Hur had toiled to pull his beautiful many-decked ship across the waters. Red worked to hose and push ugly single-decked pieces of crap down the stream. They were his burden, and Red, always the poet, had once called the burdens fardels. His partner, 'Ringo' Ringgold, had said, 'What?'

'...*who would fardels bear, to grunt and sweat under a weary life...*'

'Okay, what's a fardel?'

Ringo's expression showed he thought it was something related to passing gas. That was what working in the sewers did to a man.

'It's a word used by a colleague of mine,' Red had said. 'A fellow poet. Bill, the Bard of Avon.'

'Oh, God, not another one?' Ringo had said. 'What's he doing down here?'

'Keeping me company.'

Ringo grunted. If the subject had been World War Two Japanese, Ringo wouldn't have stopped talking. He'd been one of the first of the black Marines to be shipped off to the South Pacific to kill or be killed or maybe both. Ringo opted for survival and came back with a potful of mementos and a lot of stories.

'I admired them little yellow bastards,' he'd once told Red. 'Only they wasn't yellow. They stood up to us whites like real men.'

Red had rolled his eyes then, and Ringo had said quickly, 'You know what I mean. All us Americans was white as far as the Nips was concerned.'

Ringo was a little peculiar. That could have been blamed on

the Marines, but Red thought that it was the sewer that had done it to Ringo. It did it to all the workers, including himself. The darkness, the garbage and trash on the dark waters, the gases, the heat, these made a pressure cooker that a salesman couldn't have given away.

Red raked in a high-button shoe and looked at it before throwing it back in. Some happy young 1909 beauty had worn that. She never would have believed that she'd be wrinkled and bent and open at the seams, her breath and soul sour, and living off welfare. Out of style, out of time, just like her shoe.

Gas is the pessimism of the belly, and pessimism is the gas of the soul. Red suffered a lot from both. But he considered himself to be both a poet and the archaeologist of the living. One way to pass the time, and the gas, was to imagine he was an archaeologist. Forget what he knew about the actualities. Imagine he was reconstructing the civilization above only on the basis of what floated by and what he hosed down.

It was a strange world up there. Once there were many condoms floating by, but now there were few. This meant that they'd had overpopulation up there, and the rubber factories had been working overtime. One day, the rubbers became fewer, and in a few months where they had once been schools of little white fish, bobbing and turning and nosing each other affectionately, they were loners. No one to nuzzle or play tag with.

From this Red deduced that something terrible had happened up there. It was the Red Masque all over again, though this time it wasn't red spots on the skin but impotency. The thing in the masque walked through the streets of Golden Gate City, touching this one and that one with his wand. It made no difference who the men were: bankers, gangsters, fuzz, pushers, all-Americans, beatniks, carry-out boys, wardheelers, astrologers, talk-show hosts. They went limp as cigarettes dropped into the toilet.

Red got a lot of satisfaction from this image. He was so ugly that very few women would have anything to do with him, and those that would he wanted nothing to do with. It was a case of like repulsing like.

Red thought of himself as another Quasimodo. Where the hunchback hung around the steeple, way up there, Red chose to get down under. Heights made him dizzy, anyway.

Sometimes, he got too involved in his picture of a dwindling population. When he crawled out of the manhole at quitting time, he was surprised that the streets weren't empty after all.

'Dead and don't know it,' he'd mutter.

Today Red was working out his archaeology on the basis of the quality of the excrement going by in convoys. When he'd started working, twelve years ago, the brown gondolas that steamed on by, pushing toward their ports, the sausage-shaped gondolas floating through their dark Venice, had been of superior quality. Nothing to compare with the stuff in his grandfather's outhouse, of course, not Grade AA, but still Grade A. The stuff he encountered now, these were World War I U-boats compared to the magnificent *Queen Elizabeths*, the *Titanics* and *Lusitanias* that had, relatively speaking, graced the beer-brown seas. In those days even the bumboats, the stuff from the poor, were superior to the best from the rich of 1966. And if today's droppings were so bad, think of what he'd have to put up with in 1976.

Red didn't know what was causing the degeneracy. Was it DDT and artificial fertilizers and too much sugar? We are what we eat, and what we are includes thoughts. The stomach is the shadow of the mind, and where the mind goes, the stomach follows.

You wouldn't have got stuff like that from Socrates or Kant. They were thinkers; modern philosophers were stinkers.

'Hey, Red, what you dreaming about?' Ringo said.

'Socrates,' Red said.

'Oh, you mean that Greek cook at Captain Nemo's Submarine Sandwiches? Yeah, his food ain't what it used to be. But where the hell is it?'

'That's what I was thinking.'

'Better stop thinking and get your ass in gear,' Ringo said. 'The inspector's coming through today. Say, what's Ernie doing, anyway? He must be goofing off too. There ain't no hose going up there.'

Red looked up the tunnel. For a hundred yards it went straight as an ex-con claimed to be and then curved out of sight. The corner gave off a dim light like a glowworm in heat. It came from the lamp in Ernie Mazzeo's helmet. This helmet was like a miner's, though Ernie wasn't digging coal. Ernie dug hardly anything, which was why he would just as soon be down here as up there.

'Maybe I ought to wake him up,' Red said. 'The inspector'll fire him if he catches him sleeping.'

Red's lamp was shining down on the waters, which was why he was the first to notice the almost black stuff in the dark-brown liquid. It looked like an octopus that had been caught under a steamroller.

'What's that?' he said.

'If I didn't know better,' Ringo said, 'I'd say it was blood.'

Ernie's head floated by. His mouth was open, and his teeth shone in the beam. There was enough gold in them to make it worthwhile to mine Ernie.

2

The police came first, then the ambulance, then Inspector Bleek. The detectives questioned McCune and Ringgold, took pictures, made measurements, and put Ernie's parts in a pile. These included the head, the severed arms and legs, and the heart. The genitals were missing. They might have been thrown into the sewage and had floated by unnoticed by the two workers. Nobody thought so. Richie Washington and Abdul Y had been cut apart and their heads and limbs recovered. But their genitals were still missing. The theory was that the killer had taken them with him. No one knew why he had done this, but the sale of mountain oysters at the restaurants had dropped to almost nothing.

'You two'll have to come down to headquarters,' Lieutenant Hallot said.

'Don't you worry, boys,' Bleek said, his voice thick as dipped honey. 'I'll see that you get a lawyer and bail. I take care of my men.'

He put his arm around Red and then around Ringo to show that he played no favorites.

'They're not under arrest,' Hallot said. 'I just want them to make complete statements.'

'Take the rest of the day off when they're through with you,' Bleek said. 'God! What kind of a monster is loose down here? Why's he picking on sewer workers? Richie last month and Abdul the month before. What's he got against you guys? Us, I mean. Or is it a conspiracy by some underground outfit? Are they trying to foul up the sewer system so the city'll get sick?'

Bleek looked as upset as Red felt. He was a big man, about a head taller than Red and a head wider and almost as ugly. His mirror took a beating every morning, but that didn't seem to bother him as it did Red. He had a wife, a Chinese immigrant from Taiwan who wasn't disturbed by his lack of beauty. All Caucasian males looked the same to her.

Bleek squeezed Red's shoulders and said, 'Hang in there, pal!'

'Stiff upper lip, old chap!' Ringo jeered as he and Red walked away. 'That honey-voiced son of a bitch likes you so much because compared to him you're a wart hog's hind end and he's the peacock's.'

Red didn't say anything. They had to stand to one side then while the attendants carried Ernie by under a sheet and on a stretcher. Blood was spreading out through it like it was looking for a new home.

'I think I'll quit,' Ringo said. 'Hell, we ain't even getting combat pay!'

Red didn't say much the next two hours except to answer questions from a squad of detectives. It was evident they thought he and Ringo were guilty, but that didn't bother him. In their books, everybody was guilty, and that included the judges. By the time they'd finished the session, they were even looking suspiciously at each other. The session didn't last very long, though. The cops' red faces quickly got green, and they staggered out one by one. Red finally figured that it was because he and Ringo had brought up a lot of the sewer with them.

That's strange, he thought. They don't mind the moral atmosphere in here. In fact, most of them seem to get fat on it. Then he remembered the sewer rats and how fat they were.

3

It was still afternoon when they got out. The light was the same as everyday in Golden Gate City on a cloudless day. The brightness had the harshness of reality but made the buildings and the people look unreal. It was as if the emerald city of Oz had been whitewashed. By an apprentice painter. Or maybe by Tom Sawyer's friends.

Ringo lit a cigarette. Ringo was short and very round in head and body and legs. This, with his shiny black skin, made him look like an anarchist's bomb that was ready to go off. The cigarette was the fuse.

'Let's get something to eat,' Ringo said.

'My God, after seeing Ernie!' Red said. He wanted only to go to his room, which really wasn't anything to go to. But it was better than going any place else. He'd get into the shower with his overalls and boots still on, and wash off his clothes. Then he'd wash himself. Then he'd open a cold can of beer – the beer would be cold, too – and he'd turn the heat on very low in his oven and put the wet clothes in the oven but leave its door open. The smell of cleanliness would spread through his one room and bath. It would be like forgiveness from a priest after a long, hard confession. Repentance played no part in it, though. He knew all along that he meant to sin again, to go down into the sewers the next day. The slough of despond, he thought. Despondency was a sin, but in the tunnels its peculiar odor was overridden by all the others. Moreover, up here he got even more despondent because he had to take so much crap from everybody. He took it down there, too, but down there it was impersonal.

Then, he'd be padding around naked, passing the mirror a dozen times and avoiding looking in it. When he forgot and did look into it, he'd give it the finger. It gave him the finger back, but it never did it first. It tried, but Red was the fastest finger in the West.

By the time he'd turned the old TV set on, he'd hear a banging at the door. That'd be old Mrs Nilssen, his widowed landlady. Mrs Nilssen would cry out in her seventy-year voice that she wanted to talk to him. Actually, she was a drunk who wanted a drink. After a few, she'd want to lay him. Mrs Nilssen, poor old soul, was desperate, and she figured that as ugly as he was he'd be grateful to have even her. A couple of times she'd been almost right. But he didn't want any of her desperation. He could just barely handle his own.

After he'd yelled at her to go away enough times, she'd go. Then he'd sit down at the desk he'd bought at the Goodwill and with another beer by his elbow compose his poetry. He'd look out the window from five stories up on the hill and see other windows looking up or down at him. Somewhere beyond them was the bay and the great bridge over which Jack London and Ambrose Bierce and Mark Twain and George Sterling had once ridden in carriages. He knew that the bridge hadn't been built in their day, but it was nice to think of them rolling across it. And if the bridge had been built then, they would have crossed on it.

He had his own bridge to cross. This was finishing the poem which he had titled *The Queen of Darkness*. He'd written it on yellow second sheets and envelopes and grocery sacks and once, out of paper and funds, on the dust on his desk. The dust had inspired him; it'd kindled the greatest lines he'd ever written. He got so excited he went out and got drunk, and when he got back from work the next day, he'd rushed to the desk to read them because he couldn't remember them. They weren't there. Wouldn't you know it, old Mrs Nilssen had cleaned his room. This was the first and last time; the cleaning was only an excuse to look for the bottle that she was sure he'd hidden. She thought everybody had a hidden bottle.

He'd never been able to reconstruct the lines, and so he'd lost his chance to get his start as a major poet. Those lines would've launched him; it wouldn't be anything but *Excelsior* from then on. At least, it was nice to believe so.

Now, after a couple of millions of lines, Red had to admit that he couldn't even play in the minor leagues of poetry. His stuff stank, just as the sewers stank. Actually, it was the sewers that had ruined his poetry, though in the beginning they were his inspiration. He was going to write something as good as, maybe better than, Thompson's 'City of Dreadful Night.'

Maybe as good as Keats' 'La Belle Dame Sans Merci.' Then, ugly or not, he'd be invited to the colleges and the salons to read his poems, and the women would fall all over him. But, no, his candle had gone out in the darkness and the damp and the stink. That white wavering beauty, the muse that he had imagined moving toward him, then away, beckoning him on into distant tunnels, there to show him love and death, had died. Like a minstrel show at a Black Muslim meeting.

Still, there were times when he thought he saw her dimly, a flicker, at the far corner of the dark canal.

4

'What the hell you thinking, man?' Red said. 'I can't eat now. Let's have a few drinks first.'

This was fine with Ringo. They walked through the crowd, which gave them plenty of room, to The Tanglefoot Tango Tavern. This was half-full of winos and pushers, and the other half was narks and a drunken preacher from the Neo-Sufi Church down the street. The Reverend Hadji Fawkes saluted them as they came in. 'Is there a God in the sewers? Does he walk in the coolth of the smell?'

'Not since last Tuesday, Rev.,' Ringo said and pushed Red on ahead. Red wanted to talk; a religion that promoted intoxication as The Way was interesting. So did the other customers, as long as Fawkes bought drinks for them. But Ringo wasn't having any of a white man's faith, free booze or not.

They sat down near the jukebox, which was playing 'Show Me the Way to Go Home,' one of the church's official hymns.

They ordered a pitcher of beer apiece and a couple of hamburgers for Ringo. Seeing Red's expression, Ringo told the waitress, 'Take it easy on the catsup.'

'How's the poetry going?' Ringo said, though he could care less.

'I'm about to give up and write a book. One on the myths and legends of the sewer system of Golden Gate City.'

'Man, that's spooky,' Ringo said. 'You don't believe any of that shit, do you?'

'The Phantom of the Sewers? Why not? He could be just some wino that went ape and decided to imitate Lon Chaney. There are lots of places he could hole up, and anyway he doesn't have to spend all his time haunting the tunnels. He could live part of the time upstairs, maybe he's right here now, standing at the bar, drinking, laughing at us.'

Ringo looked quickly at the customers at the bar and said, 'Naw. Not them.'

'Has the Phantom ever done anything to hurt anybody, besides scare them half to death? And with what? A Halloween skull mask and a black robe? I don't think someone threw acid in his face and it ate his face off so the skull shows. That's right out of the old movie, Ringo.'

'I seen him once, anyway,' Ringo said. 'He was poling a long shallow boat along, standing up in it, his robes fluttering in the wind, he was near one of the big fans, and his eyes was big and white, and his face was half gone. That was scary enough but what really made me take off was his passenger. It looked like a heap of. . . something, a heap that was pulsing like a toad. It had one round eye, no lid, which was staring at me.'

'I thought you said you didn't believe in that crap,' Red McCune said.

'What I say and what I believe ain't always the same thing.'

'Lots of people are that way,' Red said. 'It sounds like the Phantom made friends with the Terrible Turdothere.'

He grinned, but the grin was only to show that he wasn't

serious. If Ringo thought he was serious, he'd never go down into the sewers again. There'd go his job and his seniority and his pension and his World War Two souvenirs. There'd go his satisfaction and contentment, too, because Ringo liked his job. No matter what he said about it, he liked it.

Every bat to his own belfry.

'I don't know,' Ringo said slowly. 'I ain't seen the Phantom since, and nobody else has either as far as I could find out. Do you suppose that the Phantom was hypnotized by the Turdothere and it had commanded him to take it to its secret lair where it could eat the Phantom?'

They were silent for a while as they watched the horror films on the picture tubes of their minds. These were the latest in a long line: *Dracula Squares Off at the Creature from the Black Lagoon, The Golem Meets the Giant Spirochete, Abbott and Costello Versus the Daughter of Mr Hyde and the Hyena Woman*. When the monsters got tired of eating people, they ate each other.

As background music, the jukebox, now off the religious kick, was bellowing country music: 'A Farmer's Daughter It Was Who Give Me Two Acres Last Night.' An old man, screaming that he was the long-lost heir to the Rockefeller fortune, was being carried out the back door into the alley. Another old man was coughing up blood under a table. His cronies were betting drinks, from his bottle, for or against his ever taking another drink.

The myth of the Turdothere went like this. It wasn't a Mad Scientist that created the Turdothere. In the old days it would have been, but people didn't believe in a Mad Scientist any more. The faith in their existence was gone. They were as extinct as Zeus or Odin or maybe even God.

It was The Mad TV Writer that was the new menace. The name was Victor Scheissmiller, a man who had really lived. Everybody had seen his picture in the newspapers and magazines and read about him in them. He wasn't something made up.

It was true that he had gone mad, his mind off-course like

Wrong Way Corrigan's airplane. After eighteen years of writing contest shows, children's shows, westerns, cops-and-robbers, science-fiction series, and soap operas, he blew the tube on his mental set. There wasn't any warranty, and he didn't try to trade in the old mind. He disappeared one day, last seen climbing down a manhole. The note he left behind said he was going to create a monster, the Turdothere, and release it on the world. After it ate up all the sewer workers, it would emerge from a storm sewer and devour the whole population while they sat hypnotized before their TV's.

The surface people thought it was a big joke. The tunnel people laughed about it when they were above. But when they were below, they did a lot of looking over their shoulders.

Nobody had seen Victor Scheissmiller in the sewers, but some had seen the heaving stinking mass of the Turdothere with its one glass eye – Scheissmiller's own, some said. Some workers said that it was the Turdothere that had killed their buddies and cut off the head, legs, and arms. But those who'd seen the thing said it had no teeth. It must gum its victims to death, or maybe it stuck a tentacle of crap down their throats and choked them. Then it wrapped itself around them and dissolved them in its juices.

How did it keep alive when only a few people had disappeared in the sewers? Easy. It ate rats, too. And it was probably a cannibal; it ate crap, too.

It grew even larger then, and it could become a colossus, since there was no end of this kind of food, unless the plumbers went on strike. Its main body, though, was supposed to be in a sort of skeleton, old bones put together by Scheissmiller. There were nerves of thread and catgut and a condom swelling and shrinking like a heart, pumping muscatel from a bottle for its blood, a jar of vaginal jelly for a liver, cigar butts embedded in the body drawing oxygen through it. And so on.

Others said this wasn't correct. The thing was a 300-pound mass of nothing but living crap, no bones or bottles in it, and it flowed along and changed shape like *The Brobdingnagian Bacillus That Desired Raquel Welch*. (Later retitled *I Bugged the Body Beautiful*.)

Everybody agreed, though, that it had one glass eye which it used to spot its victims.

'Mostly it's made of dead human hopes,' Red said.

'What?' Ringo said.

'Well, I'll be damned,' Red added. 'Look who's here!'

Ringo jumped up with a scream, upsetting a pitcher of beer, and he whirled around, crying, 'Oh, no! It's not *here*!'

'So you don't believe?' Red said, sneering. 'No, Ringo, it isn't the Turdothere. It's Inspector Bleek himself.'

'What's he doing here?' Ringo said. He sat down and tried to hide his shaking by gripping Red's pitcher with two hands and pouring out a glass of beer. He didn't make it.

Bleek drew up a chair and thrust his ugly face across the table as close as he could get it to Red's face. 'I just got the coroner's report from the cops,' he said. 'Ernie was raped, just like those other two boys.'

Ringo ordered two more pitchers. Red was silent for a while, then he said, 'Was it before or after they were killed?'

'Before,' Bleek said.

'That tears it,' Ringo said. 'I'm quitting. If I'm gonna be butchered by a sexual pervert, I'm gonna do it up in the sunshine.'

'With all the security you got?' Bleek said. 'I was afraid you two guys were thinking of quitting, which is why I am here. Hang on, old buddies. Tomorrow the police are going to conduct a massive manhunt through the entire sewer system. They need guides, so you two can help, if you want to.'

He put his arm around Red and squeezed his shoulder.

'The Public Works Department expects every man to do his duty. Besides, there'll be camera crews down there tomorrow. You might get to see yourself on TV.'

How could anybody resist that?

The hunt took four days, and it turned out just like Red McCune expected it to. Lights blazed, men yelled, bloodhounds bayed. The darkness moved in after the lights moved on, the men got hoarse and fell silent, the hounds smelled nothing but sewer gas. The hounds didn't know what they were looking for, anyway. Nobody had a glove from the Phantom to let them sniff or a dropping from a thing that was all droppings. And the Sewer Slayer, as the papers and TV called him, was out for lunch. Whoever and whatever he was, he was no idiot.

'See?' Red told Ringo.

'There's plenty of places to hide, secret exits, alcoves and old tunnels that've been bricked off, and stuff like that,' Ringo answered. 'Anyway, how do we know he wasn't hiding under the water? The Phantom of the Opera walked underwater while he breathed through a tube.'

What they did find was a Pekingese dog that'd been tortured to death and three human fetuses, all looking like Martians that had crash-landed. The usual.

They also found the rats, or maybe it was the other way around. This was when the hunters started having a good time. After trudging for miles through dark wet stinking places, getting tired and half-nauseated and bored, and in a killing mood, they had something to kill.

The rats had been running for hours ahead of them, and now there was a wagon train of them, about four hundred furry gray pioneers cornered by the Indians. Most of them had swum through canals during their flight and so looked like dust mops that had been rained on. Their eyes shone red in the beams, like little traffic lights. STOP they said, and the men did halt for a minute while they looked the squealing heaving mass over. A flashlight caught a blur that leaped down from a ledge at the far end of the chamber. It was three times as big as the others, and its one eye seemed to have its own glow. It was not gray but white above and black below.

'That must be their leader,' one of the cops said. 'Lord, I'm glad they're not all that big!'

The shooting and the clubbing started then. The .38's and the .45's and the shotguns boomed, deafening everybody in a few seconds. The rats blew up as if they were little land mines. Most of them ran back and forth instead of making a run for it through the humans. They'd heard that a cornered rat always fights, and they believed it. The skeptics among them dashed through the hunters, biting a few hands and legs. Most of them were smashed with saps or flashlights but a few got away.

Ringo jumped in with the others, swinging a Samurai sword from his collection. 'Banzai!' he'd cry, and when a rat leaped at him and he cut off its head in midair, 'Ah, so!'

Beyond him Inspector Bleek, a big grin on his face like a Halloween pumpkin's, fired a six-shooter into the horde. It was an heirloom from his great-grandfather, who had conquered the West with it. Its barrel was long enough and wide enough to make an elephant proctologist happy. It flashed out .44-caliber bullets which mowed the rats down like they were grandfather's Indians.

In his other hand he held a big Bowie knife. Red wondered if he meant to do some scalping when the last stand was over. Red crouched down against the wall. He wasn't afraid of the rats but he didn't enjoy killing them either. He wanted to hang back mostly because he knew the bullets would start ricocheting. Sure enough, one screamed by, just like in a Western, and another followed it, and then some cop yelled that the rats were firing back. Later it turned out he'd been stunned by a bullet which just touched his forehead, and in his stupor he thought sure the rats had got hold of some guns.

The men started ducking but they kept on shooting. After a while, a man was hit in the leg, and the hunters started to come to their senses. The explosions died like the last of popcorn in the pan, the echoes feebled away, and there was silence except for the running waters behind them and the faraway baying of the hounds. Their owner wasn't risking his valuable property around anything so unreliable as rats.

The blood ran down the slanting apron of concrete to the channel for a minute. Then it stopped, like an oil well gone dry, go home, boys, I'm out of dinosaurs.

The only survivor was a big old rat, the Custer of the 7th Underground Cavalry. He climbed over and slid down body after body, dragging his hind legs, which were missing their feet, his goal the waters.

'He's sure got slanty eyes,' Ringo said, and he leaped, shouting, 'Banzai!' and his sword cut off the rat's head.

'Goddamn it!' Bleek said. 'I wanted to do that!'

'I did that because I admired the son of a bitch,' Ringo said. 'He's got guts. He deserved an honorable death.'

'You're crazy,' Bleek said. He looked around, waving his Bowie as if it were a baton and the orchestra had gone on strike.

'Hey!' a cop said. 'Look at that!'

In a corner was a mass of bodies and pieces of bodies. They'd been hosed against the wall and piled up by a stream of bullets. Everything in it seemed to have been killed three times at least. But it was stirring and then it was quaking, and cracks appeared, and suddenly the giant rat they'd glimpsed when the massacre began erupted. Only it wasn't a rat. It was a cat, snarling, his one eye as bright as a hotrodder's exhaust, his back curved as if he was a bow about to shoot himself at them. Despite the blood that streaked him, his coloring, white above and black below, showed through.

'Why, that's Old Half-Moon!' Red said.

'Who the hell's Half-Moon?' Bleek said.

Red didn't say anything about his being a legend of the sewers. He said, 'He's been around a couple of years at least. When I first saw him, he was just an old alley cat. But he started getting big because rats make good eating. Look at him! He's been through a hundred fights above and two hundred below! One eye gone and both ears chewed apart. But he's a terror among the rats. I saw him take on ten one time and kill them all.'

'Yeah?' Bleek said. He took a few steps toward Old Half-Moon. The cat crouched as if to spring. Bleek admonished him with his knife but he stopped.

'I think he's become pals with the rats,' he said. 'He's their leader. After all, you are what you eat, and he eats nothing but rats, so he must be half rat.'

'You're what you breathe, too,' Red said. 'That makes us sewer workers half crap.'

'That man's crazy,' Ringo muttered.

'He got caught when they came swarming out,' Red said. 'He had to run ahead of them. Hell, even he wouldn't tackle that many rats.'

'I don't want him jumping out of the dark and scaring me,' Bleek said. He edged toward the cat, which looked as if it were going to erupt again. He was a Vesuvius of a cat, and his Pompeii would be Inspector Bleek.

'He don't pay any attention to us workers,' Red said. 'Hell, he and I've passed each other a dozen times; we just nod and go our own ways. He's a valuable animal; he kills more rats than a dozen poisoners. And he doesn't ask for overtime either.'

'We could take him in,' a cop said. Red thought he saw him reaching for his handcuffs but decided it was his imagination.

'Let him go,' Red said.

'I'm your boss!'

'If you kill that cat, I quit.'

Bleek scowled, and then, after a struggle, he put his knife in its sheath under his jacket. The smile came slowly, as if some little man inside him was working away at the ratchets connected to the corners of his lips. Finally, the big Halloween-pumpkin grin encased in plastic, he put his arm around Red.

'You love the cat, don't you?'

'He's like me, ugly and better off down here in the darkness.'

Bleek laughed and squeezed Red's shoulder.

'You ain't ugly, man! You're beautiful!'

'I got a mirror.'

Bleek laughed and let loose of Red's shoulder and slapped him on the ass. The cat darted by them, running as if he were glad to see the last of them. He'd had enough of rats for a long time, too.

6

The order came down from the Commissioner of Public Works that no sewer worker was ever to be alone while working. They must always have a buddy in sight. Red and Ringo observed this rule, if not religiously at least devoutly. But as two weeks passed, they occasionally found themselves alone. Old habits, unlike old clothes, don't wear out easily. However, as soon as one became aware that the other had gone on ahead around a curve of a tunnel or had dropped back, one started calling and didn't quit until he'd seen the other. During this time, Red had nightmares. It was always the rats. He'd see them leaping around, and then, while he stood unable to run away, they'd scurry toward him, and after a while he'd feel one run up his leg. It would stop just below his buttocks and start sniffing and he knew what it was going to do and he tightened up but those chisel teeth were going to gnaw and gnaw.

He always woke then with the rats gone, but the horror took time to melt, like a suppository that'd just come from the refrigerator.

'Nibble, nibble, nibble,' he said to Bleek. 'A man doesn't have to die by big bites.'

'Dreams can't kill you.'

'They've killed more people than automobiles ever did. Napoleon and Hitler were dreamers. Come to think of it, it was dreamers that invented the automobile.'

'Who invented dreams?' Bleek said.

That surprised Red, and he forgot what he was going to say next. Bleek seemed like a hail-fellow-well-met guy, smart enough for his job but no bargain in the intellect shop. Yet, every once in a while, he came out with a remark like this. There were a few trout among his mental carp.

Bleek looked at his wristwatch. Red said, 'Yes, I know. We got to get going.'

Ringo had started down the manhole. While waiting for him, Red looked around. The sky was, or seemed to be, the deepest blue he'd ever seen. The tall buildings along this street were like mountains themselves, banking the street, keeping it in shady trust. The manhole, however, was in a spot where the sunshine ran between two buildings, like Indians coming through a pass, Red thought. Or the Golden Horde invading the land of shadows. The patina of unreality that raw sunshine always laid on Golden Gate City was the thickest he'd ever seen. The shadows fought it, battling to keep their hold on reality, but they were retreating.

Bleek was standing near him, obviously trying to think of something to say before he got in his car and drove off. A car passed by with a young couple in it, and the girl, a lovely creature, pointed at Red and said something to the driver, a handsome fellow. He took a quick look at Red and then at Bleek, and his lips formed words. 'Oh, my God!'

'Doubled in ugliness,' the girl's lips shaped.

Red gave her the finger. The girl, her head turned to look behind her, was startled at first, but she laughed and turned to the boy and said something. Red thought for a minute that the boy might back up the car and come storming out, but after slowing down, the car speeded up. The two had thrown their heads back as if they were laughing.

Red shrugged. He'd seen this reaction many times before. People were always shocked when they uncovered the conspiracy of his genes to overthrow the human face. Then they laughed.

He started down the ladder below the manhole. Bleek said, 'How's your poem coming?'

Red wondered why he was asking him that, but he answered, 'I've given up on *The Queen of Darkness*. No, that's wrong. She's given up on me. Anyway, she was never serious. All she ever did was flirt with me. She isn't going to kiss me, like she does real poets.'

'You're a little strange,' Bleek said. 'But then I got a lot of strange ones among my boys. Sewer work seems to attrack them, but of course this *is* California. So you ain't going to write poetry any more?'

'I've had it,' Red said. 'All I've wanted for the past two years is to write four perfect lines. To hell with epics, especially epics about sewers. All I wanted was four lines that would make me remembered forever, and I'd have settled for two. Two lines to blaze in the eyes of the world so it wouldn't see the face of the man behind them. That wasn't much to ask, but it was too much. She's kissed me off for good. She doesn't come in my dreams any more. It's just the rats that come now.'

Bleek looked distressed. However, he often looked that way.

The planes of his face naturally formed themselves into a roadmap of grief.

'You saying this is the end of the line for you?'

'As a poet, yes. And since I'm half poet, though a bad one, only half a man is going to survive.'

Bleek didn't seem to know what to say.

Red said, 'See you,' and he climbed on down the ladder. He and Ringo picked up their tools and lunchbuckets and walked toward their work. Somewhere ahead of them something had clogged up the stream, and they had to find it and remove it.

They passed through areas where permanent lights blazed overhead and then through dark places where the only light was their headlamps. Like a chess board, Red thought, where the only players were pawns.

Their lamps beamed on a big pile of something indeterminable. The mass was like a dam, at least a foot higher than the water backing up behind it.

Ringo, a few feet ahead of Red, stopped on the walkway and looked down at the pile. Red started to say something, and then Ringo screamed.

The mass had come alive. It was heaving up from the channel, and two pseudopods had encircled Ringo's feet and waist.

Red was paralyzed. The tunnel had become a cannon barrel down which unreality was shooting.

Ringo fought the tentacles, tearing off big pieces of soft brown stuff. Bones wired together at the joints fell out of the stuff that struck the concrete walkway, but other pseudopods grew out of the mass and seized Ringo around the throat and between his legs. They extended, slid around and around Ringo while Red stared. His beam lit up Ringo's open mouth, the white teeth, the whites of the eyes. It also reflected on the single bulging eye on top of a bump on the side near Ringo.

Suddenly, Ringo's jaw dropped, and his eyes started to glaze like the monster's eye. Either he had fainted or he had had a heart attack. Whichever it was, he had fallen onto the mass, a little distance from the eye, and he was sinking face down into it.

Red wanted to run away, but he couldn't leave Ringo to be drawn into that sickening mass. Suddenly, as if a switch had been slammed shut inside him, he leaped forward. At the edge of the walkway he leaned down and grabbed Ringo's left ankle. A tentacle, soft, slimy, stinking, came up over the edge of the concrete and coiled around his own leg. He screamed but he did not let loose of the ankle. Ringo was being pulled out slowly, and Red knew that if he could hang on to him, he could probably get him away. He had to free him soon because Ringo, if he wasn't dead, was going to suffocate in a short time.

Before he could drop the ankle and get away, he was up to his waist in the mass. It had oozed up onto the walkway, enfolded him, and was sucking him into it.

The glass eye was in front of his face; it was on the end of a pod, swaying back and forth before him.

Red, still screaming, took off his helmet and batted at the eye. It struck it, tore it loose, and then he was in darkness. The helmet had been snatched away and was sinking into the vast body. For a second the light glowed redly inside and then was gone.

Red forgot about Ringo. He thrashed and struck out and suddenly he was free. Sobbing, he crawled away until he came against the wall. He didn't know which way was upstream, but he hoped he was going in the right direction. The thing couldn't make much headway against the waters. It had pulled part of its body away from the channel to get up on the walkway, and the waters had come rushing down the opened way. They made a strong current just now, one against which the thing surely could not swim very swiftly.

Also, with its eye gone, it was as blind as he. Could it hear? Smell?

Maybe I've flipped, Red thought. That thing can't exist. I must be in a delirium, imagining it. Maybe I'm really in a straitjacket someplace. I hope they can give me something, a miracle drug, shock treatment, to get me out of here. What if I were locked in this nightmare forever?

He heard a shout behind him, a human voice. He quit crawling and turned around. The beam of a headlamp shone about fifty yards from him. He couldn't see the figure under it, but it must be about six feet two or three inches high. Anybody he knew?

The beam danced around, lit on him once, then went back to point up and down the stream. The water level had gone down though it was still higher than it should be. The thing had gone with the current, Ringo inside it.

The beam left the channel and played on the walkway as the man walked toward him. Red sat down with his back against the wall, unable to hear the approaching footsteps because of his loud breathing and his heart booming in his eardrums. The man stopped just before him, the beam on his helmet glaring into Red's eyes so he couldn't see the face beneath.

'Listen,' Red said. Something struck the top of his head, and when he awoke the light was out. He had a sharp pain in his head, but he had no time to think about that. His clothes had been removed, and he was on his back, and his hands were under him and taped together at the wrists. His ankles were also taped.

Red groaned and said, 'What are you doing? Who is it?'

There was a sound as of a suddenly sucked-in breath.

'For God's sake,' Red said. 'Let me loose. Don't you know what happened? Ringo was killed. It's true, so help me God, he was swallowed by a thing you wouldn't believe. It's waiting out there. A man alone won't get by him. Together we might make it.'

He jumped as a hand touched his ankle above the tapes. He trembled as the hand began moving up his leg. He jumped again when something cold and hard touched the other leg for a moment.

'Who are you?' he yelled. 'Who are you?'

He heard only a heavy breathing. The hand and the knife had stopped, but now they were sliding upward along his flesh.

'Who are you?'

The hand and the knife stopped. A voice, thick as honey, said, 'I'm not worried about the thing. It's my buddy.'

'Bleek?'

'Up there I'm Bleek. In more ways than one.

'Down here, I'm the phantom of the sewer, lover.'

Red knew it was no use to scream. But he did.